The Man in the Room

A Novel

ISBN   978-0-9787484-4-9

Published 2013

Walnut Creek Press
2970 Walnut Creek Road
Marshall NC, 28753

www.walnutcreekpress.com

Cover design by the author
Manufactured in the United States of America

Dedicated to Henry David Thoreau
and Edward Paul Abbey
whose writings inspired me to try this.

The Man in the Room

by
Dennis Ruane

1

Father McGee looms large over me. I feel small in his presence even though I'm an inch taller than him. He's a stout man, although not overweight, and even cloaked in a cassock, the priest exudes strength as he paces back and forth behind his desk. I guess that he would get the better of me in a fight, and sometimes I get the feeling that he wants to give it a try. Father McGee is forty years old, and I am sixteen, a sophomore in high school.

I stand at attention, self-conscious, growing warm in my coat and tie, wondering why I'm in his office this time. He sits down and leans back in his chair.

"Why are you even attending a Catholic School if a C in religion is the best you can do?"

I shuffle from one foot to the other, stare at his desk, and remain silent. I know from experience that Father McGee doesn't want an answer yet; he just wants me to absorb the questions. I'm thankful for that because the answer to his question is that I'm attending Saint Mathew's School *only* because my parents insist that I do. I also decide it's best not to argue that an average grade is not so bad, especially in a course that I consider boring and a waste of time.

Father McGee puts on his glasses and leans over a paper that is centered on his desk. He stares at the cover for a moment and appears to be reading the words inscribed in red ink just above the title.

"Did you write this paper on Buddhism just to be funny? You knew well that the point of the assignment was to familiarize yourself with other *Christian* religions. How did you expect Sister Dorthea to react?"

He was right; I did know the point of the assignment, but I thought that Sister Dorthea might at least find Buddhism to be a refreshing alternative, like I did. I almost start to defend myself along those lines but I opt to remain silent. From the amount of red ink on the cover sheet, my guess is that Sister Dorthea didn't find Buddhism very refreshing.

Father McGee snatches up the paper from his desk, flips it open to a page he has marked, and adjusts his glasses.

"You write well, I'll give you that, but unfortunately, your literary efforts are misdirected. Allow me to quote: 'The belief that we can steadily improve ourselves through a cycle of rebirth seems to be a much more appealing ideology then the hard and fast notion of heaven or hell. Besides it seems unjust that a person should suffer eternal pain in hell for what they did in sixty or seventy years on earth. Likewise, sixty or seventy years of good living seems a small requirement for one to achieve eternal bliss in heaven'."

I shrug and look down. Those are fairly incriminating words, I have to admit. Father McGee stands and begins pacing again. I look up when he stops and faces me.

"Instead of taking advantage of the instruction you receive here at Saint Mathew's School, you obviously feel a need to spend your time questioning the fundamentals of the Catholic religion."

"No, Father, that's not what I was trying to do. I just . . ."

"Do you believe that Jesus Christ is your savior, Mr. Ryan?"

The question takes me by surprise as he intended. Father McGee's steely blue eyes look deep into my own as if he's examining my soul. He wants an answer this time. The fact is, I don't believe in God; I haven't for years. I'm a closet atheist and as such, I no longer consider questions such as whether or not Jesus Christ is my savior.

Coward that I am, I nod and manage to utter a weak 'yes', but he knows that I'm lying, and I know that my relationship with Father McGee has gone from bad to worse.

2

Good grief, I have become the geezer that I once imagined. When I let my beard grow long this summer, it developed a frostiness about the chin that adds another telling detail to the emerging picture. My older brother once warned that I would know things are getting bad when I look in the mirror and see my bald spot from the front. And there it is, as Will forebode, shining through my once proud and shaggy mane. In fact, referring to it as a *spot* is probably being naive at this point because I'm sure that a view from behind would reveal more of a bald zone.

A multitude of wrinkles underlining my eyes makes me look sad even when I'm smiling. But why not? I'm often sad or depressed, even when I'm smiling. I'm fifty-five years old now and looking in the mirror each morning only serves to remind me of that. I brush my hair back, resign myself to the doleful reflection, and turn from the mirror.

In the kitchen I pour a cup of coffee and put two slices of sourdough bread into the toaster oven. I've eaten the same breakfast every day for years now: toasted sourdough bread, coffee, and a glass of orange juice to wash down blood pressure medicine. After I follow my doctor's advice, and swallow twenty milligrams of something called lotensin, I have a second glass of orange juice, sweetened with one hundred milliliters of something called vodka.

I turn and stare over the rim of my glass at the clock on the microwave. The numbers are fuzzy, but by squinting I bring them into focus enough to see that it's eight thirty. Two weeks ago, I established a rule that I must be in my workshop by nine o'clock each morning. Considering that it's located in the basement of the building I live in, I think I'm good to be on time for work today. Outside my window, the sound of other brave souls, venturing about in the work-a-day world, encourages me to press on.

Awake, nourished, and somewhat inspired, I shuffle to the top of the stairs to descend into another day in the life. Sounds from below inform me that Hannah is in the gallery. Not that I need audible information to know that; she's always in the gallery when I come down in the morning. Hannah True has managed Duane Ryan Gallery for five years now and she's the bright spot in my day. I sometimes think that Hannah is the principal reason I look in the mirror each morning, brush my hair, and bother to come down from my apartment at all.

There's nothing romantic between us although ours is certainly more than a mere employer-employee relationship. I must confess that I did think that I was in love with Hannah once; that was shortly after I hired her. At the time, I was still adjusting to my divorce and I think that the excitement I felt in the growing camaraderie between Hannah and myself was just the tonic I needed. Infatuation passed, and a genuine, warm friendship emerged: a favorite uncle-favorite niece type relationship.

Hannah True is thirty-three years old and I am fifty-five. My policy on the older man-younger woman issue is this: after both parties have passed the age of thirty, a ten year age difference is the limit. In special cases, depending on the sociopsychological makeup of the individuals, I allow fifteen years. Hannah and I are twenty-two years apart; I'm the same age as her father. Relationships are tough enough without a built in generation gap.

If I didn't have my age policy to guide me, I wouldn't have gotten involved with Hannah even in the unlikely case that she had fallen madly in love with me. Because I like her so much, I wouldn't want her to be involved with a burned out geezer like me. In truth, the companionship I've experienced with someone happy and positive, like Hannah, is what I needed these past five years and not another romantic involvement.

But alas, Hannah is leaving me. She has resigned her position as manager of Duane Ryan Gallery. Hannah is pregnant and has decided not to return to work after the baby is born. She informed me of her decision this summer, and it will still be two months before her departure, but the weight of this change looms on my mental horizon as a dark cloud that even my morning vodka doesn't always dissipate.

Down the stairs I plod, coffee mug in hand, resigned to my fate. The door swings open and I step into a dazzling world of art: white walls, black pedestals, track lighting, and art; wood sculpture, impeccably, brilliantly, displayed. The scene surprises me every morning, reminding me of what I do and why, in spite of myself, I still do it.

"Good morning, boss."

"Good morning, Hannah."

"We had another sale from the web store last night: Caverns sold."

"Really, Caverns? That's good news. The website has really done well this year, Hannah. I'm glad you got that set up."

I know the piece that sold is already boxed and ready for shipping. Hannah is rearranging artwork on the wall from which the carving has been removed, and I walk to the center of the gallery to watch her work. Hannah is of average height with shoulder-length, auburn hair and brown eyes. She has a fair complexion and a round, pretty face that fits her personality well. Always well dressed, her clothes tend to be casual while still lending an air of professionalism.

I notice that one of my abstract carvings has been moved. I'm not surprised because I know that Hannah often rearranges an entire section of the gallery in response to the addition or removal of a single piece. I like where she's placed the sculpture, but the pedestal that it's displayed on seems slightly out of line. I go over and nudge it with my foot until the bottom is aligned with the edge of one of the floorboards. When I look up, Hannah is grinning at me.

"What?"

"I was wondering how long it would take you to do that."

"Do what?"

"Line up the pedestal with the floorboards. You always do."

"Oh, so you set me up?"

Hannah nods and turns back to the wall. She looks especially pretty today. Since becoming pregnant, she has gained weight, and it compliments her figure. Her face seems to glow with maternal happiness. The vision makes me wish, for a moment, that I had lived a more traditional life and maybe even causes me to question the choice I made to not have children. I was in my twenties then, and the fact that I aspired to be an artist for a living weighed heavily on the decision. Looking back, I still feel that it was a sound choice. My art would have suffered if I had tried to raise children and my children would have suffered because of my art.

Besides, there are too many people in the world. It's not like the species is dying out and I'm neglecting my evolutionary duty. Many of the problems that we face as a species such as pollution, poverty, and war, stem from fact that we're overpopulating the planet and competing for dwindling resources.

But I would never utter this gloomy dictum to Hannah, however much I believe it, especially now as she stands here so radiant in the bloom of motherhood. At this moment, hypocrite that I am, I would readily trade places with her husband.

"You have mail today, something besides bills or credit card offers."

"No, you mean like a personal letter?"

"Looks like it is; it's right there on the counter."

"Well glory be, an honest to goodness, old-fashioned letter. It's from my friend Dale. I haven't heard from him in a while."

"The friend from high school?"

"We go back farther than that. Dale and I met in fifth grade."

"Wow!"

"Wow is right. We've been friends since before you were born. I must say, I'm surprised that Dale wrote a letter; we've been using email as our means of communication for years now."

Besides a note, the envelope contains a newspaper article and a printed invitation. I finish a hasty perusal of the material as Hannah passes by.

"Judging from the expression on your face, it must be good news."

"I don't know if it's good news or not. He included an invitation to our thirty-seventh high school reunion."

"Really? That's neat. You went to a little Catholic school, right?"

"Yes, Saint Mathew's School in Homewood, Pennsylvania, and I went there from first grade to twelfth."

"Saint Mathew's School had twelve grades?"

"Not in one building. The grade school was a separate building, located on the other side of the church. Grades one through eight were taught there and the high school was grades nine through twelve."

"So Saint Mathew's was like a campus?"

"Yeah, a small campus: the schools, the rectory, a convent, and the church in the middle."

"The convent is where the nuns live, right? You were taught by nuns, weren't you?"

"Yes, I was taught by the Sisters of Saint Francis."

"That's hard for me to imagine. I'd never have guessed you went to a Catholic School if you hadn't told me. And you went there for twelve years?"

"I sure did. Well get this, my first grade class had thirty-six kids, my graduating class had thirty-four, and twenty of the people I graduated with were the same kids I started first grade with."

"You're kidding me. My graduating class at Janesville High had over six hundred students, and there were many people in my class that I didn't even know."

"Oh that wasn't a problem at Saint Mathew's. I knew everybody alright, and everybody knew me."

"I think that's nice, though. Are you going to go to the reunion?"

"I don't know, probably not. I've never gone to one before."

"With such a small class, how do they ever get much of a turnout?"

"It's not easy. Besides the classes being so small, the high school closed down thirty years ago, so no classes have graduated from there in decades. The reunions have evolved into a coming together of all Saint Mathew's alumni, not just one class, so that helps. But they still aren't overly crowded from what I'm told. This one could draw a better attendance, though. According to this newspaper clipping that Dale sent, the high school is slated to be torn down in a few months and the space will be used to expand the church parking lot."

"Oh no."

"It's not that big a deal. The building has been in bad shape for years now. It's been used for offices and storage ever since the school closed, and my guess is it's not worth the maintenance costs anymore, even for that. I have to admit though, I'm surprised they're tearing it down. Many members of Saint Mathew's Church are graduates of the high school and I would expect some sort of protest against the idea."

"How do you feel about it?"

"Ah, surprised, but not upset. I couldn't wait to get away from the place when I was there and I haven't thought too much about it since. My parents went there though, in fact, they met there, and even my grandmother Ryan graduated from Saint Mathew's. So I guess if it were up to me, I'd keep it around."

"Well, I think you should go, Duane; a road trip might be good for you. Who knows, maybe you'll hook up with an old high school sweetheart."

"Oh no, I told you, Hannah, no more relationships. I'm devoting the rest of my life to the things that are most important to me: art and drinking."

Hannah's smile disappears. I know that she worries about my drinking and I'm sorry I made the remark. I speak hastily in an attempt to get past it.

"Maybe I just *will* go, then. You're probably ready for a break from me."

Hannah's smile reappears, and she doesn't rush to disagree with my presumption.

3

It's an inspiring journey from Janesville, North Carolina to Homewood, Pennsylvania. The entire drive entails interstate highway, no stop lights for hundreds of miles, and much of the route traverses the Appalachian Mountains of Virginia and West Virginia. Don't knock interstates around me. I can't stand traveling back roads anymore; they're so slow and aggravating. If you want to get from point A to point B, you travel the interstates. I've come to like everything about them: the speed, the scenery, the idiotic billboards, the semis roaring by, the danger, the road rage. It's all good. Interstates are both the rat race and the human race, coming at you fast, and it's the only way I travel.

This road trip is a good test for my new Toyota truck. The Ford had served my cause well, transporting me and my estate to the mountains of North Carolina and then hauling tons of wood in the fifteen years that followed. But in the end, the poor old machine was literally falling apart around me, and even my buddy, Lonny, at the local service station was reluctant to pass it on inspection anymore.

With a tear in my eye, I drove my aged truck across town to the salvage yard, sold it for eighty-seven dollars, and then walked away without looking back. That's the best way to end such a relationship. I thought it was only fitting that on the way home, I stopped at a bar named *Headlights*, a sixties retro place with a vehicle theme, to hoist a few beers to the memories and the miles.

The fact is, I probably could have done without a truck at this stage of the game. I rarely fetch my own wood anymore, and that was the principle reason I've driven one these many years. When I do venture out of my studio to get wood, it's only because I'm in the mood, or to prove that I can still do it. However, when the old truck was giving out and I considered downsizing to a car, my machismo genes started firing—I had to have a truck. My truck had to be four wheel drive, too, even though Janesville gets about an inch of snow a year and I never go too far off the road in any season.

Elaine would be shocked to hear that I'm going to my high school reunion because she tried often to get me to be more sociable during the decade that we were together. I wonder what she's doing these days, and more specifically, if she's still with Professor what's-his-name. She definitely moved away from the bohemian artist type when she left me for that guy. Elaine lives in Asheville, only twenty miles from Janesville, but we've had no contact for over a year now.

When I was young and just starting out in this dubious profession, a wise old man cautioned me that art and relationships don't mix. At the time, I knew he couldn't possibly be right, for I was in love with Cynthia Morris, and it was a feeling that I knew would never die. I suspected that he'd just never found true love like I had; he hadn't met his soul mate.

Cynthia and I split up about a year after that, and now, two divorces and half a dozen soul mates later, I appreciate what that wise old man was trying to tell me. He would probably approve if he could see me now, free as a breeze and determined to stay that way. Even better, I'm on the road again, just like Willie Nelson sings about, except that Willie's rich and famous and I'm neither, but that's beside the point.

The point is that I'm actually going to a Saint Mathew's High School reunion. I'm a little shocked, myself that I'm being so sociable. Why am I doing this? I guess I'm going mostly because Dale prodded me to. Dale's been a better friend to me than I've been to him, and he's the one who has made the effort to keep in contact over the years as I've wandered my crooked path. Even though he's followed a traditional track in life with regards to family and career, Dale never questions my lifestyle or my motives.

Dale and his wife, Jenifer, began dating when they were students at Saint Mathew's High School and have now been married for twenty-five years. Dale is a partner in a successful architecture firm; Jen teaches at a small college. They have three grown children, the youngest of which is in her sophomore year at Penn State. The course of his domestic life is a model for what many people aspire to when they're young, and what many look upon as a success when it comes to fruition.

Yet my friend has never judged me for my failed marriages, my lack of progeny, or my financial ineptitude (not to mention my shifty and unpredictable behavior). I sometimes wonder why. If anything he seems to be a bit intrigued by the path I've taken, like one might be with a former companion who has wandered off into a foreign land.

While Dale's letter is the main reason I'm driving north today, I have to confess that I've developed a strange curiosity to see Saint Mathew's High School again, especially since it could well be the last time. Yet I feel no sentiment for the building, and can muster only a slight concern that it's slated for demolition. The truth is that while I was a student there, I often wished that Saint Mathew's High School had been demolished before I ever walked through the doors.

It's hard for me to believe that it's been over thirty-five years now since I last walked those musty halls. In fact, since graduation, I've only ventured onto the Saint Mathew's campus a handful of times, and that was either for a wedding or a funeral.

The last time was twelve years ago for my Grandmother Ryan's funeral. Dear old Grandma Ryan, she was happy and laughing right until her death at the age of eighty-nine. Decades before her timely demise, Grandma had requested that her eight grandsons serve as pallbearers for the funeral. At the time we were all in our teens and it seemed like a charming and appropriate idea. However when the time came, we were larger people, some of my cousins quite portly in fact, and the casket was small, such that four of us on each side proved to be a crowd.

The problem became most obvious when we carried the casket up the stairs of Saint Mathew's Church and found ourselves bumping into each other and kicking each other's heels. We tried to maintain a solemn demeanor, but were forced to take awkward, tiny steps to continue our forward progress. When one of my cousins likened our operation to a giant centipede creeping into the church, we struggled instead to keep straight faces as we escorted Grandma to the altar. She would have loved it.

My first memories of Saint Mathew's Church are vague in my mind, which is not so surprising since I typically slept through much of the service. When I was awake, there was little to see except tall people all around that blocked my view. What I remember most are the mysterious sounds: the singing from up in the air behind me, the booming voices from the front that seemed to be from people in charge, the bells and chants, and then everyone, including my parents, talking or singing the same thing all at once.

In another two years, church became something my older brother and I did with our father on Sundays. That came about when Mom and Dad started going to church in shifts so that my infant brother could stay home. This was an arrangement that suited Will and I just fine and I think my father preferred this as well—just the guys hanging out.

One advantage of going to Mass with Dad was that he liked to attend the earliest possible service, the one that began at seven in the morning. For us it meant that we could get it out of the way first thing and have the rest of the day to play. I can still picture the three of us cruising to church in the big Chevrolet station wagon, Will and I sitting in the front seat beside him, dressed in suits and ties, looking like miniature versions of our father.

Andrew Ryan, wasn't an outwardly religious man, but he was very much a Catholic and firmly believed that a Catholic should go to Mass every Sunday. My father practiced what he preached, even years later when he was too ill to do much of anything else.

I don't remember many details about Mass from this era either. Dad was not one to sit up front, and short people such as Will and I were at a disadvantage in the crowd. For the most part, my brother and I would entertain ourselves to whatever extent we could get away with and anticipated the trip home because we often stopped at Duval's restaurant for doughnuts.

By the age of five, I appreciated that there was some great importance associated with Saint Mathew's Church and it was somehow tied into the idea of God that I was learning more about every year. But I still only went to church because I was taken there by my father, just like I went to the barber shop when he took me there. While I could easily understand the reason I needed to go to the barber shop once a month, it was still not clear why I needed to go to church every Sunday.

At age six my perception of church would change because that was when I entered the first grade at Saint Mathew's School, and the age of religious innocence came to an end.

4

I don't believe that Sister Timothy was an inherently mean woman, but I do know that she wasn't a person that should have taught first graders. She was too stern, and loud, and impatient for children as young as we were. I was intimidated by everything my first days at Saint Mathew's School and especially by her.

Sister Timothy was a member of the Sisters of Saint Francis, the order of nuns that taught at Saint Mathew's School. She wore the traditional dress of the Sisters of Saint Francis or the *habit*, as it was called, a bizarre and intimidating costume to a six year old. The main features of Sister Timothy's attire were a long black gown with many folds that hung down to the floor, a stiff, white bib that covered her entire chest, and a mysterious flat cap draped in black cloth that flowed onto her shoulders. At the front of the cap, white material made up a wide strip across her forehead, and her face was framed in a stiff white band that looped under the chin.

The only parts of Sister Timothy that weren't covered were her hands and face. It seemed to me that the white band around her face was too tight and I wondered if that was why her face was always puffy and red.

For jewelry, a silver cross hung from a black cord around Sister Timothy's neck, and was centered just below the bib; and the long gown was cinched at the waist by a large set of wooden rosary beads that made a clicking noise when she walked.

Saint Mathew's School didn't have a kindergarten, so I was

introduced to academics at Haywood Elementary School, a public school. My kindergarten classroom was big and colorful and cheerful, and so was my teacher, Mrs. Schafer. I loved her and I knew that she loved me. However, as a result of my kindergarten experience, I came ill-prepared to Saint Mathew's Grade School. I knew right away that Sister Timothy didn't love me; she was too strict and loud for me to believe that. On the wall behind her, Jesus hung on a cross, bloody and dead. What a difference a year made.

Sister Timothy taught us the rules of Saint Mathew's School, from how our coats should be hung in the cloakroom to the correct way our pencils should be sharpened. She showed us the proper way to fold our hands when we prayed, that is with the palms pressed together, the fingers perfectly straight, pointing upward, and the thumbs folded, the right one over the left. She taught us what to pray and when to pray. We prayed every day, in fact, three times a day: upon arrival, before lunch, and at dismissal.

Sister Timothy was a fanatic about neatness and order. My mother liked things to be neat and orderly, too, and one of her favorite expressions was *a place for everything and everything in its place*, but in first grade I experienced that philosophy at a whole other level. Sister Timothy applied it to everything: pencils, rulers, chalk, erasers, books, desks, hands and feet. She put particular emphasis on the fact that in each row our desks should always be lined up precisely with the floorboards.

We went to church often that year and from Sister Timothy I learned things about Saint Mathew's Church that I hadn't appreciated before. Up to that point in my life, the Church had been a big, bright, intriguing place for me, a crowded place where people go on Sundays. Although I didn't fully understand why I was there, and I couldn't see what was going on, I felt welcome and secure. Sister Timothy introduced me to the darker side of the building.

She took our class to the church during off hours when it was empty, and mysterious. We first-graders were introduced to the confessional booths imbedded in the wall at the back of the church and Sister Timothy informed us that we would be in them soon. She took us up the winding staircase to the choir loft to view the monolithic organ that resided there and told us that in two years, some of us would be members of the boy choir and would sing there during Mass.

Perhaps the most poignant memory of those shadowy excursions into Saint Mathew's Church was that of a marble statue of Jesus that stood in the vestibule at the back of the church. Although the image was of Jesus as a young boy, there was something about the statue that gave me the creeps.

The statue portrayed Jesus dressed in a brightly colored robe with shiny gold trim, and with a magnificent, jeweled crown on His head. His right hand was raised with the index finger pointing upward toward His heavenly home. The ornate robe and loud colors weren't at all in line with what I had learned about Jesus in religion class. Typically images of Jesus as a boy depicted Him in very plain clothing and often He would be helping His stepfather, Joseph, in the carpenter shop.

But it wasn't so much the garish costume as the expression on the face of the statue that was the problem. I thought there was something sinister and malevolent about it from the first time I saw it. The statues large, bulging eyes seemed to follow me as I moved, and little white teeth, distinct through parted lips, gave the impression of a condescending smirk.

Sister Timothy assembled us around the intimidating statue, and used it as a backdrop while making the point that even as children, we had responsibilities as Catholics and members of the church. Perhaps she thought an image of Jesus that was closer to our age would help impress her message upon us, never realizing that the sculpture frightened us instead. Looking back however, I wonder if Sister Timothy brought us before the statue for that very reason, to instill the fear of the Lord in us at an impressionable age.

The creepy statue aside, by far the most affecting memory I have of first grade is an incident that occurred about midway in the school year, the details of which are still distinct in my mind fifty years later. That afternoon, Sister Timothy paddled two of my classmates. I can't remember anymore what it was that these boys did to warrant her action, which is interesting to me now, since that seems like something you wouldn't want to forget, for your own good.

What I do remember is that Sister Timothy had been in a bad mood all day, leading up to the incident. Late in the afternoon, she suddenly became very angry, called the names of the boys and instructed them to come to the front of the room. Then she stormed to the closet at the back of the classroom and returned to the front, holding a wooden paddle.

The paddle was the standard model of that era: about eighteen inches long, three inches wide, and half an inch thick. Sister Timothy ordered the boys to lean over, and then hit each of them, three times, on their rear end.

To this day, I remember the names of these classmates, and I can still see the looks on their faces as they returned to their seats. Joe bawled all the way to his, and once there, covered his face with his hands and continued to cry. Mike hurried to his seat and was struggling not to cry, but once there, put his head down and sobbed.

After the boys returned to their seats, Sister Timothy asked in an angry voice if anyone else thought they needed the same. We sat deathly silent. She went back to her desk and didn't say anything else to us until the bell rang for the school day to be over.

Looking back, I don't judge Sister Timothy for what she did or think of her as an unusually mean woman. She just wasn't a person that should have taught first grade or perhaps any grade for that matter, and of course it was acceptable back then to punish children by hitting them. *Spare the rod and spoil the child*, and, *reading and writing and 'rithmetic, taught to the tune of a hickory stick*, were popular verses.

My parents had a red ping pong paddle that I had personal experience with, and even my grandmother Ryan had a paddle on hand in her house. I was no stranger to that form of discipline when I had done something wrong, but what I witnessed that day in first grade was different in my experience and I've never forgotten it.

It's a sad fact that of the many milestones that were attained that first year at Saint Mathew's School, not the least of which were *reading and writing, and 'rithmetic*, this is the event that stands out in my memory. I'm glad to this day that Sister Timothy never singled me out to be paddled, and also thankful that Sister Timothy was replaced the following year by Sister Malcolm, a wonderful first grade teacher, who arrived before my younger siblings entered Saint Mathew's School.

Everything changed when I entered second grade because my new teacher, Sister Mary Sean, was the perfect person to teach second graders. To this day, she remains as one of the nicest people registered in my memory. Sister Mary Sean was young and pretty and happy, and I can't recall her ever being angry or of ever being intimidated by her. She never hollered at us and never, ever, hit us. If at times she was disappointed by our behavior, she would become quiet, and her silence was all it took for us to mend our ways. We second graders loved Sister Mary Sean and we knew that she loved us.

Under Sister Mary Sean, we spread our little wings and soon left first grade far behind. My anxieties over Saint Mathew's School quickly dissipated, and I became confident, gregarious, and somewhat mischievous—traits that would characterize my personality for years to come.

Once a week in music class we were encouraged to perform for our classmates by playing an instrument or by singing in front of the room, an opportunity I never missed. I entertained my classmates with my rudimentary skills on harmonica, recorder, and even an old set of bongo drums that a neighbor loaned me. For my grand performance, I surprised everybody with a rendition of the Elvis Presley song, *All Shook Up*, complete with an imitation of Elvis' posturing and gyrations. I had been given a forty-five RPM record of *All Shook Up* by an uncle, who was correct in assuming that I was ready for rock and roll. I practiced in secret for weeks just for music class and told no one at school of my plans.

Sister Mary Sean was so delighted that she went next door, returned with the third grade teacher, Sister Saint Hubert, and then insisted on an encore. Sister Saint Hubert was an elderly woman who was very sweet and friendly, and who I'm sure never expected to be introduced to rock and roll that morning. I can still see the two nuns, standing in the doorway, red-faced, with their hands over their mouths, watching my performance. Sister Saint Hubert was so impressed that she had me repeat it for the third grade. It was the pinnacle of my musical career and I owed it all to Sister Mary Sean.

Yet as wonderful as that year was, one of the memories that stands out from my second grade experience is of a confusing and upsetting incident that has haunted me ever since.

1963

Art is my favorite class. Sister Mary Sean is showing us how to make a turkey drawing by tracing our hand. After we get the turkeys done we're going to cut them out and hang them on the bulletin board for Thanksgiving decorations. I'm coloring the feathers on mine when Sister Saint Hubert comes to the door and talks with Sister Mary Sean. They're whispering, so I can't hear what they're saying, but it looks like both of them are really worried about something.

Sister Saint Hubert leaves and Sister Mary Sean shuts the door. She looks at us and doesn't say anything for a little while. She folds her hands like she's going to pray, but touches the corners of her eyes with her fingers. Her face is real red; I think she's trying not to cry.

Something must be really wrong to make Sister Mary Sean this sad. The room is the most quiet I've ever heard it. Nobody is even moving. Sister Mary Sean gets a tissue from her pocket and wipes her eyes before she talks.

"Children, I have some bad news."

Sister Mary Sean stops and takes a breath. Then she talks in a real soft voice that's shaking a little.

"President Kennedy has been shot and is hurt very badly."

She stops again and looks down for a little bit. Then she raises her head and talks more normal.

"I'm going to lead you in prayer, so that we can ask God to help our president recover from his wounds. We will say a decade of the rosary."

I can't believe that the president has been shot. At Saint Mathew's School we're proud that John Fitzgerald Kennedy is the first Catholic president of our country. I like President Kennedy; I like the way he looks and the way he talks. I know that he's a smart man and a nice man. I don't know why someone would want to hurt him.

We make the sign of the cross. Sister Mary Sean says the Apostle's Creed, because it's really long and we haven't learned that yet. Next comes an Our Father and then three Hail Marys. We just start the second Hail Mary and Sister Saint Hubert taps on the door again. Sister Mary Sean talks to her but only for a little while this time. Sister Saint Hubert leaves, and Sister Mary Sean is crying a little bit. She takes another breath and then tells us.

"Children, President Kennedy has died. I will now lead you in a full rosary to ask God to accept his soul into heaven."

5

Hannah reserved a room for me at the Expresso Inn, a motel located on the west side of Homewood, just off the interstate. She urged me to try one of the bed and breakfasts in the Homewood area, but she knew well that I wouldn't stay in one and had looked up the information on the internet just to harass me. Hannah knows that when I travel I like to be anonymous, and that's impossible at a bed and breakfast where camaraderie is part of the package. Who wants to start their day by chatting merrily with strangers over breakfast?

An Expresso Inn is the *anti* bed and breakfast. During your entire stay, you don't even have to make eye contact with a human being if you don't want to. Everything is done *express*, on a computer screen, and on your way out, there's a complimentary Espresso waiting at the door. Can't beat that.

I arrive in Homewood earlier than anticipated and I'm not in the mood for my express check in, so I decide to meander through town in the direction of my alma mater, Saint Mathew's School. My plan is to travel there by a circuitous route, one that will allow me to visit other scenes from my past and gradually work myself into the proper frame of mind. I exit the interstate on the south side of town rather than in the area where I grew up, so that I can steer clear of the most familiar scene of all, the old family home. I don't want to get depressed so early in the weekend.

Merging onto Haywood Street, I join the evening traffic

and mingle with impatient drivers, lurching along from light to light, anxious to be home after the days toil. Before the interstate came through this area, Haywood Street was a lazy, tree-lined, road that bisected family farms and led into a quiet, working class neighborhood on the outskirts of Homewood. Now Haywood Street is a four lane highway with so many new, shiny, commercial structures lining it that I would hardly know where I was, if I didn't know where I was.

The sad truth is that along most major highways, where this change has progressed to the commercial extreme, I could be anywhere in the United States and still have the same hyper-sensory experience. It all begins to look the same *and* smell the same.

Country roads transform into four lane gateways to huge plazas that require their own four-lane roads complete with traffic signals. Family farms are paved over so that megastores and fast-food restaurants can contend for consumers on land where cattle once roamed. Not that I'm a defender of cattle over consumers; I think the countryside would be best without either.

Fortunately the noise and confusion of Haywood Street melt away quickly at a given distance from the interstate, and after a turn to the left and another to the right, I find myself back in familiar territory. The changes here are minimal and understandable: a different color of paint on this house, a fence instead of a hedge around that one, new names on some of the mail boxes. Perhaps because of my own disconnected life, I find something reassuring in this continuity.

This is how I choose to enter my home town, not with a grand entrance down the main boulevard, where the fancy business types congregate, but rather, to make an unobtrusive passage through one of the city's back doors, an arrival more in character with the humble, hand laborer that I am. Now I have to confess, I didn't choose just any back door, but one that opens into a neighborhood that I was once as familiar with as my own.

I navigate another two blocks, take a right onto Beaumont Circle, and park my truck just past my long lost, high school girlfriend's house. I gaze across the street at a white, two-story structure that is nestled so comfortably into the shrubbery and trees that it appears to be a natural outcrop of the land. Now this may seem like a strange thing to do, considering that Nancy Bundy and I haven't communicated in over three decades, but if one is in the mood to dabble in nostalgia, as I apparently am this afternoon, the memory of a one's first serious romance is in a hallowed class.

Nancy Bundy transferred to Saint Mathew's High School during my freshman year and the attraction between us was immediate. We were both cute, and cool, and outsiders at Saint Mathew's for different reasons. I, because I had gone through some changes and no longer wanted to fit in, and Nancy, because she transferred from a large public school in Pittsburgh and never could fit in.

For the next two years we were inseparable to a degree that led some to suggest that we might be joined at the hip. Sister Dorthea knew better, however, and one afternoon when she was in a bad mood, she not only physically separated us, but in a loud voice for all in the hallway to hear, she exclaimed, "please leave some room for the Holy Spirit."

However, my first serious romance ended with a serious thud that, psychologically, I still feel today. Nancy cheated on me. The summer before our senior year, she started seeing somebody else (*seeing* is the polite way to put it), and not just anybody else, but Hal Davenport, quarterback of the Homewood High School football team—Hal the hunk.

I was crushed, devastated, humiliated, and last but not least, put in my place by the kid from the big public school, something that was always a rub with us Saint Mathew's boys. How could I hope to compete with Hal when Saint Mathew's School didn't even have a football team? I was a member of the Saint Mathew's Eagles cross country team, but no matter how fast I might run or what race I might win for the blue and gold, I was no match for Hal out there on the gridiron, weaving and dodging tacklers, throwing for another touchdown, leading the Homewood Blue Devils to victory.

Nancy was remorseful, embarrassed, and apologetic, but in the end she stuck with that old Blue Devil, Hal Davenport, and even transferred to Homewood High School for her senior year. Hal and Nancy married while they were in college and divorced when their children were in college. I felt no gratification when their relationship ended, but even as I sit here now, thirty-five years later, I feel a loss when I remember how wonderful ours was in the beginning.

Perhaps that's the reason why, in spite of my jaded opinion of relationships, I come by here, to imagine Nancy and I together as we once were, young and naïve and happy. For a little space in time, all we wanted or needed was each other and our future happiness together seemed certain. For me, love would never again be that sweet and innocent and scary all at the same time. Now it's just scary.

It doesn't look like anyone is home and I'm tempted to walk around back to see if the old wicker swing, upon which Nancy and I passed so much time together, is still hanging on the porch. I wonder if the basketball hoop, where I played one-on-one with her kid brother, is still hanging on the side of the garage.

On second thought, I decide against venturing from the truck. What if someone calls the police? I can see the headlines now: *Decrepit Old Homewood Native Caught Lurking Around High School Girlfriend's House*. Besides, I read somewhere that nostalgia is really just a form of depression. Who needs it in another form? So I leave the back yard as it exists in my memory, take a drink from the flask in my coat pocket, and drive on.

Beaumont Circle borders the Beaumont Country Club at one end and passes through the swankiest neighborhood in Homewood, named, as you might guess, Beaumont Heights. The *Beaumont* part I can understand since much of the property that makes up the club and the adjacent neighborhood were once part of the estate of a family named Beaumont. It's the *heights* part that never made much sense to me since the neighborhood seems to be at the same level as the surrounding area.

It's interesting to me that in Beaumont Heights I see little change in the houses and yards. I guess once you've achieved swankiness, you don't mess with it. Everything looks much the same to me as it did back when Nancy and I walked her family's disagreeable little dog, Mica, along this street. One of the few things that I liked about Mica was that she liked to poop on well manicured lawns.

Perhaps my jealousy was just showing through to some extent, having grown up in the Crawford Street neighborhood, an area that apparently never achieved such heights. Was my neighborhood considered *Crawford Depths* then, even though it was every inch as high above sea level as Beaumont Heights? I'm just being facetious now, of course; it's the vodka talking.

Whenever we kids would complain about what we didn't have in life, our father had a standard response. He would assume a thoughtful expression and in a solemn voice say, "I cried because I had no shoes, and then I met a man who had no feet."

Needless to say, the philosophical insight of this statement was lost on us, selfish brats that we were, and we complained all the more, even about having to hear that old saying yet another time. I never forgot those words, however, and they've served me well over the years, especially in times when buying a pair of shoes was a hardship for me.

Along the way, I've heard different variations of the same adage and recently I've learned that its origin dates back to 1259 CE where it's part of the works of the great Persian poet Sa'di. Now with all due respect to Sa'di, I still credit Dad whenever I think of the saying. When I recall his slow, measured recital, the solemn tone of voice, and the timeless expression on his face, I feel he put his personal stamp on it.

Looking back, I have to wonder about this young man who was my father, dealing with complaining children, paying for the shoes on their feet, working hard each day at his coal business to support a family. Perhaps it's time for me to compose my own variation of Sa'di's proverb: I cry because my life is screwed up; because my dreams have failed to come true, and then I remember a man who had his life in order, whose dreams *did* come true, and then his dreams and his life were snatched away from him.

I descend (in a manner of speaking) from Beaumont Heights, take a left on Dunham Avenue, and drive toward the heart of Homewood. Weariness from my journey is beginning to overtake me, so I opt for a more direct route to Saint Mathew's School.

With a population that hovers around fifteen thousand people, Homewood is not a large city, but more of a big town. Main Street stretches through the heart of town from east to west for about a mile, fronting a business district that extends a few blocks north and south. Beyond that, residential areas expand the city limits for another mile or so in every direction.

At the first light, I turn onto Main Street, and I'm struck with the degree to which Homewood has changed since I last traveled this route. That was just before my mother moved to Florida, and I had come through to help her prepare the Ryan homestead for passage into other hands. The sad state of Homewood at that time meshed well with the melancholic mood I was in for having a hand in letting go of the family home.

The town's decline had actually begun many years before when the great coal seams in western Pennsylvania started to run out. Homewood, the town that in the early twentieth century grew with an abandon that caused some to predict it would one day rival Pittsburgh, simply ran out of fuel.

I was fortunate to have lived here during the tail end of the golden era (albeit the tip of the tail), but as fond as my memories are, they're nothing compared to my parent's experience of bustling sidewalks full of people, two glittering theaters, and a Main Street lined with vibrant businesses.

As I cruise the boulevard now, it seems that some of the vibrancy has returned. Many of the old building have been renovated, revealing marvelous architecture and ornamentation that have long been obscured by the soot of the preceding industrial era. Small public parks are interspersed among the buildings, adding greenery amid the concrete and glass. Dale has been telling me about these changes, but to see them for myself is to really appreciate what's happening.

Best of all, there are people out and about. People shopping, sitting on benches, walking dogs, and people conversing. These activities had all but disappeared in the seventies when the colossal, enclosed shopping complex, otherwise known as *the mall*, came into being on the edge of town. After settling in amid much pomp and circumstance, the mall proceeded to siphon the lifeblood from Homewood.

What I'm seeing now suggests that the glitz of the colossal enclosed shopping complex might be losing its appeal, a transformation that is a welcome development to this native son. I haven't lived in Homewood since I left for college in 1973 but its downward spiral still affected me. Even from a distance, no one likes to hear that the home team is losing.

So with a lightened heart and renewed hope for the future, I turn my steed toward Saint Mathew's School. At the west end of Main Street, I turn onto Pennsylvania Avenue, a road that skirts the edge of the Saint Mathew's campus, and as I make the next left onto Jefferson Street, Saint Mathew's High School comes into view.

When I was a student here, I always parked in the same spot: in the center of the parking area, facing the building and backed up to the very edge of the lot. Nobody could park behind me there, and because there were many spaces, other students rarely parked so far from the building. Even though there are only half a dozen vehicles here today, I maneuver into that same position now.

I'm surprised to see that the old school building looks the same as it did when I last saw it. In fact, it looks much the same as it did on that day when I first saw it. That was on an Easter Sunday when my brother and I went to Mass with our father. Attendance was high as it typically was for a major church holiday and as a result the parking area around the church was full. We had to park in the High School parking lot, and Dad took the opportunity to introduce Will and me to his alma mater. I was three or four at the time, chilly in my new dress pants, holding my father's big, calloused hand, and looking up at the school as he talked. I couldn't quite grasp what significance the building held for me, but it was obvious that Dad liked it.

Saint Mathew's High School was built in 1910 to serve a Catholic community that, like Homewood, was growing rapidly as the coal mines boomed. The three story brick structure is quaint in design, especially with the bell tower at one corner, but it was never in the running to be an architectural statement. Basic and functional are the adjectives that best describe the building; tall and long portray it fairly well, too.

I must admit, to find the school so well preserved after all these years, saddens me somewhat and I don't know exactly why. Perhaps it would be easier to accept its impending demolition if it were in a more dilapidated state: broken windows, a sagging roof, a few missing bricks.

Wait a minute here, could there be some slight sentiment for this old building lurking in the murky depths of my conscious? *Come on, old boy, snap out of it.* What real difference does it make to me who lives far away in North Carolina, whether there's an old abandoned school that I once attended *against* my will, taking up space on Jefferson Street in Homewood, Pennsylvania or an asphalt parking lot? At least the parking lot would have a practical use: a frugal man such as myself could park his truck here and walk downtown, thus avoiding parking fees.

Nonetheless, Saint Mathew's School is still here and I'm here, so I might as well appreciate the moment. Not only am I here, but I'm parked on the spot where Dale and I sat in the mornings during our high school tenure, gathering our wits to face another day of instruction at the hands of the Sisters of Saint Francis. In high school, I drove an old jeep, a vehicle that Mom and Dad bought for Will and me, and I picked Dale up on the way here.

How nice it will be to see Dale again and discuss the vagaries

30

of life over a beer or two or ten. Eh, what's this? Even as I entertain the notion, a sporty, maroon BMW, is slowing down on Jefferson Street and looks to be turning into the lot. It does turn and I can see Dale grinning as he pulls in beside me. He exits the car wagging his head from side to side.

"Hey Duane, old habits die hard, eh?"

"Well speak of the devil. I was sitting here, wondering what was missing, and then you show up."

We shake hands and chuckle at the sight of each other: two aging men who have known each other since we were teenagers.

"How are you doing, old man?"

"Growing old and grumpy right on schedule, how about you?"

"I'm doing well, better now that you're back in town. How long have you been here?"

"I got in about half an hour ago."

"Well you know your welcome to stay with Jen and me, but I assume you've already made arrangements."

"Yes, my gallery manager has already made motel reservations."

"Hannah right? She's still with you?"

"Yep, Hannah and I are still a team. I don't know what I'd do without her."

"I don't either. All I can say is the woman must have the patience of Job."

"Watch it there buddy, I know the Bible and that wasn't a compliment."

"All right, I'll back off for now. After all, I've finally got you to a reunion and I don't want to drive you away. I can't believe that you're actually here. Tell me, why *did* you decide to come this time?"

"Why? You know me, how sentimental I am. I wouldn't miss an opportunity like this to see old friends. And now when I say *old* friends, it's not just a figure of speech."

"I'm touched, Duane, but excuse me if I'm skeptical. That was never enough of a reason before."

"Yah, well, I guess I needed a break, too. I've been in a rut and seem to be just spinning my wheels these days. I thought a road trip might do me some good; maybe get the old creative juices flowing again. And for some strange reason, the fact that the school is going to be torn down got me moving. I got this urge to see this old place one last time before it got demolished by the powers that be."

"Do you know who the powers that be are?"

"No, not really. How would I know?"

"Oh, I'm sorry, I forgot that you don't subscribe to the diocese newsletter. Actually, I was going to use that information as my final tactic to get you to come to the reunion, but after I knew you were coming, I decided to tell you face to face. The Bishop of Greensburg Diocese has set the stage for the demolition of the school, and that would be none other than His Excellency, Bishop Thomas McGee."

"Are you kidding me, *the* Thomas McGee?"

"I kid you not. And now he's *Bishop* McGee."

"Well I can't say I'm surprised that he's a bishop now, but I'm shocked that he would want the high school torn down? It seemed to be his heart and soul back when he was pastor here. Why is he doing it?"

"Just not worth the cost of maintenance anymore."

"But I thought they were using the school for offices."

"Apparently it's still not worth the cost. Just like all old buildings, there's always a new expense cropping up just to keep it up to the safety codes. That's why the top floor isn't used anymore; it was condemned because there's only one stairway."

"No, not the auditorium. What did they do?"

"The cheapest thing possible: blocked off the stairs to make it inaccessible. The stage was never used anyway, but the fact that an entire floor is abandoned rather than making the necessary changes to keep it functional is a sign of the underlying problem. But hey, let's face it, the building wasn't the greatest design from the beginning. It's not surprising that problems are becoming obvious as building codes improve."

"So you think demolition is a good idea?"

"I wouldn't necessarily call it a good idea, but it's a practical idea. The price to bring this building up to code is astronomical."

"Well that settles that."

"Not entirely it hasn't. There is talk among some alumni of raising the necessary money, even though at this point, it hasn't gone beyond the talking stage. From what I've heard, no number that has been mentioned comes near to the amount that's needed, and any proposal that's reached Bishop McGee's desk thus far has been dismissed out of hand. He argues that there are many buildings in the diocese that are more functional and practical that also need to be maintained. Also, to renovate an old structure like the school would not just be a one time cash outlay; it would be a constant monetary drain."

"Is he right?"

"Yes, he is, but there are many structures that are financial burdens and yet are maintained anyway, say for their artistic or emotional appeal. Frank Lloyd Wright's *Fallingwater*, up in the mountains, comes to mind. But, let's face it, this ain't no *Fallingwater*, and old Father McGee was never big on art or emotion."

"That's for sure. Pompous, that's how I remember him; Mr. Macho priest. *Duke*, the nickname that we gave him, was perfect."

"Yah, it did fit him. Duane, do you remember that time he fell over backwards in his chair in study hall?"

"How could I forget that? He was mad anyway because he had to fill in for Sister Charles, and was taking it out on us. What was he thinking, leaning back on a chair with coaster wheels? He was furious that people laughed. Remember the look he gave me?"

"Oh man, I sure do. But he always had it in for you, Duane. You never should have written that paper on Buddhism."

"Oh, it wasn't just that or even the fact that I converted to atheism on his watch. I think that it was my attitude that bothered him most. He knew that he couldn't get to me. Whether it was sins on my soul or marks on my permanent record, I didn't care, and he knew it."

"What's up? You suddenly got a serious look on your face."

"I think I saw someone looking out the rectory window, the right, window of the second floor. That's Duke's old office, isn't it?"

Dale turns and looks toward the rectory, a building located sixty yards away on a hill that rises on the opposite side of Jefferson Street. The two story brick structure is nearly overshadowed by Saint Mathew's Church and hemmed in from the road by three ancient maple trees.

"That's Father Walsh's office; he's the pastor now. I don't see anybody in the window."

"Whoever it was, they moved right after I looked up. Could it have been Duke? Is he here?"

"I don't know if he's here yet, but I know he's coming sometime this weekend. He's going to say Mass, and he's the guest of honor at the closing banquet on Sunday."

"Why is he the guest of honor? Why not Sister Mary Agatha? She was the principal for more years than he was the pastor."

"True, but the Catholic Church is a patriarchal system, Duane. Even if she had been pastor and he had been principal, he would probably be the guest of honor. And after all, he *is* the Bishop now."

"Is Sister Mary Agatha coming this weekend?"

"Last I heard, she might be here. She's in her eighties now, you know, and I was told that her health isn't good."

"Well, I would much rather see her as the guest of honor."

"Little wonder, Mr. teacher's pet."

"Oh come on now."

"You were her favorite Duane, don't deny that."

"Well, maybe I was. I wonder why? I never could quite figure that one out."

"Oh, I think she relished the challenge: the silent intellectual, the still water that runs deep, the moody . . ."

"Alright; that's enough. Sister Mary Agatha wasn't always so easy on me though. How about the time in Latin class when she called me *The Great Sphinx*."

"That was terrific. She hit the nail right on the head that time. It's no wonder that the name stuck."

"What do you mean, stuck? You're joking, right?"

"No, it's the truth; we still call you that sometimes. And now, Mr. Sphinx, even though I could stand here and talk all evening, I need to run. I have a few more items to pick up for the party. That's why I'm out and about right now. You want to come along for the ride?"

"No, but thanks anyway. I need time to decompress after my journey. I'm going to be around through the weekend though, so we'll have plenty of time to catch up on things."

"You *are* coming to the party tomorrow aren't you? Jen is really whipping up quite a spread, and she made some vegetarian dishes with you in mind. She told me to order you to attend."

"Wouldn't miss it for the world."

"Good. Glad you finally made it to a reunion, Duane. You're going to enjoy it, and I guarantee this weekend will get you out of your rut."

6

Alone in my motel room, a shot of vodka in hand, a beer nearby, I ruminate. Under usual circumstances, I prefer a stout beer to chase vodka, but I couldn't resist buying a six pack of Coal Country on the way back to the motel. Coal Country is the quintessential western Pennsylvania beer, a legendary, pale, crisp lager that was the choice of my father and his father before him.

Coal Country Beer is the first alcoholic beverage I ever drank. We were just kids when my brother and I spirited away a bottle from the case that our father kept in the pantry and shared it among the boughs of the maple tree in the backyard. Back then, I couldn't understand the appeal it had for Dad as opposed to more tasteful beverages such as soda pop, or artificial orange juice, but before long, I would understand too well.

Dale looks good for his age, but like me, he looks his age. That saddens me for obvious reasons. I first saw his face when he was a boy, a handsome, eleven year old who had transferred to the fifth grade of Saint Mathew's School from the Homewood public school system. He was having some behavior problems there, and his mother decided it was time to go against the wishes of her husband, who was not a Catholic, and place their son in the hands of the Sisters of Saint Francis.

I liked Dale from the moment I saw him. I liked his looks, his attitude, and the cool shoes he wore: shiny, new penny loafers (without the pennies, of course). Like most of us who were schooled within the sheltered confines of Saint Mathew's, I was drawn to that aura of mystery that surrounded kids from the public school system.

Interestingly enough, Dale was never a behavior problem at Saint Mathew's School, and was actually rather quiet and well behaved. For some reason, however, his arrival and our subsequent friendship triggered my own behavioral issues.

In the beginning, my behavior was undoubtedly born of a desire to make an impression on Dale, an attempt to be cool in my own way, but before long, it went beyond Dale. I became a rascal in my own right and loved the role.

I wasn't the belligerent kind or one to openly challenge the authority of the nuns or priests. We did occasionally have those types at Saint Mathew's, but never for long. Typically, they would not show up in the fall when school started, and we would learn that over the summer, they had transferred to the public school. I wasn't a rebel without a cause type either; I always had a cause. It's just that my cause was usually frivolous, often just the intention of showing off.

One incident that stands out in my mind is the matter of my discharge from the Saint Mathew's Boy Choir. I became a member of the choir in third grade, at the age when boys were encouraged to either join the choir or to become an altar boy. Because my older brother was already in the choir, I followed his footsteps into the small brick building near the convent, known as the Music Room, and became a choir boy.

To be a member of the choir was cool at first. I felt holy and important in my cassock and surplice, hovering above the congregation in the choir loft, like a member of a celestial host. However, it wasn't long before the angelic feeling wore off, and I began to suspect that signing on with the choir wasn't such a good idea.

Sister Marguerite, the choir instructor, was a tiny, elderly woman, with a very even temperament: she rarely became angry with us or voiced her displeasure, and she rarely seemed pleased or complimented us on our performance. I can still picture her, a droll little face in a starch white frame, peering at us over the piano. After we sang a particular piece, she would often sigh and in a melancholic voice say, "let's try it again, boys."

The choir practiced every school day at noon recess while our classmates were outside screaming and laughing and having fun. The Music Room was near the recess area such that we could hear the noise they made, the sounds of freedom and happiness. We sang at seven o'clock Mass every Sunday morning, midnight Mass on Christmas Eve, and practically lived in church during Easter week.

By the time I reached seventh grade, I was desperate to get out of the choir, but by then, I was well aware of the fact that there was no easy way to get out—something that wasn't mentioned when I was being recruited. However, clever lad that I was, I came up with an ingenious plan.

Some of my older friends on Crawford Street were going through puberty; their voices were cracking and squeaking as their vocal chords lengthened and thickened. My vocal chords were still short and thin, but the idea came to me that if I faked that my voice had changed and could convince Sister Marguerite, she would have to let me go. Over the weekend, I rehearsed a squeaky, pubescent voice, and the following Monday, at the start of choir practice, I raised my hand.

1967

"What is it Duane?"

"Sister Marguerite, my voice is changing and I don't think I can sing in the choir anymore."

She stares at me for a moment, and her expression stays the same. Sister Marguerite looks down at the piano before she speaks.

"Come to the front of the room, please. Turn and face the choir. I'll play, and you sing. We'll *see* how much your voice has changed."

What can I do? I have to sing or else admit that I'm lying. If she's making me sing, she mustn't believe me. I know my chances are slim now, but if I don't try, there's no chance.

Sister Marguerite starts playing *Old Folks At Home* by Stephen Foster, which is strange because in the four years that I've been in the choir, we never sang a song like that. We always sing religious songs. She's probably doing it to throw me off, but I know the words. I just have to sing like my voice has changed.

"Way down upon the Swanee River, far, far away.

That's where my heart is turning ever; that's where the old folks stay."

I sound bad enough, but I know that it sounds like I'm faking it. Any second Sister Marguerite is going to stop and yell at me. Why isn't she stopping? She's not even looking up at me. I have to keep singing.

"All up and down the whole creation, sadly I roam."

Now the other guys know what I'm trying to do, and they're making faces at me to make me laugh. If I laugh, I know I'll be in worse trouble. I look up in the air so I can't see them, and I keep singing.

How long is this going to go on? Why is she dragging it out? Oh, now I know what she's doing. Instead of yelling at me, Sister Marguerite is embarrassing me for trying to get out of the choir this way. She's making me look like a fool in front of the other guys, and in the end, I'll still be stuck in the choir. Why did I ever try this stupid idea?

My best bet is to just stop singing and apologize. I'll still be in trouble, but at least I'll get it over with sooner.

"All the world is sad and dreary, every . . ."

Sister Marguerite stops before I have a chance to. She just lifted her fingers from the keys, right in the middle of a line. She still not looking at me, and not saying anything. I guess she's thinking of the best way to tell me off. Look at those guys grinning. They know what's coming and they can't wait.

Sister Marguerite finally speaks, and she says something no

one expects to hear.

"All right then, Duane, I've heard enough. *Get out.*"

I can't believe my ears. Am I really free? I expect Sister Marguerite to say more, so I hesitate, but she doesn't even look up. I go out the door and run straight to the recess area to tell Dale what happened. I'm laughing and making it sound like my trick worked, but something bothers me. Sister Marguerite wasn't fooled; she knew I was faking that my voice had changed. I'm glad that I'm out of the choir, but I can't understand why she let me go.

Three years later, I'm a sophomore in high school, and while crossing the church parking lot, I see Sister Marguerite walking toward the convent with an armload of books. From the time a boy enters first grade at Saint Mathew's, it's ingrained in him that whenever he sees one of the sisters carrying anything, he must make a beeline to her and offer his services. Thus in spite of the history between us, I approach Sister Marguerite.

In the time since my departure from the choir, I haven't spoken with her again. Sister Marguerite is an obscure personality on campus, who rarely attends school functions, and passes most of her time at the convent or in the Music Room. I do know that she no longer directs the choir and her only duty outside the convent is to teach piano lessons.

As I come up alongside her, I'm surprised at how small she is. When I first met Sister Marguerite, she was taller than me, and now I'm nearly a head taller than her. I'm also struck by how friendly and gracious she is. She thanks me and gladly transfers the books to my arms.

Sister Marguerite addresses me by my first name, so I assume that she hasn't forgotten my infamous performance of *Old Folks at Home*, but if she does remember, she isn't mentioning it. Instead we talk about the coming of spring, about the convent gardens that she cares for, and about her ongoing war with dandelions. I think that Sister Marguerite has smiled more in this brief encounter than she did during the entire four years I was in the choir.

Looking back, my guess is that Sister Marguerite hadn't enjoyed teaching the choir anymore than I enjoyed being a member of it, but she had no choice. As a nun, she'd taken a vow of obedience, and so in spite of what her personal aspirations might have been, she was doing her duty. Perhaps that's why she often stared listlessly from behind the piano and was gloomy much of the time.

Since then, I've met many people with the same vacant look in their eyes, people who are doing their duty in spite of what their aspirations might be. Oddly enough, these folks aren't even bound by a vow of obedience.

As I refill my shot glass, and open another Coal Country, I hum the melody to *Old Folks At Home*. I don't know what became of Sister Marguerite after I left Saint Mathew's but I think about her on occasion. At the least, I like to believe that whenever she heard *Old Folks At Home,* she thought about my rendition with amusement, like I still do today.

Maybe Sister Marguerite let me go that day because she could relate to my desire to be released from doing something I didn't want to do. Or perhaps when she realized that I would carry my ruse to such an extreme, she knew that she might as well let me go, that I would stop at nothing to be free—and she was right.

7

Is this where it happened, here in this sad old building? Is this where we were born, where we lived and laughed and cried, learned to love and hate and everything in between? Brothers and sisters, cats and dogs, birthdays, holidays, and one funeral. Then we wandered out the door with abandon.

I stare at the house I grew up in, a run-down, two story stone building that stands at the corner of an unkempt lot. A realtor sign looks as if it's been hanging in place for years, adding to my dreary perspective of the property: besides being neglected, it's unwanted. The front porch sags under the weight of time, untrustworthy boards are evident through chipped and peeling paint, and clouded windows with broken down blinds give the impression of sad old eyes looking wearily out from the past.

Such an introduction to the Ryan home place should convince me not to explore further, but I wander down the side alley anyway, enticed by memories of my past. Upon viewing the back of the property, I wish I had resisted the temptation. A collection of furniture and appliances covers the rear porch and spills off one end into the yard. A large, overstuffed couch is the centerpiece and beside it, sits a rusted washing machine.

Both couch and washer are piled with boxes, in a way that suggests some sort of order, but I can't decide at first if someone is moving out or moving in. Judging from the weathered condition of everything on the porch, the most likely explanation is that these items are simply being stored here.

The yard is hardly recognizable for what it used to be. Where are all the trees? Where is the magnificent maple that grew beside the garage, the one that was the best climbing tree in the neighborhood? Old and stout, with a thick web of branches, spread in all directions, we actually played catch in that tree, scampering around its boughs like monkeys. Other times we would just sit up there and talk for hours, especially when we had friends or cousins over. For we kids, the maple tree was an extension of the house, an arboreal living room of sorts. Could that weathered stump, standing dark and lifeless in a clump of weeds, be all that remains of that grand old tree?

Where is the boxwood hedge that surrounded the yard and framed our little world? My father was proud of that magnificent old hedge, which was planted by the builders of the house half a century before he arrived. Dad spent many hours caring for it and introduced Will and me to hedge clippers at an early age to help with the cause.

I don't know why these changes bother me now; I was never sentimental about the old home place before. My philosophy has always been that time moves on and it's best to leave the past where it is. I unscrew the cap of my bottled lemonade and drink to that wise principle.

A clever tactic that I've employed for some years now is to buy a sixteen ounce bottle of lemonade, drink about a third of its contents, and then bring the bottle back up to full measure with vodka. Little do people suspect as they hurry by on their way to some respectable engagement, that this forlorn looking man, skulking about the alleyways, is actually having a little private party. I admit, there's not much to celebrate, but I never let that stop me.

My father was so proud of this property, that I'm glad he'll never see it in such a sad state. Too bad one of us offspring didn't take it over in the end and maintain the old place. What nonsense am I thinking now? My siblings were as anxious to get out of Homewood as I was, and with good reason. The town was scraping bottom at the time, with no sign that it would right itself soon. We're scattered in all directions now, and hardly think about each other anymore, let alone consider this old house. My brother, Will, lives in Virginia, and yet I haven't seen him in years.

I was dying to get away from Homewood after my claustrophobic years at Saint Mathew's School, anxious to get out into the wide world, where nobody knew me and where I could be anonymous. I didn't know exactly what I wanted to do, only what I didn't want to do, and I knew that I didn't want to stay around here and be like everybody else. Since then, I've been so focused on my career, that where I was from or what happened to this old place hardly affected me—until now. Could it be because I'm scraping bottom now, with no sign that I'll right myself soon?

Looking around, I see Pittsburgh Steelers bumper stickers on cars going by and Steelers flags, hanging off porches, and it takes me back to those golden years in the early seventies when the Steelers were winning Super bowls. I was in my twenties then as were my siblings and friends, and we often returned to Homewood for special occasions such as holidays and Steelers football games.

Weekend parties, arranged around a Steelers' Football game were common and our house seemed to be the natural focal point. If the weather was nice, we would play football in the yard before the game, then throw some burgers on the grill, drink a beer or two on the back porch, and go inside to watch the Steel Curtain shut down another hapless team.

How nice it would be to see this old place as it was back then, with the magnificent trees and the boxwood hedge. What a joy it would be to have a Steelers Football weekend again with my brothers and sisters and the old gang. I hear the Steelers are pretty good these days, too. Listen to me, I haven't watched a football game in twenty years; I can't even name one player on the Steelers team. I better get away from this place; it's playing with my head.

I take one more drink for the memories and turn to go when

I'm startled by a voice close beside me. I turn to see a small, elderly man, smiling and staring at me.

"Mr. Liston?"

"Hah ha, I thought it was you, Duane, but I wasn't sure. Didn't recognize me at first either, did you?"

"I'm sorry, Mr. Liston, but you caught me off guard. I was daydreaming. How did you guess it was me?"

"I noticed a truck with North Carolina plates across the street from the house here, and I remembered that was where you moved to. Then when I saw someone standing here, looking at the old place, I guessed it might be you."

"You spotted my plates from your house?"

"Well, binoculars helped. When you see a sign around here that says 'neighborhood watch', you better believe it's true when I'm doing the watching. How long you in for?"

"Until Monday. I'm here for my class reunion."

"That's right I read in the paper about the Saint Mathew's reunion. Well good to see you again, Duane. Say you in a hurry? Want to come over for a beer and catch up on things?"

"You still make your own?"

"Sure do."

"Can't turn that down."

Moments later I'm sitting in Tom Liston's living room, his dog, Pepper, hovering near me. She seems beside herself that I'm in the house. For as long as I can remember, the Listons have had a dog like Pepper, some sort of beagle mix, and always with a name like Pepper, or Missy, or Happy.

Mr. Liston returns from the kitchen and soon I'm sampling one of his fine porters. Beer making has been a hobby of his for over half a century now, and needless to say, his product is very good.

The Liston house is much as I remember it, which is just the tonic I need to offset the shock of seeing the Ryan home place. When I was growing up, Tom Liston and his wife, Martha, were a small town couple straight out of a Norman Rockwell painting. A little older than my own parents, they were delighted when Mom and Dad moved into the neighborhood with an infant son and even more so as four children followed.

The Listons only had one child, Max, who was five years older than me and had Down syndrome. We all liked Max and he was at our house and in our yard often. He was the man of a thousand jokes, and one year, after he took up the harmonica, became the man of a thousand tunes as well. His health was never good: heart trouble, kidney failure, and diabetes, to name the worst of it. Max died one night in his sleep at the age of forty and we were all devastated at the news.

Mr. Liston is becoming more familiar to me as we talk. I can see now that he's a shrunken version of the man I once knew, but he looks good, healthy and alert, for his age, which I calculate must be around ninety.

"Marty's been dead eleven years now, Duane."

"Yah, I know; Mom told me about that. She used to get the Homewood paper in Florida."

"I never thought I'd get over it, let alone live this much longer. I think about her everyday. I hear her voice sometimes. Cancer got her, lung cancer. She couldn't quit smoking; smoked right to the end. You know we put her favorite ash tray in the casket with her."

"No."

"Yeah, we did. It was Marty's request."

We both have a chuckle and sip our beers for a moment.

"How old are you now, Mr. Liston?"

"Turned ninety-one in the spring."

"Wow, you look good. How does it feel to be in your nineties?"

"To tell you the truth, Duane, sometimes when I think about it, I don't know if I should laugh or I should cry."

"Laugh then. Being ninety is one thing I don't have to think about. Ryan males don't tend to live long."

"You never know, sometimes it runs in families, but other times it's a chance thing. Nobody else in my family got out of their

46

eighties. You can't go on what happened to your father though, Duane, that was just bad luck. It still bothers me, the way Andy died."

"Me too. I think it's bothered me more as I've gotten older and can imagine it from his point of view."

"You know, Duane, your father and I were good friends. He was like a younger brother to me in some ways, and we talked about a lot of things. Did you know that he thought you might take over the coal business one day?"

"No, he did?"

"He said it more than once, just not to you. He didn't want to pressure you into it and he wanted you to give college a try. But he saw the way you took to it, the way you fit in with the crew when you worked there."

"I had no idea."

"Well, it wasn't to be. Fate had other things in store for both of you. I still miss your father after all these years. He had his own way of looking at things and I always liked hearing his point of view. You remind me of him, Duane. You're different than him in a lot of ways, but like him in basic ways."

"Well thanks, Mr. Liston. Nobody has ever said that before, but I consider it a compliment."

"It is. Boy oh boy, your father loved that old house over there."

"I know. Just before you came up behind me, I was thinking that it's good he can't see it now. Who owns it, anyway?"

"Some big shot lawyer from out in Fairdale; last name's Thompson. I think he bought it mostly as a tax write-off; puts almost no money into it. Cut all the trees and bushes down so he wouldn't have to pay someone to do trimming or rake leaves. Divided it up into apartments that he'll rent to anyone, so it's little wonder that the place has been trashed.

Rather than make the repairs it needs, Thompson's trying to sell it now. Friend of mine has the real estate contract, but she said it's been no easy sell. Hasn't had any good offers, and Mr. Fancy

Pants is griping at her about it all the time, like it's her fault."

"Well, maybe the right person will come along, someone like Dad."

"I don't know if those kind of people exist anymore, Duane. If they do, they don't come around here.

Say you need another beer there, young man? Your bottle's nearly empty and I'm heading to the kitchen."

"Uh, yah, thanks. I have to take it easy here though. I'm going to a party this afternoon and I want to at least arrive sober."

"I'll cut you off in time."

Mr. Liston goes to the kitchen and I take the opportunity to look over the pictures that hang above the couch. One that catches my attention is of Martha Liston when she was young, maybe in her early twenties. She's standing on the bumper of an old car, a Packard I think, laughing and apparently just acting silly for the photographer.

Next to this is a picture of Mr. and Mrs. Liston with their son, Max, when he was an infant. Max is grinning and his parents are beaming with pride. I focus on another picture of Max, taken when he was older, the way I remember him. He was such a nice guy, always excited and happy to be a part of our activities. When we played football, he wore an old leather helmet that an uncle had given him. I still remember the sound of his voice as he charged along the sidelines with the football tucked under his arm, laughing and shouting out that he was Franco Harris.

I turn from the photographs and sit back down as Mr. Liston comes into the room and hands me a beer.

"How's your work going, Duane?"

"Uh, pretty good. Well, not real good. I went through a rough period a while back, a divorce and all. I'm having trouble getting going again."

"I'm sorry to hear that. I didn't know you and Cathy divorced."

"Yah, we divorced, too, but this time it was Elaine and I."

"Oh, sorry, I'm afraid I'm behind the times."

"Ah, that's okay. This was still five years ago, and I should be over it by now. But it's not just that; there are other things going on, too. I haven't lost my enthusiasm for carving—at least I don't think I have—but I can't seem to push myself like I used to. I don't know which direction to go now, and I used to never think about it. I just kept on going. I'm sorry Mr. Liston, I know I probably sound like a whiner, but it's just. . ."

"How old are you now, Duane, mid fifties, right?"

"Yes, fifty-five."

"Duane, your fifties can be a rough time, if you let it get to you. You have a pretty good feel for what life's all about by now, and you realize that in spite of the good things, it's not all it's cut out to be. Some religious types rationalize the disappointments as our worldly trials, preparing us for the eternal reward, but I don't buy that. I believe in God, but I don't think He meddles in our daily affairs like that.

What I think, Duane, overall life is about loss, and there's no getting around that. How you deal with the losses determines how happy you are and what you're going to accomplish. You've got to let people go and push on with your own life. Lordy, lordy, everybody I had once is gone now: Max, Marty, Mom and Pop, my brothers and sisters. It hurts, but hurt wears away with time. A person can't just curl up in a ball and feel sorry for themselves. As long as your still alive, you have to keep living.

I'm ninety-one now, and I know I don't have much time left, but I wake up every morning with plans in my head, some new project to work on. Maybe that's what you need, Duane, some new project."

I listen to Mr. Liston's advice much as I might have many years ago and recognize the same simple logic that has guided him through his long life. I smile and raise my bottle.

"Thanks, Mr. Liston, cheers."

"Cheers, Duane."

8

I purposely drive by the house. Why the hell am I so nervous? The party seems to be well attended; cars are parked everywhere. Why wouldn't it be? Dale and Jen are both popular. I was popular once, too, back in my youth. I was often class president and had a wide array of friends. Back then, I was downright gregarious and extroverted, not to mention, spontaneous, trendy, and mischievous.

But everything changed by the time I entered Saint Mathew's High School. Over the course of the preceding summer, I became a different person: quiet, aloof, detached, and indifferent, to restate some of the adjectives used by those who attempted to describe my personality.

My grades slid to average, I never held a class office again, and rarely participated in school activities. Two major events led to my transformation during the summer of 1969: the Woodstock Music Festival and the Vietnam War.

I loved music from an early age and was an avid fan of many of the musicians who performed at the Woodstock Festival: Crosby, Stills, Nash, and Young, The Who, Joe Cocker, Janis Joplin, Sly and the Family Stone, The Band, Jefferson Airplane, and Jimi Hendrix. And I was introduced to new and intriguing personalities like Joan Baez, Arlo Guthrie, Ritchie Havens, Ravi Shankar, and John Sebastian.

Before 1969, the Vietnam War had been an abstract event that

I'd been vaguely aware of since I was ten or so. I never questioned the foundations of the war or doubted the righteousness of my country's involvement in this tiny country that I had never heard of before. Like many Americans, I assumed that it was just a matter of time before we won and it would be over. I would listen to reports of the war on nightly television news and since the body count for the Viet Cong was always higher than for us, I felt confident that we were winning.

The Woodstock Festival and the words expressed there by my musical heroes altered my view of the Vietnam War and of my country. I began to question all that I had been told, and my opinion of society and religion began to change soon after.

The summer of 1969 was a watershed in my life, the repercussions of which, affect me even now, as I cruise by Dale's house for the second time. I was too young to go to Woodstock or Vietnam. I've always regretted that I couldn't attend the Woodstock Festival and have always been thankful that the war ended before I had to worry about being drafted. Both events are many years in my past now and while I didn't became a musician or an activist, I never again settled comfortably into society.

Now as far as my current popularity is concerned, the truth is that in spite of my unsocial tendencies, I'm fairly well liked, albeit not popular like Dale. I'm not a surly or a mean person, and that counts for something. I'm not a hothead, even though I do have a temper. Not a short fuse, but I definitely have a fuse, one that's hard to put out once it's burning.

"It's just the Irish in you", Grandmother Ryan would say matter-of-factly. Whatever it is, I've never liked it; I've worked at it. One approach that has proven to be effective is to simply avoid people, and as I get older and grumpier, the circle of people that I choose to avoid is expanding.

After I pass Dale's house for the third time, I veer to the side of the road and park behind a charcoal-colored Jaguar. I take note that one of my former schoolmates has done well or at least likes to splurge on pretentious, impractical vehicles. I bet if I put my truck in four wheel drive, I could run right over the car without even noticing.

It's time to be sociable. I withdraw the flask of vodka from my coat pocket and take a few long sips. There's nothing like a little bottled self-confidence before committing to an uncertain social situation.

I step away from the truck and steer myself in the direction of the house, convinced that I can face these people. After all, I've done something different than any of them, no matter how much money they make. I'm a professional artist, and there's no denying that, no matter how little money I make. I straighten my tweed jacket, smooth my hair back, and place myself in sociable mode.

As I draw near, I hear familiar music: *Street Fighting Man* by the Rolling Stones, a song that has long been a favorite of mine. To the casual listener, the song's lyrics seem to be a rare political statement by the Stones, a call to revolution, but I've always interpreted the words as a call to take action, while at the same time, questioning whether it will really make any difference. Now there's a conundrum I can relate to.

I hear voices and laughter intermingled with Mick's boisterous poetry, and I recognize the unmistakable clink of ice against glass— now that's music to my ears. The party is in the backyard, and I stroll around the south side of the house, foregoing the paved pathway to the north to avoid unnecessary attention. I weave my way through shrubs and trees and follow my olfactory senses to locate my friend who I suspect will be manning the grill. I emerge from the drooping branches of red pine and spy Dale, spatula in hand, talking with a stout, bald man.

"So what animal are you serving up today, old man?"

Dale turns in my direction and grins.

"Pigs, well their ribs at least. Where's your plate? You look like you need fattened up a little. Duane, I'm sure you remember Mr. Robert Macy? How long has it been since you two have seen each other?"

I struggle to contain my shock. Could this be Bob Macy, my

skinny high school classmate with the curly hair that he relentlessly tried to straighten? He obviously no longer has concern about his curliness, or his skinniness for that matter.

In high school, Bob was a common friend to Dale and me, although closer to Dale, as evidenced by the fact that they have remained in touch over the years while aside from an occasional telephone conversation, Bob and I have not. He grins and shakes my hand.

"Duane, it's been a long time. Don't look so surprised. I know the years have taken their toll on me, but to be honest with you, if you hadn't come sneaking around the house like that, I would never have guessed it was you either. What have you been up to?"

"Oh, same old, same old, Bob; still have the gallery in North Carolina. How about you, are you still in Newport News? Dale usually keeps me up on these things."

"Well he's a little behind this time, because Darlene and I moved back to Homewood last year. We got a place over on Mayflower Drive near the Country Club. We're semi-retired right now, but want to start another business here: computer software again, but on a much smaller scale."

"That's good news, Bob. It's nice to hear that someone has moved back to Homewood. The trend is usually in the opposite direction."

"Not anymore, Duane. Homewood's changing and people *are* moving back. You remember Nick and Lisa Smathers from high school don't you?"

"Oh yah, are they still together?"

"They sure are. They've lived in Philadelphia for years now, but they've decided to move back to Homewood."

"Really?"

"Yes indeed. They're in for the reunion this weekend, but for the last six months they've been back and forth, looking for land to build on. In fact, Nick was in just a few weeks ago checking out some land up on Laurel Ridge. I went with him to walk the property and on the way back through town, we stopped for a beer at Mutt's Place."

"Mutt's, that place is still in operation? God, we used to buy beer there when we were in high school."

"That's why Nick and I decided to go there, mostly for old time's sake. But hey, that reminds me, and I didn't get to tell *you* this either, Dale. Neither of you will guess who Nick and I saw at Mutt's. We ran into Carmen."

"Carmen, as in Carmen the janitor?"

"Yes Dale, the same old Carmen, he was at the bar, and fairly drunk I might add. Why, what's wrong? Why are you looking at me like that?"

"Carmen was found dead in his apartment yesterday morning."

"No."

"Yes, I read it in the paper, Carmen Vincenzi. They even mentioned that he was a former janitor at Saint Mathew's High School."

I had nearly forgotten Carmen, the cantankerous janitor at Saint Mathew's School. I remember him as a short, plump man in his late forties with a dark complexion, greasy, slicked back hair, bib overalls, and a low, raspy voice. He was usually grumpy and often complaining out loud, but at the same time, he was trustworthy and loyal to those of us he liked. We often hid in the custodial room to skip class without worry of being given away, and for years he knew that we smoked cigarettes in the boiler room, a small room behind the oil furnace.

"I'm stunned. He didn't look good, but I didn't see him at death's door either. What did he die from?"

"The article didn't mention that. Did you talk to him?"

"Yah, I did, and it seemed like he remembered me, too. I was in a good mood and I thought I would tease him a little about how he bricked up the entry to the boiler room."

"That was strange, wasn't it? At the end of our senior year, to have the boiler room sealed up like that. It was a neat little hangout while it lasted. I ask Carmen back then why he did it, and he just said that Father McGee told him to."

"That's what he said at Mutt's the other night, Duane, but I kept after him about it, just joking, of course, complaining that he ruined our hangout. Then, all of a sudden, he started acting weird."

"Carmen always acted weird."

"I know, but this was different. It seemed like he drifted away and was thinking about something else and not even listening to me. He started mumbling to himself and saying how sorry he was that he did it."

"That *is* weird, even for Carmen."

"Yes, that's what I thought. This is what he said: 'I should never have done it. Father McGee told me it was for the best, but it was a damn sin. I shouldn't have done it'."

"All he did was close up a weird little room that was used by delinquent high school boys as a smoking parlor. Why should he be so remorseful or sin-struck?"

"That's exactly what I tried to find out, Dale, but when I asked him, he got angry and yelled at me: 'leave me alone; get away from me'.

Other people at the bar were giving us the eye by then, so Nick and I took our beers to a table and left him alone. But, hell, I would never have bothered him at all, if I'd known he had such a short time to live."

"Now Bob, don't be too hard on yourself. It took a few weeks before your interrogation did him in."

"Thanks, Duane. I feel better now."

"I'm kidding, Bob, you know that, but, how strange. Why would Carmen get so upset over something that seems so simple and stupid?"

"Ah, maybe just too much drink over the years and he got a little batty in the end."

"That's what Nick and I decided that night, but I guess we'll never know, now."

"Well, I feel bad about Carmen. I guess not so much because

he died since I had nearly forgotten that he ever lived, but I'm sorry that he was drunk and angry in the end. That's a fate I sometimes fear for myself."

Dale is silent as he turns a pork rib on the grill. Fat drips onto hot coals and a crackling, sputtering sound accompanies a small plume of smoke that rises between us toward the sky. I wonder if I said too much with that statement, and so I speak quickly to keep the focus on Carmen.

"Wasn't his relationship to Duke interesting? He would do anything Father McGee asked. Carmen adored the man."

"He sure did. I think I understand it though. Carmen was gruff and crude, but he was an unwavering Catholic, and religious, too. Father McGee was his kind of priest: a little rough around the edges, a hard-ass, John Wayne type priest. Duke was Carmen's kind of link to God, or at least back then he was. After what happened at Mutt's, I can't quite figure what Carmen thought about the guy."

Dale remains silent as Bob speaks, and then he decides to end the conversation.

"Say Bob, can I trust you to take over the grill while I reintroduce *El Longlosto* to his fellow alumni?"

"I will do my best, master chef. I promise to leave no rib unturned. Now don't overdose Duane on society."

I'm surprised at Bob's remark, but a part of me hopes that Dale will take his words to heart. Dale and I move along the perimeter of the crowd as he leads me toward the house and eventually into the kitchen where his wife, Jen, is preparing food. Jen is an excellent cook and loves her craft such that the ribs will have stiff competition.

When we enter the kitchen, Dale and Jen's daughter, sees us first. She hugs me and gives me a kiss on the cheek. I've known Lisa since she was born and now she's a sophomore in college. Jen notices the commotion and comes across the room in her apron to greet me.

"It's about time you made it this way," she shouts playfully as she throws her arms around me. We chat briefly, but Jen is obviously distracted and needs to return to her preparations. Before she does she grabs a plate and serves up a large portion of spinach lasagna with a creamy pea salad on the side.

"Here, I thought of you when I made these, and I want to make sure you get some while I've got you here."

Dale grabs two bottles of Coal Country from the refrigerator and ushers me back outside to introduce me to former classmates. What a shock! I remember these people and they seem to be basically the same, but now, like me, they have older faces. All are surprised to see me and most seem genuinely happy that I'm here.

I'm in the mood now: the music is good, the food is excellent, I have a cold beer in hand. I'm enjoying the stories and marvel at the variety of careers and lifestyles that resulted from a common beginning. In return, I accommodate with sweeping summations of my own experiences in life (of course, leaving out the gritty details for the sake of politeness).

I learn that similar festivities are taking place at other locations in Homewood this evening, each representing a different class that graduated from Saint Mathew's High School. This is a tradition that has evolved for Friday of the reunion weekend and is followed by a formal dance, Saturday evening, when all the classes come together. I hadn't really planned on going to the dance, but at the moment, with so much good cheer and lively conversation swirling around me, I feel that I just might. I'm glad I came to the party now.

Then I turn to find myself face to face with Mark Peterson, someone I tended to avoid in high school, and in the spirit of reunion, I try to forget what a boor and braggart he was back then. Mark politely allows me to sum up my life and career in a few lines, smiling and nodding in a way that causes me to wonder if perhaps I judged him too harshly in the past. Then he counters with an exhaustive account of his exceptional life, his remarkable family, and last but not least, of his courageous career, working as a psychologist for the pentagon—same old Mark.

While I'm thus engaged, Dale is called away to attend to a logistical problem, so that by the time I'm finally able to extricate myself from the verbal onslaught, I'm alone, adrift in a pool of voices, standing apart from the crowd and observing. An old familiar scene where everybody seems to fit in effortlessly, moving from conversation to conversation while I struggle to find a slot to fit into without Dale nearby to act as my social liaison.

Just as I'm approaching my threshold for human crowd tolerance and the thought enters my head that I might go back to the motel and zone out with a movie and some vodka, I feel a light tapping on my shoulder. I turn and peer into pale green eyes and the face of a beautiful female who is smiling as if she knows me. The woman has brunette hair that hangs in rivulets to her shoulders and she wears a dress that is elegant but in a casual, earthy way, a style that is akin to my own taste in fashion.

Instantly, computer-like, my eyes scan the woman's face in an attempt to calculate her age. When I meet a younger woman these days, I usually hope that she's older than she appears so that she might be in my ten year, younger woman-older man ballpark or at least make the fifteen year exception. However, I needn't play that game this time, because this woman is clearly too young to make the cut.

"Are you Duane Ryan?"

"Y-yes, I am."

"My name is Brittany Schuster. It's nice to meet you. First of all, I want to tell you how much I admire your work."

I shake her soft, inviting hand, marveling at the refreshing change in company from Mark Peterson.

"It's nice to meet you Brittany. Thank you for the kind words about my work."

"They're not just kind words. I work in an art gallery in Santa Fe and I've followed your career for a number of years now. I was hoping to finally meet you."

"Schuster; why does that name sound familiar to me? You couldn't have attended Saint Mathew's High School."

"No, I didn't, but you knew my sister, Sally Schuster."

"I did?"

"Sister Sally."

"Sister Sally? Oh, *that* Sally Schuster. Your sister was Sister Sally?"

"Yes, well, half-sister. My mother was married before. Sally is the daughter of her and her first husband."

I'm stunned; Brittany seems to know it and smiles. Memories of this mysterious personality from my past, who we referred to at Saint Mathew's as *Sister Sally*, begin to flood my mind, so that it's with great effort that I keep my thoughts focused on the person in front of me.

"Well, Brittany, this *is* a surprise. Is Sally here?"

"No, I came alone. Actually, I came because I was hoping you would be here. Could we go somewhere to talk?"

"Uh, sure, why not? As a matter of fact, I was just leaving."

9

1973

"So, are you surprised that the statue was stolen?"

"Yes Sister, I am."

"Duane, don't do that. Please call me Sally. I'm not a sister yet, and besides, I like to hear you say my name: just Sally, not Sister or Sister Sally."

I smile, knowing full well that Sally Schuster isn't a nun yet. In spite of her objection, the truth is that *Sister Sally* has become a nickname of sorts for Sally Schuster, everybody's favorite nun-in-training. I'm in love with Sister Sally, and it's a pleasure just to hear the sound of her voice. I say 'Sister' sometimes just so she'll correct me. Perhaps it's part of some kinky syndrome I've developed over twelve years of instruction under the Sisters of Saint Francis that I especially like to hear her scold me.

Sally Schuster is a beautiful and charming twenty year old woman who has certainly charmed me, an eighteen year old senior at Saint Mathew's High School. She has recently entered her novitiate, a period when a young woman who aspires to be a nun learns about religious life and the ways of the sisterhood. Sally lives in the convent and participates in the day to day life of the Sisters of Saint Francis, but is not a full member of the order because she hasn't taken the vows of sisterhood: poverty, celibacy, and obedience.

During her novitiate, Sally has a novice director, an experienced, older sister who is responsible for her development as a nun, and in my opinion, she has the very best of novice directors in Sister Mary Agatha. Sally is supported by the sisterhood and does not have to work in the outside world, so she helps in the school library, where we are talking now.

"So, *Mister Ryan*, are you surprised that the statue was stolen?"

"I sure am. I'm surprised that anyone would want it. I just hope Renata Barlow doesn't offer to replace it."

"Who is Renata Barlow?"

"A wealthy member of the parish. She and her husband donated the statue to the church about fifteen years ago. Mr. Barlow just died, but you may have noticed them together earlier this year, sitting up front during Mass. She's a lot younger than him and dresses real wild."

"Yes, I know exactly who you mean, but she's so different from him that I didn't think they were married."

"She's different all right. I guess he met her when he was traveling in Brazil, sometime after his first wife died. Giving the statue to the church was her idea and she brought it back after one of her trips home. Nobody wanted to question the gift and risk offending Mr. Barlow because of all the money he gave to the church over the years, but the statue gave everybody the creeps right from the start—those big eyes and funny little teeth. I'm sure that even Monsignor Schroeder didn't like it, and that's probably why it was back in the vestibule all these years."

"Well, whatever the story on the statue is, I hate to see this sort of thing happen; it changes the whole atmosphere of the church. A church shouldn't have to be locked and some people are pushing for that now."

"Namely, Father McGee, right? What a surprise. He's probably wanted the church locked ever since he came here. He's the paranoid type anyway; used to be at some big church in Phoenix or somewhere out west. You know he belongs to the NRA, don't you? And I heard, he has a collection of guns in his office. *From out of the wild west, came the gun slinging priest to clean up Saint Mathew's parish.* I never read in the bible that Jesus carried a gun."

"Come on Duane, stop it. Why do you have it in for Father McGee?"

"Me have it in for him? Sally, he's been on my case ever since I got to high school. The man just doesn't like me."

"Father McGee is on your case because he thinks you have great potential; he doesn't think you try like you should."

"What, how do you know? Did he tell you that?"

"N-no, not really; that's just what I think."

"Hmm, I sure have never seen it that way."

"Well, whatever, I won't miss the statue. It always gave me the creeps, too. It's not the way I want to picture Jesus as a boy. You know, there's a rumor that Bob Macy was behind the theft."

"Really, why?"

"Because of something else he did. Something about hiding someone's car and they thought it was stolen."

"Oh yeah, I was there that day. That was a brilliant joke, Sally. Bob got fifteen of us to pick up Phil Pantalo's VW bug from the high school parking lot and carry it halfway up Tuesday Alley, the little alley between the parking lot and Shady Lane. Phil was fooled and reported his car stolen. If it hadn't been for the fact that fifty people witnessed it, Bob might have gotten away with it. The police weren't too upset over the incident, but Sister Mary Agatha sure was.

I don't think Bob's behind the statue disappearance, though; it doesn't really seem like his style to me. I do know he's the one who put the sunglasses and the Grateful Dead tee shirt on the statue a couple years ago."

"Why are you smiling? Do you think that's funny, to desecrate a statue of Jesus?"

"No, not at all. I think it's a despicable thing to do, and Bob deserves hard time in purgatory for it. I'm smiling because, uh, I'm just happy. I'm always happy when I'm here in the library."

"Are you happy because you're here with me?"

"Y-yes, I am."

"Duane, could I ask you something? Why don't you go to the dances or date anyone?"

"I date, or I did, and I used to go to the dances. I just split up with someone last summer, that's part of it. Why are you asking?"

"Because I was wondering, if I were a girl in your class would you want to go to a dance with me?"

I sense that Sally is asking more with this question than just whether or not I would want to accompany her to a dance and I can feel my face reddening. My hunch that Sally has the same feelings for me that I have for her is gaining credence by the second. I step closer before I answer because I perceive that this is the moment I have been waiting for.

I smile and respond to Sally's question by simply nodding, and that seems to be romantic enough for her. She smiles and takes the last step that separates us; her eyes tell me what she wants me to do. I encircle her waist with my arms and press my cheek gently against hers, inhaling the wonderful fragrance of the woman I'm in love with. Sally sighs; we hold each other for half a minute, trembling.

I move my hands up and down her back, caressing and exploring. She places her hands on each side of my head, we look into each others eyes, and then I kiss her. Sally Schuster and I as a couple is a crazy idea, but so what? Everything about life seems crazy these days. We'll make it work somehow. I'll quit high school and she'll quit the sisterhood, and then we'll run off to California and become children of the sun, living on the beach, kissing and holding each other for the rest of our lives.

Our lips meet again; two bodies press together in perfect complement. I know that we shouldn't be doing this here, but there seems to be no turning back. Then suddenly, I am turned back and pulled away from Sally by a forceful heave on my arm.

Father McGee's face is crimson. He's breathing in short, hard bursts, exhaling through his nostrils like an enraged bull. He releases my arm, grasps the lapels of my coat in a powerful, tight fist, and pulls me close. Father McGee glares into my face but speaks to Sally.

"Sally, go to my office. I'll be there shortly."

"F-Father McGee, we, I , it's not really . . ."

"Sally, go to my office, *now*."

Sally hesitates, but leaves the library. Father McGee's gaze grows more menacing the moment she closes the door. He tightens his grip on my coat and pulls me closer.

"You asshole, I ought to beat the crap out of you. What the hell is wrong with you? How could you do this?"

"It wasn't just . . ."

"Shut up. You've been a disappoint to me ever since I met you, but this beats all. How dare you take advantage of Sally?"

"But I . . ."

"Shut up."

Father McGee continues to hold me, but with diminishing force. His breathing slows, and the threatening stare gives way to an expression of sadness and introspection. He maintains his hold on my jacket for a few seconds more and then lets go with a sigh. Father McGee turns and walks away, leaving the door open.

I'm embarrassed, ashamed, mortified, and I'm scared for Sally and me. I know I'm in big trouble and I don't know what will happen to her. This is what Father McGee has been waiting for, the big screw-up that will enable him to kick me out of school. He doesn't want an atheist to graduate from Saint Mathew's School anyway. What bad timing with only two months left until graduation. Two more months and I would have been out of here and free of him.

Well, screw you, Duke. I don't believe in you or your God and you know it. You have no power over me and that's why you hate me. I don't need your damn diploma. Sally and I will run away to California. We'll be children of the sun, living on the beach, and you'll still be a stupid priest, here at St Mathew's."

10

"So Duane, what made you choose wood as a medium?"

"I didn't really choose wood; I think it chose me. I started carving wood when I was about eleven years old, as a Boy Scout. In fact, the first merit badge I received was Woodcarving."

"How interesting! And you've never looked back since?"

"Oh yes, I've looked back many times. In fact I have a crook in my neck from looking back."

"But I mean, it's been your passion ever since."

"Passion, I don't know if I'd call woodcarving a passion. Addiction is probably a better way to describe it. I can't seem to give it up."

"I can relate to that. It surprises me though that you've stuck with wood all these years. Wood is such a primitive and unpredictable medium for a contemporary artist."

"Those are some of the reasons I like wood as a medium. I don't think of it as primitive; it's historic. Woodcarving was one of earliest art forms. Jesus Christ was a woodcarver, did you know that?"

"I thought He was a carpenter."

"Nah, that's what they teach in Sunday school, but after studying ancient biblical texts I came to a different conclusion. Jesus was actually a woodcarver."

"Really, I never heard that before."

"Actually, Brittany, I read that a long time ago in a woodcarving manual, and it was just speculation by the author. I often repeat it as fact, but I've never found any historical evidence to back it up. On the other hand, there's not much evidence to back up anything about Jesus, so why couldn't He have been a woodcarver?"

Brittany and I are drinking wine at the East Side Tap, one of my old haunts. As the name implies, it's located on the east side of Homewood, in a neighborhood that has obviously benefited from the city's revival. I was hoping that the place might still be in operation after all these years, and I'm delighted to find that not only is it open for business, but the old East Side Tap is doing well. The bar is full and we're actually lucky to get a booth.

Brittany Schuster is more alluring with each passing moment and more desirable with each sip of wine. I'm trying to control myself, trying to be professional and sophisticated, but just as the Roman philosopher, Pliny the Elder foretold when he said, "*in vino veritas*", the wine is converting me into my true, decadent self.

I have a feeling that Brittany is flirting with me. It's probably just wishful thinking, but whether it is or not, the old corpuscles are firing like they haven't fired in years. Instinctively, I commence to lay the verbiage on a little thicker.

"Now as far as wood being an unpredictable medium, I think that's one of the reasons it's continued to be my medium of choice. Early on in my career it was a problem, because I planned out every piece carefully. I did sketches and a clay models before I began a piece, but rarely did the finished carving match my plans.

I'd run into a knot or a hollow area or some other problem hidden in the log and would have to change my idea to work around it. Over time, I've not only come to accept the imperfections, I relish the challenge of dealing with them. These days, I start working on a piece of wood with only an outline of an idea and allow it to develop while the work is in progress."

"So in a sense, you're making the piece up as you go."

"Yes, with every piece to some degree; with abstract pieces, most definitely. For me, an abstract piece is an interaction between inspiration and a piece of hardwood."

"That's really awesome."

Uh oh, I wish Brittany hadn't said that. For one thing, I've never really accepted the word 'awesome' as a suitable replacement for 'cool'. I don't mind the word, but save it for something really awesome, like a tornado, and when the discourse simply calls for agreement or appreciation, use the more subtle expression, 'cool'.

Besides the semantic problem I have with 'awesome', Brittany's use of it informs me that she's a member of the *awesome* generation, which could date her as much as twenty years my junior. I've never really been in a situation before when a woman, who is this much younger than me, showed such interest, and that puts me in an ideological quandary. Abiding by my older man-younger woman rule was easy in theory.

Brittany turns in response to boisterous laughter from the crowd at the bar and her right leg abuts against my left knee. When she turns back her leg doesn't. It could be nothing; she may think that the hard, knobby protuberance that she is up against is just the leg of the table. But something about the way she's looks at me makes me think otherwise. I take a long, slow sip of my wine and give her a look of my own.

Winds of the old days begin to stir around me, awakening memories of when I was young and in my prime, recollections of other pretty women in dark and intimate settings. I wonder if this young lady realizes that she's playing with fire?

But is she playing with fire or just stirring up old ashes? Why would somebody this pretty and young be attracted to a burned-out geezer like me? Surely she's noticed my bald spot. Maybe she's insane, a pathological geezer chaser. What do I know about her other than that she claims to be Sally's Schuster's sister?

"Duane, I love this place. It's so different from the bars in Santa Fe. It has an old fashioned look and feel to it and yet at the same time it's really, um, what's the word I want . . ."

"Cool?"

"Ah, yes, it's cool"

"I agree."

"Oh, by the way, I want to tell you that when I mentioned your name to the woman I work for in Santa Fe she said she was familiar with your art, and when she heard that I might meet you, she asked me to mention that she would be interested in featuring you in a show sometime."

Brittany leans close to me and smiles as she says this and it's obvious that she's impressed with her boss's commendation of my work. *Ah, now I see what going on here.* Trapped in the Santa Fe art world with its contemporary, meditative style, and pale, bleached-out, color schemes, Brittany is irresistibly drawn to me, a dark and brooding artist from the eastern mountains, who carves his emotions into primitive forest hardwoods. I smile at that notion, absurd even by my standards.

"What are you smiling about?"

"I'm just in a good mood. I'm always like this when I'm on vacation."

"How often do you go on vacation?"

"About once every ten years."

"You're joking, right?"

"Yes, I'm joking, but it's true."

"Well, I'm in a good mood, too. Let's have another glass of wine."

"Excellent idea. Would you order please? I need to powder my nose."

"I sure will and these are on me. Hurry back," she says with a smile and a wink.

The men's restroom at the East Side Tap has improved by at least a thousand per cent since I last visited it. Clean and bright with two urinals, a toilet, and two sinks, instead of how I remember it, a dingy, one light bulb room with an antique toilet and a matching sink. Soap and towels are a luxury unheard of in the old days. I like the new look, although I must say, I miss the old graffiti.

How am I to respond to this unfolding situation with Brittany? What am I even doing here with her? Who is this brazen woman who lured me from the warmth and companionship I was experiencing with my fellow alumni with the claim that she is Sally Shuster's sister? On the way here, I asked her about Sally and her response was vague; she said we could talk about it over a glass of wine. Well we've had our glass of wine, young lady, and now it's time to talk.

While washing my hands, I view a face in the mirror that I recognize: not so bad looking, just older looking. I know from experience that if I shave, I look younger, but it's too much to hope that the East Side Tap would supply razors along with the other amenities. Uh oh, I seem to have made a decision regarding involvement with Ms. Schuster if I'm thinking such thoughts. Am I really this weak? And the answer is, yes, of course I am. I've always been weak in situations such as this—that's been my downfall.

I rough up my hair with both hands to give the appearance of more body and then smooth it back to each side. I'm taller than Brittany; if I keep my head high and don't let her get behind me, she might not see the bald zone. One last look in the mirror and I accept that what's reflected back is the best I can do.

As I approach our booth, Brittany smiles. Two glasses of a white wine are on the table. I'm not much of a wine drinker these days—not enough alcohol content to stand on it's own, and wine can't compete with beer as a chaser after vodka. However, in a situation such as this, a pleasant conversation about art, with a pretty woman, a crystalline glass of wine, served in an elegant, long stem glass, is the only acceptable beverage. I pity those poor ruffians at the bar, grappling their clumsy beer mugs, while they discuss sports and other crude subjects.

I sit down and reach for my glass, but before taking a sip and getting distracted once more in pleasant conversation, I decide to get to the point.

"Now Brittany, I'm really curious, how is your sister, Sally?"

"To be honest with you, Duane, I have no idea."

"What do you mean?"

"Nobody has seen or heard from Sally since nineteen seventy-three."

"What, seventy-three? That's when she was at Saint Mathew's. Are you talking about a missing person type thing?"

"Y-yes, I guess it was."

"Were the police or FBI involved?"

"I think so, but I don't really know for sure."

"I don't understand; what do you mean by that?"

"Well, there are a lot of things that are sketchy from that time period. My mother isn't the most reliable source of information, mostly because she doesn't like to talk about it. From what I know, she drank a lot for a while, she and her first husband both did. She's straight as an arrow now, believe me. Mom and Dad are bible-thumping, Southern Baptists."

"*You* don't remember?"

"No, when Sally disappeared, I was only a few months old, so I never really knew her. Everything I know about her, my mother told me."

Hmm, what do I make of this? Of course Sally disappeared from my own life, but I guessed that after the incident in the library, she was reassigned to another parish, and then continued with her novitiate. After Father McGee let go of my collar in the library, he never spoke to me again about anything, let alone Sally, and no one else who I could talk to in confidence seemed to know where Sally went.

Brittany continues to speak about her mother as I drift in thought and while I'm not catching all of what is said, it's apparent that she has a tenuous relationship with the woman. Of the many questions that come to mind as a result of the information Brittany has given me so far, one suddenly stands front and foremost.

"So, Brittany, I have to ask. Why are you here then? If you never even met Sally, then why did you come to a reunion at a school where she was a nun-in-training for only a year?"

"Oh, yes, I bet that does seem a little strange, doesn't it? Well, I've worked at the Art Gallery in Santa Fe for five years now, and

70

I love my job, but I really want to be a writer. I want to write a novel."

"Don't tell me, the great-American-novel type novel."

"Yes, exactly. What other kind of book does a serious writer write? Why are you grinning? What's so funny?"

"Nothing; I can appreciate your avocation; I can relate to long-hour, low-pay professions. So you're working on a novel, is that why you're here?"

"Well, yes, that's part of the reason. The mystery surrounding Sally is something I've wondered about since I was little, but I mostly forgot about it as I got older and moved away from home. Once I got into writing, and started playing around with ideas, I came up with a story based on Sally's disappearance, and that got me wondering about her again. I don't really need to know all the facts about what happened with Sally to write a novel, but now I want to know, just for my own curiosity."

"And that's what led you here?"

"Yes, I knew that Sally had been at Saint Mathew's in 1973, so I decided to look up some of the people that graduated the same year. That's how I found out about the reunion. I thought a good place to start was by talking to some of the people that knew Sally last."

"*Last,* you talk as if she's dead."

"She might be. Why would she cut off all contact with her family?"

"Oh, I can think of less dramatic reasons why a person might do that."

"Well, I really hope Sally isn't dead, but it's possible. I don't want her to be dead, but in my novel, a nun *does* die. She gets murdered by a priest. The idea of the nun getting killed by a priest is actually based on a true event."

"Sounds like a cheery story you're putting together there, Brittany."

"It has a good ending, trust me. In my story, the priest is older, in his forties, and he falls in love with a beautiful young nun. She resists his advances and finally threatens to expose him. The priest has high aspirations for a future position in the church hierarchy and kills her to protect his reputation and career."

"I like the story line so far, and I think I have the perfect character for the priest: Father Thomas McGee."

"Who?"

"Father Thomas McGee, he's currently the Bishop, but he was a priest at Saint Mathew's when Sally was here. He'll fit the bill for your villain."

"Father McGee, why do I think I've heard that name before? Let me think. I heard my mother talk about a Father McGee, that's it."

"Your mother knew him?"

"She must have, or else another Father McGee, because I'm sure I've heard his name. I was real young, maybe three or four. She was talking about him to my father in another room and they didn't know I was listening. She was mad about something he had done and called him a son of a bitch. I never heard my mother say anything like that before so that's probably why it stuck with me."

I'm surprised at the remark. I wouldn't argue with Brittany's mother on that point because Thomas McGee is a son of a bitch, or at least back then he was, but I had reason to think that of him. Why would Sally's mother have such an opinion? How did she come to formulate that impression over the short period that her daughter was associated with the man?

Father McGee did seem to hover around Sally, now that I think about it. That's no doubt why he caught Sally and me in the library that day. Should I tell Brittany that part of the story? No, better not; I still don't know anything about her. She could be a private investigator working for Duke as far as I know.

"Was that the only time you remember hearing his name?"

"I think, but maybe not. Actually, the more I think about it, the more familiar it sounds to me. If I remember, I'll tell you."

"Please do. I'm really curious now. Shall we have another glass of wine?"

"No, I don't think so, Duane, I'm tired all of a sudden. I love this bar, but I'd like to go back to my motel now. Would it be too much to ask for you to take me there?"

"But your car is back at the party."

"So what; it's not illegally parked. I can get it tomorrow."

Brittany smiles.

Egad, can this really be happening? Back in my reckless youth, I would be beaming at a development such as this, but now in my cautious maturity, an edgy grin is the best I can muster.

On the way to the motel, Brittany and I don't talk about Sally or art. Our route runs through the center of town, so we talk about Homewood with me doing most of the talking. You never realize just how vast your knowledge is of the place you grew up in until you describe it to someone who's never been there. Brittany is an avid listener, and by the time we arrive at her motel, she seems as enthused as I am about the revival that is taking place in Homewood.

Brittany is staying at the Oak Park Motel, located on the south side of town. I was familiar with the establishment and tried to hide my surprise when she told me she was staying there. I remember the Oak Park Motel as a run-down, mom and pop establishment that seemed behind the times even when I was young. She told me she booked her reservations on line, and I was certain Brittany was in for a revelation when she experienced the place in the real world. But as we pull into the parking lot, it is I who am surprised at the extent to which the old inn differs from my memory of it.

The Oak Park Motel is a cluster of cottages, characteristic of early twentieth century accommodation that emerged to provide lodging for a new class of traveling motorists. Situated close to the highway and having rooms easily accessible from the parking area they were the first *mo*torist ho*tels* or *motels*. It's hard to believe that such a simple entity could still coexist alongside modern, motor hotel behemoths such as the Expresso Inn.

The parking lot circles five enormous oak trees that are

illuminated by lights beaming up from a cluster of rhododendron bushes that surrounds them. Brittany senses that I'm impressed by this majestic, arboreal centerpiece, so she informs me that many more oak trees line the perimeter of the property behind the cottages, forming a small oak forest. Suddenly, a revelation comes to me.

"You know, it's funny, in all the years that I lived in Homewood and drove by this place, I never associated the name of the Oak Park Motel with the fact that it's actually located in a stand of Oak Trees."

"It's nice, isn't it? Don't you love this place?"

"Well, it's no Expresso Inn, but I can understand the appeal of the trees if what you're used to are cactuses."

"Hey even with cactuses this place would have more charm than an Expresso Inn. You're just jealous. Wait till you see the rooms."

Brittany is right, as I enter her room, I do feel a tinge of envy. The rooms are small but neat and simple, with furnishings that remind me of my own home during the time I was growing up. By comparison the furnishings at the Expresso Inn seem mass-produced and artificial, more in line with the businesses that line Haywood Street.

Brittany removes a bottle of Chardonnay from a refrigerator below the television. I sit down on the bed, peering about the room and wondering why the experience of visiting this little motel is affecting me so. Perhaps it's because I identify myself with the same era, and see it as representing a time when the pace of life was slower, the world was less crowded, and life was not so complicated.

When Ms. Schuster sits down close beside me on the bed, I suspect that she's a bit inebriated and I'm not sure if this a good thing or a bad thing. If Brittany was an infant when Sally disappeared, than she's at least twenty years younger than me. The voice of reason sounds in my head: *remember the age policy Duane; for your own good, stick to policy.*

But wait, perhaps an amendment to the policy is in order to

74

cover rare circumstances such as this, a situation when the younger woman is coming on to the older man. After all, the original guidelines were drawn up under the reasonable assumption that just the opposite would be the case. Yes, a policy adjustment is in order: moved, seconded, ratified.

No sooner is the amendment enacted when Brittany's arms encircle my neck and her lips approach mine to kiss me.

Here we go, old man. You know what to do. It's been a while, but it's just like riding a bicycle; you don't forget some things. But now that I think about it, I used to wreck on my bicycle.

"Brittany, uh, wait, let's stop for a minute."

"Duane, what's wrong?"

"Nothing's wrong; something just isn't right."

"Come on, Duane, we're both over eighteen and we're on vacation. What isn't right? I'm attracted to you, that's all. I feel like I know you. I don't believe in holding back when I feel this way. Life's too short for that."

"I agree; life *is* too short, but *this* is too fast. I'm attracted to you, too, and I'm getting to know you quickly, but let's sleep on it for tonight—in separate beds."

"What? Are you serious?"

"Yes, I need to think about it."

"Okay, Duane, I'm sorry."

"Don't be sorry, Brittany, it's my hang-up. The older you get, the more hang-ups you drag along with you. In fact in my case, that's pretty much what I am now, a collection of hang-ups, creeping along the road of life. I need to think this through, that's all."

"But my car is at your friend's place."

"I, I'll pick you up. Let's have breakfast in the morning."

Brittany smiles.

"I'd like that," she whispers. She pulls me close and kisses me.

"Duane Ryan, *you* are a complicated man.

11

Complicated, so that's what I am. It's not the first time that someone has used that adjective to describe me. *Complicated*, I might as well take it as a *compli*ment. I drink to the notion of being complicated: a shot of vodka followed by a swig of Coal Country Beer.

At least it's better than being simple—I think. Of course it is. I'll drink to that, too. Another hit of vodka, followed by that legendary Pennsylvania lager, and my mind lets go of its moorings. I'm adrift in thought, and ready to analyze the events of the day.

Why didn't I stay with Brittany tonight; what's wrong with me? What red-blooded, human male wouldn't have stayed? Wait, don't tell me, I know the answer, it's because I'm not a red-blooded, human male, I'm me, the mutant, the eccentric, the idiot, always cautious and on alert, hesitant at every step so that I don't get tripped up again. That's because I've learned the hard way that life will get in the way of art, and an artist must be vigilant: observe life, but don't let it get complicated. Relationships are life in its most complicated form.

And besides, I know from experience that one night stands are never just that. I believe that if I had been the cold and calculating type, that could have been true, but when I tried to be that type during one misguided era, it didn't mesh with my rudimentary sense of right and wrong. Basically, I don't like to hurt people, even when they seem to ask for it.

Once upon a time, I was involved with a woman who was more concerned with sex than romance—the feminine cold and calculating type. I knew almost from the start that she was enlisting me for that purpose, but I was young and reckless and decided to go along for the ride anyway. That relationship lasted less than a year and left me feeling cheap and debased by the time I finally got away.

I don't think about Vera often, and memories of our affair don't bother me now. Instead, I'm troubled by memories of the women who cared for me, the women who thought I was an answer to some dream, and then were sorely disappointed.

I've never been the warm and romantic type, either. I tried to be that type, too, but it didn't mesh with my sense of detachment and individualism. You might say that I'm the tepid and pragmatic type when it comes to romance—not exactly the stuff of great love stories. *Love means you never have to say I love you.* See, that just doesn't work.

I declare here and now that nobody should believe in an artist. We are indifferent creatures with respect to life; true artists always are. That's my problem, I'm a bona fide artist, and whether or not I've been outwardly successful with my art does not change that fact. In my little world, nothing matters but art: not money, not family, not friends, not love, and not even life. I realize, however, that one needs to be alive to work, so I try to hang on to that last attribute—for now.

Sister Mary Agatha was someone who believed in me. I first realized that she did when I was a sophomore in high school, and while I was certainly no star pupil at that stage of my career, she watched over me and encouraged me as if I was. I often wondered why she didn't focus more on the A students who were always slobbering all over her, and I have no doubt that they wondered, too. Despite what Dale might say, I was not teacher's pet material. I respected Sister Mary Agatha, and I was always polite to her, but I never sought her attention.

I believe she called me the Great Sphinx that day because she expected great things from me, great things that never materialized during her tenure. Sister Mary Agatha taught Latin, a course that was required at Saint Mathew's School. I hardly excelled at Latin I, and Latin II was optional, but I signed on because I knew Sister Mary Agatha wanted me to. I followed along for half a semester, but I never really applied myself and I was in way over my head by mid year.

Sister Mary Agatha entered the room one winter day, late, red-faced and flustered. Considering what a punctual person she was and how much she seemed to enjoyed the class, her demeanor suggested that she was dealing with some school problem that overshadowed the day's lesson in Latin II.

At this point in the year, Sister Mary Agatha had come to realize that even though I was sitting at my desk each day in my jacket and tie, with my eyes open, I wasn't really there anymore. I never volunteered an answer, and I rarely had one when called upon. This apathy was evident in most classes by my junior year but perhaps most obvious in Latin II. After all, if I was having a hard time convincing myself that trigonometry and chemistry held some relevance for me out in the world beyond Saint Mathew's School, imagine what a task it was to attend to Latin, a dead language that wasn't even used in the Catholic church anymore.

For weeks Sister Mary Agatha let me slide, but this particular session, in her agitated state, she suddenly ask a difficult question of me, one that she surely knew I couldn't answer. I had scarcely admitted as much when she threw her hands in the air in an expression of exasperation and exclaimed, "ah yes, Mr. Ryan, *The Great Sphinx.*" She didn't dwell on it. She just hurled that one spear at me to let me know she didn't approve of my attitude and then turned her attention to the rest of the class.

I felt some embarrassment, but I was really more surprised than humiliated. Sister Mary Agatha believed that if she was patient with me, at some point I would click into gear and live up to the potential that she seemed to think I had. For that reason, she always cut me too much slack, and on that particular day, her patience having already been taxed in another arena, she decided to take up some of that slack.

Sister Mary Agatha's patience returned and I never perceived a carry over of this incident into our relationship. Because the story spread beyond the walls of the Latin II classroom, The Great Sphinx moniker carried on, apparently even to this day.

To some extent, I managed to rehabilitate my reputation in Latin II before the year ended by winning first place in a Latin project competition at the Buhl Planetarium in Pittsburgh. Sister Mary Agatha was shocked that I entered because there was never a great rush to enter this competition, even from among the motivated students. When Sister Mary Agatha announced the contest, my mind clicked into gear, and I was thinking of possibilities before the class ended. The Great Sphinx came to life and not only submitted a project, but won first place.

For my entry, I employed woodcarving knives from my Boy Scout days to construct a model of a Roman siege tower. For materials, I utilized twigs from the yard, and bound them together with string and tiny wooden pegs. The tower moved on wooden wheels and was complete with pulleys and draw gates that actually worked. I passed many hours in the basement at home, absorbed in siege tower construction—far more time than I ever spent studying Latin II.

My motivation with respect to this project surprised everyone, including myself, but looking back, I have some perspective on what drove me to participate. My enthusiasm for this project emerged not so much from a desire to explore the details of a Roman war machine or to experience the thrill of Latin competition, but rather, in response to an opportunity to express myself as an artist, and more specifically, to do so in three dimensions, as a sculptor. Whatever my motivation, Sister Mary Agatha was delighted.

I've often thought about Sister Mary Agatha over the years and wondered why she made such an effort on my behalf. She was a good woman and she believed in me. I have no doubt that she's still a good woman, but doubt she would believe in me still, and I wouldn't blame her for that. After all, what grand result has come to pass as a consequence of my eccentric ways and unorthodox lifestyle, my reckless pursuit of some artistic dream? It seems that Sister Mary Agatha's patience was all for nothing.

Not that I'm a total loser or a burden on society. I may not have garnered fame and fortune or changed the world with my vision, but I've managed to support myself as an artist all these years, and that constitutes some measure of success. And even though there were never any great moments, I've had my share of good moments. Yet, I have to admit to myself, that I've never reached the artistic plateau I once imagined, and now, the window of opportunity is small and steadily closing before my bloodshot eyes.

In my twenties, I expected to blaze a brilliant, artistic trail, exceeding the expectations of the believers, such as Sister Mary Agatha, and silencing the critics, such as, well, *they know who they are*. But alas here I am, in my fifties, the fire going out, trudging onward, mostly by momentum from the past. I no longer tease myself with great expectations; I hope, at best, for an outside shot to hit home. The right piece in the right place at the right time is all it takes. Isn't that what I used to tell myself?

Fortunately, my material ambitions are small at this stage of the game. I don't think about financial success beyond enough income so that I can relax in my old age, and I don't need fame anymore or even think I would appreciate it now. I just want a little space to myself and then for everyone to leave me alone so that I can work (and drink) in peace.

Someday my audience will discover and appreciate my work; I've got to believe that. In fact, I'll drink to that. I empty my shot glass, follow with the last of the Coal Country, and effectively reign in my conscience for another day.

I do hope Sister Mary Agatha comes to the reunion.

12

"Whoa, hello, hey Dale, hi. What time is it?"

"It's seven-thirty. You mean you're not up?"

"You must have forgotten that I never get up before ten when I'm on vacation."

"I didn't forget anything. You've obviously forgotten that we talked last night."

"We did?"

"Yes. You wanted to know if Sister Mary Agatha was coming to the reunion, remember?"

"Oh yeah, sure, I remember now. What did you answer?"

"The same thing I answered when you asked me yesterday afternoon. Last I heard, she's might come. Now get washed up and go to breakfast."

"What?"

"Breakfast with Brittany, remember? You asked me for this wake-up call because you hate those chipper, motel, wake-up calls."

"Oh no, breakfast, that's right."

"Hey, don't give me that. Last night you were crowing about it. She's Sister Sally's sister, eh?"

"I guess, Dale. That's what she says. I don't know what I'm getting into here."

"Well, be careful, old man."

"I'm always careful; the problem is I can be stupid at the same time."

"Hah, I think we all have that problem. Hey, I know you got to get moving, but before I forget to mention it, let's head out to Sileo's this afternoon, you and me and Bob. He's up for it."

"Sileo's still exists?"

"You better believe it. I passed by Springville a few months ago and detoured through town to see if it was still there. It was, and I couldn't resist stopping in for a beer to check it out. Mike Sileo is dead, but his wife, Rose, and Mike junior run it now."

"What about Grandma?"

"Long gone, Duane. She would be about a hundred and ten by now."

"She was the greatest. Nobody could pour a draft like Grandma."

"That's for sure. Are you with us? A couple drafts, a couple chili dogs sound good."

"Of course. Let's go for our record: seven chili dogs and seven drafts."

"A couple drafts, a couple chili dogs."

"Okay I'll be good. You guys pick me up?"

"Yep, around noon."

Brittany looks ravishing in the morning light. She would look ravishing in any light, but since the morning light is something rare and exotic to me, she looks particularly ravishing. She's wearing faded blue jeans, a cream colored blouse, and a brown leather vest, buttoned up the front. Blue denim and brown leather, one of my favorite color combinations.

We're eating breakfast at Polly's, a little restaurant that I often frequented back in my high school days. Polly's was the first place I ate a charbroiled hamburger with lettuce and mayonnaise, and in spite of my recent efforts toward vegetarianism, I still think back fondly on the experience. On one of my passes through town, yesterday, I noticed that Polly's was still in operation and made a mental note to eat here sometime this weekend. Much to my

82

delight, the original signboard hangs outside, bearing the same slogan: *Where the home folks eat.*

Brittany and I aren't exactly *home folks*, but we're enjoying our omelets nonetheless. We both agree that the food is excellent and the ambiance of this old diner from another era is priceless. I can't believe that Polly's isn't running those imitation food joints on Haywood Street out of the county. I'm just about to express this opinion when Brittany surprises me with a direct question.

"So where's the party tonight, Duane?"

"What?"

"Where's the party tonight and what should I wear?"

"Uh, well, Brittany, the party, if you want to call it that, is at the Grand View Hotel tonight, but it's a formal type thing and I hadn't really decided . . ."

"I can be formal."

"Well, I, um, I'm sure that you can, but I'm not sure if I can be formal. Actually, to be honest with you, I was considering going to the formal, but I never thought I'd be taking a date. That would change the whole dynamics of the situation and I may have to think this through again."

"Oh come on, Duane; it'll be fun, and I could pick up all sorts of information for my book. Let's go. I'll help you dress."

"Uh, well now, that does sound like it could be fun. And to be honest with you, that's one reason I was considering not going: I actually hate to dress myself."

"Did you bring a suit?"

"Yes, I brought a suit."

"I can't wait to see you in it. What time should I come over?"

"Around five will be fine I guess. I'll be there most of the afternoon; I need some time to get ready. I want to trim my beard and practice tying my tie."

"Wow, it sounds like you have a really busy day planned. What are you doing for lunch?"

"Well actually, for lunch I'm traveling with two gentleman to the city of Springville to partake of the culinary delights and quality spirits at an establishment known as Sileo's."

"Sileo's sounds like fun. I wish I could go."

"Brittany, you can come, but this is pretty much a guy thing. I'm going with two former classmates—both guys. One of them, Dale, hosted the party you came to last night. He's going and we're taking this other poor guy, Bob Macy. The man has more problems then you can imagine. Dale wants me to talk to Bob and try to straighten him out a little. I'm not really looking forward to it, but I owe it to both of them."

"I understand. That's okay, because I can't go anyway."

"You can't?"

"Nope; I'm going to Pittsburgh."

"Pittsburgh? Why?

"First of all, because I've never been there. Second of all, because a cute guy from your class asked me to have lunch with him in Pittsburgh."

"What? Who?"

Brittany stares at me for a moment and then smiles.

"I'm just teasing. I wanted to see if you would look jealous."

"Did I?"

"A little, but you could have done better. Actually, I have an aunt who lives in Pittsburgh, my aunt Shirley, and I'm having lunch with her. Don't worry, I'll be back in plenty of time to dress for the formal."

"Why do I have this feeling that you're always a step ahead of me? Alright, then, I'll be there. You better be careful in the big city."

"I will be. And you be careful in Springville. Is that a city?"

"Uh, no, Springville is a small town, and Sileo's is actually a little dive of a bar that would serve minors back when we were in high school. That's how we became acquainted with it. I doubt I'll need a fake idea to get served this time."

"Sileo's doesn't sound like a good place to take your friend if he's having problems."

"Yah, well, I, uh, pointed that very thing out to Dale, but he said it's sort of a reverse psychology type thing, to make Bob appreciate what he *has* in life."

"You're lying aren't you?"

"Not about going to Sileo's."

"What are you doing this morning, then? Do you have any openings in your busy planner?"

"As a matter of fact I do. You see, my day usually doesn't start until an hour from now, so I happen to have time on my hands that I don't know what to do with. Would you like to go sightseeing around the greater Homewood metropolitan area?"

"I'd love to."

"Well then, *Ryan's Cheapo Truck Tours* is at your service."

13

"This is it, Brittany, the Ryan family home place. Inspiring isn't it?"

"How long has it been this way?"

"The property's been on a downward spiral almost since my mother moved out, fifteen years ago, but it's definitely taken a turn for the worse since I saw it last."

Brittany and I are sitting in the truck, staring across Crawford Street at my old home place. I wanted to focus on the more popular tourist sights for Brittany's first tour of Homewood, but she didn't seem so interested in the historical or architectural as she was the human interest side of town, me being the human of interest. She wasn't even that impressed with the log house on the edge of town, where legend has it that George Washington slept one night. She seems more interested in seeing where I used to sleep.

"What's changed since you saw it last time?"

"The windows didn't have paint peeling off like that and the porch wasn't collapsing. The boxwood hedge that was my father's pride and joy was still here, or at least it was in the front. It used to go around the whole yard, but was torn out when the parking lot for the apartments was put in. At least the last time I was here, the hedge still blocked out the cars and the dumpster.

It was a fantastic yard when we were young, Brittany, closed in by the hedge, and there was a great climbing tree that we'd play in for hours. The stone building in the back is the garage and the upstairs was our hangout and a meeting place for many clubs over the years. We used to play football in the yard and all the neighborhood kids would play. Mr. and Mrs. Liston, neighbors from up the road, came over often, they and their son, Max, and, uh . . . I'm sorry, I'm running at the mouth now."

"That's okay, I don't mind. Those are the sort of stories I like to hear. I love the house, especially the stone work. Even though it hasn't been kept up, it's neat and sturdy looking. Is it old?"

"Yes, it was built in the late nineteen hundreds. As the story goes, an itinerant stonemason cut and laid the stones for this building and a number of old places in Homewood. There were ten of his buildings left when I was a kid and now there are only six."

"Well it must have been wonderful in it's day."

"It was, and I can still picture exactly how it looked, inside and out."

"Do you want to walk around back?"

"No, I did that yesterday, and I still haven't gotten over my depression."

"At least it's for sale. Maybe someone will buy it and fix it up again."

"I hope so, but I doubt it. The property has sold twice since my mother lived here and the decline has been steady over that time. Where are you from Brittany; where's your home place?"

"I, uh, don't really have one. We rented and moved around a lot. The closest thing to a home place I have is a big white house where we lived when I was really young. It's the first place I remember, and I have happy memories of living there. It's somewhere near San Francisco, but I've never been back there."

"I'm sorry. You probably wonder about me, whining about this old place."

"No, I think I understand, and it doesn't bother me that I don't have a family home. I wish I did in a way, but on the other hand, I don't have to watch it be neglected or get torn down. Having roots can be a nice thing, I think, but it seems to me you can get tripped up on them too."

"Brittany, my dear, that is so profound."

"Don't make fun."

"I'm not making fun; I wish I would have said it. You've hit the nail right on the head. I almost cringe when I hear that old catchphrase, 'getting back to my roots'. I think people like talking about getting back to their roots more than actually having to deal with them. You never hear someone say, 'Hey, my quest is finally over, I got back to my roots, my life is in harmony again. Now I'm going to quit talking about it and leave everyone alone'."

"Duane, has anybody ever told you that you're cynical?"

"Yes, just about everybody that's known me for any amount of time."

"So what do you think of me? I want to know."

"I, uh, don't know what I think. I've only known you for, let's see, about eighteen hours. I need at least ten years to formulate an opinion of someone."

"That's not true; you have an opinion. What do you think, Mr. Cynical? Do you think I'm loose? Do you think I'm flaky?"

"I don't think you're loose. No more loose than I am and that's just the right amount in my opinion. You don't strike me as flaky either. I knew you were intelligent since our first talk. Okay, here goes, my eighteen hour opinion: you're a free spirit, open-minded and curious about the world, confident, easy to talk to, and you're kind to cynical old men. To be honest with you, you're the type of person I wish I would have met when I was younger."

"Really?"

"Yes, I mean that. Not that it would have worked out. I was a crazy man when I was young, too full of ideas and too full of myself. No relationship was going to work out."

"I think that's one of the intriguing things about artists, how they're obsessed with their ideas."

"Yes, and as long as you keep your distance your intrigue will remain intact. I think that in the case of my first wife, Cathy, the very things that intrigued her about me in the beginning were what she hated about me in the end. She wasn't a demanding or unreasonable person, but she wanted to live a somewhat normal life at some point. She wanted to have children."

"Did you and she have children?"

"No, but she did, eventually. After our divorce, Cathy married a high school teacher and they had three children. Cathy probably has grandchildren by now."

"And you got married again? Was it the same story?"

"No, Elaine was a whole different story, but I guess it was the same basic problem. She knew what she was getting into with me; she just got tired of it and wanted to try something else.

Hey Brit, let's drive somewhere. I've seen enough of the old home place, and we can continue this discussion in the truck. Now that I know what your tastes are, I've adjusted the tour itinerary."

I steer the truck in what must seem to be a random pattern to Brittany, through a variety of neighborhoods, representing different levels of prosperity, but we are steadily moving west with each turn. I have my window partially down, and cool, sweet air, tinged with fall aromas, circulates through the truck. A brilliant sun is full in the sky behind us, lighting a perfect autumn morning and illuminating scenery that becomes all the more magnificent as we leave the city.

Moments like this cause me to wish I could drive along forever, exploring the world as I once did, open-minded, free, and happy. Such a glorious landscape causes me to envy painters who command such a versatile medium with which to describe what they're seeing and feeling.

Then again, maybe that's the trap we all tend to fall into. Instead of appreciating these moments for all they are, including the acceptance of their fleeting nature, we strive to capture them with our arts, or more often, try to re-create the mood with our homes and the objects we fill them with. It's an effort that's doomed to fail and in the process we grow old and inflexible and are less prepared to experience the next grand moment of life.

"Excuse me, could I ask where we're going *Mr. Silent Tour Guide?*"

"Oh, I'm sorry, of course. I, uh, was just going to tell you that. We are headed toward the Walnut Grove Cemetery."

"Really, you're kidding."

"Brittany, I never kid about cemeteries."

"I happen to like cemeteries. Is it an old one?"

"Yes, it *is* old, but the population is still growing. Since we were on the subject of family roots, I thought you might find this particular cemetery interesting."

Half a mile along a road aptly named, *Cemetery Lane,* I turn onto a gravel driveway and pass under an arched sign that reads: Walnut Grove Cemetery, est.1885. A hundred yards down this lane, amid a landscape of tombstones, I pull to the side of the road and turn off the engine.

"We go on foot from here."

"Good, I'm in the mood to walk. Before we get started though, what was that you were saying about you and your second wife?"

"Elaine, yes Elaine. My, you have a good memory. I was hoping we had left Elaine back in town.

Elaine asked for it with me. Her first marriage was fairly normal: both professionals, good money, one spoiled child, a cozy, suburban, mini-mansion. At the age of forty, she had it all but felt that she needed more. She needed to do something wild and crazy, like get involved with an eccentric artist, and that's what she did. Our relationship was her design from start to finish."

"In the end did she hate you for what intrigued her in the beginning?"

"No, Elaine didn't hate me in the end. She just got bored again and moved on to someone different, a college professor this time. I didn't see it coming, even though I should have. Actually, we kept in touch for a few years, but not in recent times. I held out hope she would change her mind, but I don't anymore, and I guess it's just as well. It was never going to work, whatever changes we might have made."

"I'm sorry, Duane, I . . ."

"Hey, there's no need to feel sorry for me. I was no victim, even if my story implies that. I knew the odds for success were long and I could have stopped going along with her plans at any time. Besides, it's water under the bridge now; I've moved on with my life, etcetera, etcetera. But if you still can't help but feel sorry, you can make it up to me by telling me *your* story."

"What do you mean?"

"I mean, are you married, were you ever married, do you have children? I just bared my soul here, and I think I deserve a little *quid pro quo*."

"Really, I didn't think you would be that interested."

"Ah yes, the age old dilemma of the sexes: men have this inherent need to express their emotions and discuss what their feeling while women are so reluctant to open up and talk."

"Okay, I'll talk then, even though I wouldn't exactly say that you *bared your soul*.

I've never been married, and no children. There was one guy I was with for about twelve years; we split up about a year ago. Donny and I lived together for the last eight years of that time, and it was really nice for a while. Sometimes I really thought we would be together for the rest of our lives.

Then it just grew old, I guess. Donny wanted to move to San Diego and I didn't and that's pretty much what ended it. But if we'd really wanted it to work, then I would have gone or he would have stayed, or else we would have worked something else out. His wanting to go to San Diego was a convenient reason to end the relationship.

I haven't been seriously involved with anyone since and I'm not in any rush to get involved. I enjoy being single again. I don't think people are really meant to be together for long periods of time, like decades, I mean. People change too much to make that a reasonable expectation. How can you promise a lifetime to somebody who may be somebody else ten years down the road?"

"Well said; I agree entirely. I don't know of one couple that has had the long and loving relationship we were taught to expect from storybooks. It looks good when there's a picture in the paper with the announcement that Mr. and Mrs. So and So are celebrating their fiftieth wedding anniversary, but it's usually been a long and rocky road for them to get to that point. Most of the couples I know who managed to stay together that long, just hung in there for at least part of the time, mainly because getting out would have been such a hassle.

Now on the other hand, look at us. We've been together for only a day and we still get along great. That proves that short relationships are the key."

"Duane."

"Yes?"

"Let's walk."

Brittany and I pass the next forty-five minutes walking the grounds of the Walnut Grove Cemetery. In spite of its sprawling nature, the cemetery is a beautiful, well kept necropolis, covering four rolling hills that are located two miles from downtown Homewood. Expansive lawns with orderly rows of gravestones are interspersed with magnificent stands of evergreens and hardwoods.

I've been fascinated with cemeteries since I was young and particularly so with this one where many of my relatives are buried. I know the Walnut Grove Cemetery well and give Brittany my exclusive tour, including the oldest and most interesting tombstones, statues, and mausoleums.

It seems only fitting to begin the tour at the grave of John Home, founding father of Homewood whose mortal remains lie in a cove surrounded by an ever-encroaching forest of oak trees. A faded American flag flutters in the breeze next to a commemorative marker that outlines John Home's exploits in the American Revolution. In appreciation of his service he was given the tree-covered parcel of land that became Home's woods or *Homewood*. His grave is surrounded by those of family members, representing successive generations, right down to the present.

While not as comprehensive or localized, my own family

has a respectable representation at Walnut Grove Cemetery. Three generations of both my mother's family and my father's family are buried here. I work the various family plots into the tour in chronological order, beginning with great-grandparents.

Brittany proves to be a very attentive listener, which makes for a pleasant stroll among the graves. We have nearly completed a lengthy circuit of the cemetery and are approaching the area where the truck is parked, when I lead her to a plot that is of more recent vintage. A large central stone with the name 'Ryan' engraved on it is surrounded by six smaller stones.

"Who's buried here?"

"My grandparents, my Uncle Tim, Uncle Martin, Aunt Maureen, and here beside this hemlock tree, my father, Andrew Ryan is buried."

"Your father? I didn't know your father was dead."

"Well that's one of the cemetery tour surprises, and I always save it for last. Yes, Dad's been dead for a long time. He died right after I left for college."

"Andrew Ryan, 1929 to 1973. Wow, he was only forty-four."

"Yes, if I was him, I would have been dead eleven years ago."

"That's sad."

"It was sad. I remember the day that we buried him here, like it was yesterday. It was a pretty day in September, like today, and everybody was crying."

"What did he die from?"

"Oh, some artery trouble that appeared out of nowhere and got him. All Ryan males eventually die from heart or artery trouble, but usually not the way he did. He suffered for about a year and was in a lot of pain before he died."

"Does it bother you to come here?"

"No, it's been too many years now. I still think it's sad and sometimes wish that he was alive and I could talk to him, but I stopped grieving long ago."

"I've wondered what it must be like, when someone that close to you dies. I've never really gone through that."

"Well, from my experience, when a person dies, from that moment on, they drift back in time, forever. There's no holding on to them, no matter how hard you try. You have no further interactions with them and they, slowly but surely, become less and less a part of your life. As sad as that sounds, it does eventually get you past the grieving. I guess that's the basis of the old saying, *time heals all*."

"But still, you have your memories of the person; your family has memories of your father forever."

"Yes, that's true, and actually for a while, the memories kept him close. Dad still seemed like part of the family in the years right after his death because the memories were so fresh. But the family kept moving along, and many other things happened that started crowding the memories out. Marriage brought new people into the family, then came grandchildren, and at the same time, other people died or moved away.

So much changed that as the years went by Dad became a personality from another era. None of the grandchildren ever met him; to them, he's always been an image in an old photograph and a character in stories from the past."

"That's too bad."

"Yes it is in a way, but it happens to everybody. It'll happen to us sooner or later—sooner for me, later for you. Nonetheless, whenever we die, a couple generations go by and nobody will remember us. Perhaps it's for the better. Life is for the living."

"You know, Duane, you're pretty profound yourself, in a depressing way."

"Thank you, and with that bit of profundity, I officially conclude the Walnut Grove Cemetery Tour."

"I enjoyed the tour very much, but I have one last question. Are you going to be buried here?"

"No, as much as I like cemeteries and despite my *roots* in this one, I plan to be cremated. There are too many cemeteries in the world and with the human population growing like it is, I think it's impractical and even sort of selfish to use up space this way."

94

"What do you plan to have done with your ashes?"

"I don't know; I haven't really decided yet. I've heard of people having their ashes dispersed in exotic ways like sprinkling them above Niagara Falls in the spring time, or releasing them over the Himalayas just as the monks begin their evening prayers, but I don't really want my ashes outdoing me. They can be used for some practical purpose like adding them to a compost pile. Actually, I haven't given it much serious thought, although I guess I should start thinking about it."

"You should; everybody should. I want to be cremated, too, but if I had lived my life in one place like Homewood, I can see the appeal of knowing that I would be buried in a peaceful spot like this among family members. Have you ever thought about having your ashes spread here?"

"No, I never have, but now that you mention it, I like that idea."

14

"Nice car, Bob."

"Thanks Duane. Hey, good to see you're still with us after your disappearing act yesterday. Dale has filled me in a little. He tells me that you eloped with . . ."

"I can imagine what Dale probably told you, and you know it's best to believe only half of it."

"I only told him what I know, Duane, and as tempting as it was, I didn't embellish. So come on, *you* embellish. What's the story here?"

Bob is driving Dale and me to Sileo's Bar in a metallic-gold, Mercedes Benz sport-utility vehicle. He drives a Mercedes, Dale drives a BMW, and I drive a pick-up. What can I say?

"I don't know what's going on, guys. It all happened so fast. This woman, Brittany Schuster, shows up out of nowhere. She's half my age, or, uh, let's say, about sixty percent my age—that sounds better. She's real nice; easy to talk to, and smart, too. She's smarter than me. But I've never been one to go for younger women; it's against my rules. Actually, I'm afraid of younger women."

"Dale said she's Sister Sally's sister."

"That's what she told me, Bob. She said she's Sally's half sister: same mother, different fathers."

"Why do you suppose such a pretty young woman latched on to an old codger like you? That's the real question."

"Well, Dale, she probably sized up the codgers at the party and decided I was the best of the lot, which I am. Before you come back at me on that one, let me tell you something interesting Brittany told me. When Sally Schuster left Saint Mathew's back in 1973, she disappeared."

Bob looks at me in the rear view mirror. "What do you mean, disappeared?"

"I mean that nobody has seen her since then. Brittany told me that her family hasn't seen or had contact with Sally since 1973."

"Well that's weird. I often wondered what ever happened to her and why she cut out of Saint Mathew's so suddenly. She was so nice; everybody liked Sister Sally."

Springville is a four mile drive from Homewood, so we had only begun to share our memories of Sally Schuster when Bob steers into the parking lot of Sileo's. Only Dale knows of the library happening between Sally and me, and sworn to secrecy many years ago, he keeps well away from mentioning it in his recollections.

We cross the gravel parking lot and enter Sileo's to the raspy clang of a bell above the door. Our eyes adjust to the dim light as the few patrons that are scattered about the room, look our way with indifference. However, the bartender, who I assume is Mike Sileo the younger, welcomes us in a loud, friendly voice and tells us to sit wherever we like. To our delight, the same booth we preferred decades before is available.

Springville was never a thriving town even when it's main street was the primary road from east to west, but after the interstate circled the area in the seventies, the town all but withered and died. Places like Sileo's just hang on mostly for the sake of hanging on.

"Is that the same television that was here?"

"Come on Duane, that's impossible. It's a Toshiba. I don't think Toshibas existed back then, did they Bob?"

"How would I know? It's in the same spot though, so give Duane a break. His memory's not entirely gone. Remember watching the NCAA playoffs here?"

Dale and I smile and nod—those were the days. Sileo's is so similar to my memory of it that I find it comforting. If I don't look too closely at Bob or Dale, I can almost imagine it's 1973 again. When I do study my two old school chums, aged gentlemen that they are now, I have to smile to think that we're here once more, all these years later, at the same table, doing the same thing.

A young woman soon appears to take our order and serves us nearly as fast. Before we are halfway through our beers, the chili dogs arrive.

"Mmm, delicious as ever. As bar food goes, Sileo's is as good as it gets."

"I agree, Duane, but, did we ever try anything besides chili dogs with coleslaw?"

"Not that I remember, but why *would* we try anything else? What a combination: hot, spicy chili and cool, sweet slaw on top of a good old American hot dog. To complete the picture, a cold, sparkling Coal Country Beer on the side."

"Hey, I thought you were a vegetarian."

"I am, Dale. Haven't you ever heard of an ovo-lacto-chili doggo vegetarian?"

"No, I can't say I have."

"The terminology stems from the Latin 'ovum', meaning egg, 'lac', meaning milk, and from the English term 'chili dog', meaning chili dog."

"Oh I understand now; that makes perfect sense, so I think I'll change the subject. I want to hear more about Sally Schuster's disappearance. Was it a missing person type thing?"

"Doesn't sound like it became as official as that. I did get the impression it was a dysfunctional family type thing. Actually Brittany only knows what she's been told by her mother since she was an infant at the time. As far as she knows, Sally hasn't been seen or heard from since she left Saint Mathew's School in 1973."

"Wow, that's crazy. So is that why she's here, to try to find out what happened to Sally?"

"It's part of the reason. Brittany has aspirations to be a writer and she's working on a novel based on Sally's disappearance. That's what got it all started, and get this, her story has to do with a nun getting murdered by a priest. The priest falls in love with a beautiful young nun and when she resists his advances and threatens to expose him, the priest kills her to protect his reputation and career."

"I can see that."

"So can I, Bob, and while I listened to her, the prospect for a villain came to me: Father Thomas McGee."

"There you go. Did you tell her that?"

"Yes and that's when it got really weird. Brittany is fairly certain she's heard his name before."

"She heard of Duke?"

"Not 'Duke', but she heard the name Father McGee before. When she was a little girl, she heard her mother say it and refer to him as a son of a bitch."

"It *must* be the same Father McGee."

"Exactly what I thought, but how or why would Mrs. Schuster have that impression, considering the short period of time that her daughter was associated with the man?"

"Well now, I can think of one possibility. There is some reason to think that something was going on between Duke and Sister Sally."

"What are you talking about, Bob? Come on now, that can't be true; I never heard anything about that."

"It's something that surfaced after we graduated, Duane, so you wouldn't have been around to hear about it. Do you remember Agnes Rueben, the woman who volunteered at the rectory? She cleaned and kept the place in order."

"Saint Agnes, you mean? She took care of the priests, went to Mass everyday and twice on Sundays."

"Right, that's her. Well, Saint Agnes wasn't above a little gossip, and since she was a good friend of my Aunt Helen, my aunt was privy to some interesting information about the goings-on inside the rectory.

Mrs. Rueben told her that Sally was in Father McGee's office a lot, and even though she insisted that she never intentionally eavesdropped, Mrs. Rueben said that she couldn't help but overhear that Sally was sometimes crying. So one day when . . ."

"Why would she be in *his* office so much? Sally was training to be a nun not a priest. She should have been in Sister Mary Agatha's office if she needed to be in anyone's office. And why would she be crying?"

"I know, Duane, it seems odd, but on the other hand, Duke *did* tend to hang around Sally, even when they were out and about on campus."

"Yah, you're right; he did."

"Well listen to this. One day when Mrs. Rueben was upstairs dusting, the rectory was so quiet that she assumed no one was there. When she passed Father McGee's office, the door was partially open, and she almost went in to dust. When she peeked in, she saw Sally with her head on Duke's shoulder and he had his arms around her."

"No."

"That's what she said, and Mrs. Rueben wouldn't make something like that up."

I'm stunned. A romantic connection between Father McGee and Sally Schuster is the last thing in the world I would ever have imagined. Was that why he was so furious when he caught Sally and me in the library? Even though I knew at the time that Father McGee disliked me and that I'd committed a serious transgression, his reaction that day seemed harsh. Was it the response of a jealous lover?

I can't accept the thought that Sally and Father McGee were romantically involved and struggle not to give my thoughts away. Dale senses my aggravation and since he's knowledgeable of the history behind my feelings, he steers the conversation in another direction.

He's learned of a renewed effort to halt the demolition of the high school and opens up a discussion along those lines. During another round of beer and chili dogs, I try to attend to the conversation as best I can, but I'm so distracted by Bob's revelation about Sally and Father McGee that I miss most of it.

On the drive back to Homewood, Dale and Bob continue to converse about the high school in the front seat while I scowl and ruminate in the back. When I was young and rash, I sometimes wanted to punch Duke in the nose, and now, here I am, old and rational, and I want to kill him. Imagine the nerve of that self-righteous, pompous, overbearing, hypocritical, jerk. At the same time he was lording over us, and dared to question my attitude, he was breaking his priestly vows, philandering and deceiving, not to mention, taking advantage of Sally who probably looked up to him.

I have to wonder how Sally could have liked him, and she must have to some extent. It puzzled me back then that she defended him whenever I talked about him. She told me that he was on my case because he thought I had potential that I wasn't using, but how would she have known something like that if he hadn't told her?

I wonder if she ever kissed him. Ugh, the thought of it, Sally and Father McGee kissing and then Sally and I kissing. If it's true, I could be one pair of lips removed from kissing Duke. I don't even want to think about that; I've got to change the subject, quick.

"Are you guys going to the formal tonight?"

Dale and Bob stop talking and Dale turns.

"My goodness, Bob, there's someone in the back seat. Hey it's Duane, our long lost schoolmate. You've been so quiet that I forgot you were with us, old man."

"I'm just very moved by the whole Sileo's experience, being there again with you guys and all. I needed some quiet time to reflect on it. Are you going to the formal tonight?"

"Of course, we always go. Don't tell me you're going."

"Yes I am."

"I'm shocked. I didn't ask before because I assumed there wasn't a chance you'd go. To what do we owe this honor?"

"I was thinking about it anyway, believe it or not, and then this morning, Brittany let it be known that she would like to go, and that settled it. Can you believe it, I've only known this woman for a day, and she's already calling the shots?"

"Yeah, I can believe it."

"I believe it too, Duane. That's the story of your life, isn't it?"

"Very funny, Dale."

"So we'll get to meet the mysterious new woman in your life."

"I guess so. She wants to meet you guys, too, anybody who knew Sally. To tell you the truth, I'm anxious to hear what people think of Ms. Schuster."

"Did you bring a suit?"

"Yes, Dale, I brought a suit. Why do people keep asking me that?"

"Not the tweed jacket. I mean a real suit with pants."

"Yes, Dale, matching pants a black belt, and shiny patent leather shoes."

"Wow, I'm impressed and shocked. You didn't pick that up just for the occasion did you?"

"No, I bought the outfit for my grandmother's funeral about twelve years ago. I think this will be about the third time I've worn it."

"Well that makes more sense. You had me worried about you for a minute."

15

Alone at last, propped up with pillows, mentally exhausted. Even the best of company can wear me out, and I need to be alone in my own space to mull over what I've learned out in the world. I'm having a drink with the man across the room. I wonder if that's the reason large mirrors are placed on the wall opposite the bed in motel rooms, so that people who drink alone feel like they have company. It works for me.

Sileo's was fun, like old times in some ways, but it's too bad that Bob dropped a bomb on me. Not that he knew he was doing it, since Bob knows nothing of my amorous relationship with Sally Schuster. The fact that he still doesn't after all these years is surprising because what happened in the library that day is the type of gossip that would typically have spread around the parish like wildfire.

I only told Dale, so I know that from my direction, the story stopped with him. But what about Sally and Father McGee? Am I to believe that they told no one? In Sally's case, it's understandable since she disappeared from the scene soon after, but Father McGee didn't go anywhere. In fact, he's been around ever since.

At the time, I was surprised he didn't shout about what I'd done from the pulpit at the next Mass and expose me to the congregation for the sinful, amoral wretch that he thought I was. I expected, at the least, to get kicked out of school, but not only didn't I get kicked out, I received no form of punishment, and nothing else was ever said to me about the incident. Father McGee never said another word to me about anything, not even my attitude, and hardly looked at me during those last months before graduation.

For years, the best explanation I could come up with was that his snub was just the response I should have expected after what happened that day in the library. Father McGee already had it in for me and then after catching me, *taking advantage of Sally*, as he put it, he wanted nothing else to do with me.

Yet, this interpretation never quite settled the issue in my mind. The Duke that I knew would have relished the opportunity to skewer me, if not publicly, then at least in his office, and he definitely had that opportunity. But if he and Sally *were* involved with each other, his reluctance to punish me or kick me out of school could be seen as an effort to avoid wider scrutiny of the matter.

I refresh my glass and gaze at digital numbers on a clock at my elbow. As I watch, a one and a zero flip into place to mark the time at ten minutes after two. It seems that it should be later with all that's happened today, but time seems to slow down when I'm under the influence of vodka. Another benefit I experience from vodka is that it serves to mellow me out—unlike some drunks I know. For instance, I don't want to kill Father McGee anymore, which is a good thing. After all, it would detract from the positive mood of the reunion if I murdered the Bishop.

Who am I to be so judgmental, anyway? How would I have conducted myself if I were in the position he was back then: forty years old, still young and virile, and with his back up against a vow of chastity? I probably would have had a fling with Agnes Reuben.

And he's still at it, still a priest after all these years, and not only is he a priest, but Thomas McGee is now the Bishop of the Diocese. Needless to say, it's not exactly the career path I would have chosen, but he's stuck with it, and he's been successful.

How successful have I been after all these years? What have I really accomplished along my career path? My work isn't on display in any major galleries, and I haven't even made so much as a ripple in the mainstream art world. I'm poor: one accident or IRS attack from bankruptcy. I drink too much; I think too little. I'm a ten-time loser when it comes to relationships.

At least I'm still an artist. I haven't given up, and that counts for something. I haven't thrown in the towel and gone the way of the world like my long lost bohemian friends. I don't care if they *are* more wealthy and more sane than I am now, they still gave in. When the going got tough, they took the path of least resistance, they joined the establishment, became part of the system, went to work for the man, or worse, *became* the man—all those things we vowed not to do when we were young and free.

Not me; I didn't give up. I plodded on without them, determined to go my own way, to make some artistic statement, certain that I was destined to change the world with my unique point of view. Money, awards, social status, none of those were a concern. Art for art's sake, that's what drove me. I'm still at it, still going for it, still out on a limb, old and crazy now, and for some reason, still betting on myself.

Exactly why I wandered down this *less trodden path* back there in my youth isn't so clear to me anymore. After I graduated from Saint Mathew's, I went a fairly conventional route by going to college. In fact I was delighted to be at a large public university and out of the confines of a small Catholic high school. West Virginia University wasn't far from where I grew up, but it could just as well have been another country for the freedom that I experienced.

My unorthodox attitude, which for some was a problem in high school, now seemed to be a character trait that intrigued a new and wider audience. Although I never fit in with any one crowd, I felt at ease with any crowd and grew confident and comfortable with a position on the fringes of conventionality.

While in college, I had an interest in art, but only as a hobby. I kept a sketch pad handy and did some drawing on the side, but I never considered art as a possible career. I chose psychology as a major instead, a path that I believed would enable me to help others while learning to understand myself in the process. *Ah, the idealism of youth.*

I made good grades my first year and my advisor, Ernie Knoll, was pleased. I remember Ernie well to this day, because he was one of the first truly paradoxical characters that I met along the road of life. He had a neatly trimmed mustache and thinning brown hair that was pulled back into a wispy ponytail. Ernie always wore faded, bell-bottom blue jeans, and a dress shirt of either flowered or paisley design. I guessed that he was about forty years old, but his mannerisms and demeanor, suggested someone younger.

Ernie took a long drag on his cigarette as he perused my record. He blew the smoke toward the ceiling in long continuous stream and then looked across the table at me with a gap-toothed grin.

"Ya done well, Duane, real well. But let's face it, lots of psychology majors do well. You need something to beef up your resume and give you an edge over the others. How about if we throw in some science courses? I'm going to put you down for Bio 101 and Chem 101. You can handle them."

Ernie was right. Not only did I handle them, I enjoyed them and mastered them. I found the factual nature of these courses to be refreshing after the vagaries of psychology. A year later, I changed my major to Biology and when I continued to do well, and encouraging words began to sound in my ear, I became convinced that I was on the right career path. The fact that I didn't know exactly what I expected to find at the end of the path didn't concern me as much as proving that I could walk it.

I graduated at the top of my class, *magna cum laude*; it seemed my potential had finally broken through. Phone calls were made, doors opened, and within months, I was a graduate student in the Biochemistry Department at the University of Wisconsin, with a whole new slate of classes, and my very own research project: *The Effects of Single and Combined Deficiencies of Manganese, Selenium, and Vitamin E in the Rat and Chick*. I'm not kidding, that was actually the title.

To be a graduate student was cool at first; I felt scholarly and important roaming the halls of the biochemistry building in my lab coat, test tube in hand. As a scientist, I was contributing to human knowledge, improving the lot of humankind, changing the world. However, it wasn't long before my academic engines started to cool off, and that rationale failed to muster much of a charge in me. The fact was, I spent my days taking slow, measured steps toward scientific details, while the world changed rapidly, not affected by or even aware of my efforts.

About this time, I was home visiting my mother, and I found myself staring at the Roman siege tower that I created for the Latin contest eight years before. The project had sat on a shelf in my bedroom since its first place finish at the Buhl Planetarium. I had always been pleased with the piece, but now in light of my disillusionment with the career path I was walking, I found it especially intriguing.

Memories of the joyful hours I spent working on the sculpture came back to me, compelling me to look for the carving knives I used in its construction. I took the knives with me to Madison and my woodcarving career resumed.

I tried to live a double life at first, dividing my time between carving and science. I would rise at six in the morning to carve for an hour or two and then go to the biochemistry building to become a scientist for the rest of the day. I experienced ever more pleasure in my growing ability as a woodcarver creating wooden spoons, bowls, duck decoys, and a growing assortment of simple wood sculptures. At the same time, I faced mounting regret for the decisions that led me to graduate school and an employment that was becoming intolerable.

The conflict would have come to a head under any circumstances, because my lack of enthusiasm, *my attitude*, was not going unnoticed by my colleagues, but it was actually an external influence that brought my academic career to an abrupt end.

The year was 1981 and the United States was gripped in the cold war with the Soviet Union. At the urging of a female acquaintance (and soul mate), Cynthia Morris, I attended a rally outside the Wisconsin Capital Building, sponsored by the Nuclear

Weapons Freeze Campaign. In the course of the program, a most eloquent and enthusiastic speaker detailed what would happen if a twenty megaton nuclear bomb detonated where we stood that beautiful spring day.

Twenty megatons was the bomb size of choice for the Soviet Union, and at the time, the Soviets had an arsenal large enough to deliver such a bomb to every city in the United States that had a population of fifty thousand or more. As frightening and insensible as it was, there we were, eyeball to eyeball with the Soviet Union, and what's more, the nuclear arsenal possessed by the United States was even larger than that of the Soviets.

If a twenty megaton nuclear bomb had detonated on the Capital Square that day, a fireball would have formed in every direction, reaching out for two miles. Temperatures would have instantly risen to twenty million degrees Fahrenheit, and everything within that zone, buildings, cars, and of course, all organic matter like me, would have vaporized. Two to four miles away, the blast would have ripped buildings apart and leveled everything, including concrete and steel structures. Even as far away as thirty miles, the heat would have been so intense that all exposed skin, would have suffered third degree burns.

The speaker's words awoke me from a naïve dream world I had been living in. Until that moment, I had managed to delude myself with the notion that I was in a relatively safe place on earth in the event of a nuclear war. Now, it was clear to me just what this nuclear stare down amounted to: if either the United States or the Soviet Union blinked, there was no safe place; we were all going to die.

With that possibility, churning in my head, I found it difficult to be overly concerned about *The Effects of Single and Combined Deficiencies of Manganese, Selenium, and Vitamin E in the Rat and Chick*. The prospect of vaporization at any moment made me reluctant to commit any more of my remaining time as solid matter to a PhD program. I wanted to live for whatever time was left, doing something that I loved, something that I believed in.

I avoided the biochemistry building for a few days, spending the time at my workbench, carving and pondering humankind's bleak future. Then late one night, I crept to my office, dropped my notes in the trash, arranged books and data on a shelf for my successor, and walked out.

But the nuclear war never happened; the cold war ended. I lived for whatever time was left, but now it seems that too much time was left. I didn't vaporize in an instant, instead I burned out slowly.

I glance at the clock again, wishing now that time would stop altogether and leave me alone. I stare across the room at the man in the mirror. He knows that I must get up off this bed and do something. That's what I've read about this sort of thing: when I feel myself sinking, I need to focus on some simple, practical task, something that will pull me back. I don't want to think the suicide thing today. I must get up.

16

When one is required to tie a tie only once every decade or so, it's not so easy to do Fortunately, my years of training at Saint Mathew's School provide me with a strong background of experience to draw on. Usually after half a dozen tries, I can get the look I want.

The knot is no problem: a loop in and around this way, a loop in the opposite direction, a wrap around the outside, and then the wide end down the middle. The tricky part is getting the two ends to be the proper length when the knot is complete and pulled taut. I don't care what the current trend is, I like the wide end to hang an inch above my belt with the narrow end three inches shorter and tucked neatly behind.

This curious piece of wardrobe, the tie, originated in the 1630s and is of military origin, tracing back to the time of the Thirty Years War, when Croatian mercenaries in French service wore small, knotted neckerchiefs around their necks. This aroused the interest of the fashion-conscious Parisians, and before long, the new article of clothing started a fashion craze in Europe that continues to this day in Homewood, Pennsylvania.

I must confess, I don't just carry around such facts in my head. I became so engrossed in this tie-tying activity that I took a break after the third practice run and did some necktie research on my laptop.

I was pleased to learn that the knot I'm working with, the

very one my father taught me to tie when I was six years old, is known as a Windsor Knot. This particular method of knotting one's neckerchief was invented in the early twentieth century for the Duke of Windsor who preferred a thicker knot. The Windsor Knot is described as a knot that looks especially well on men with longer necks as it tends to shorten the perceived height of the neck. Now, being of long neck, that's a reassuring thing to know.

Everything I learned from my research was positive until I read that James Bond never trusted a man who wore a Windsor Knot. He felt it demonstrated too much vanity and was often the mark of a cad. *That Bond,* he sure knows how to bring a guy down.

I actually enjoy getting formal when the occasion calls for it, be it a funeral, a wedding, or a bona fide formal. I'm sure this traces back to my years at Saint Mathew's School as do many incongruent character traits. I certainly can't imagine wearing a suit every day like I did back in high school, but once in a while it's fun—like wearing a gentleman costume.

I get the tie right at last, make a mental note of the exact point where I made the turn for the first loop and then untie it. That's the key to a well-balanced Windsor knot, hitting that first turn right.

A knock sounds on the door, and I open it to find Brittany staring at me with an impish grin on her face. She looks very nice, wearing a light green cotton shirt over a denim skirt, and with her hair tied back in a loose, frizzy, pony tail.

Without warning, Brittany wraps her arms around my neck and kisses me.

"Surprise," she says.

I grin. I *am* surprised and also delighted to see her.

"Hey we have to have some ground rules for this relationship, like no pop-ins."

"Sorry, I don't play by the rules."

"I've noticed that. Did you have fun in Pittsburgh?"

"Yes, it was a lot of fun. I haven't seen Aunt Shirley in years and we really had lots to talk about. We've always had an easy time talking to each other."

"Is Aunt Shirley your mother's sister?"

"No, she's my father's sister, younger by five years. Actually, Mom and Aunt Shirley had a falling out a while back and haven't spoken much since. They never really did get along too well from what I remember. Aunt Shirley's very liberal, especially compared to my mother, and she's not big on religion either. I sometimes think Mom tried to keep me away from her so I wouldn't be corrupted."

"Did your aunt corrupt you?"

"No, of course not."

"Who did then?"

"Devious artists like you."

Brittany still has her arms around me and is edging me backwards toward the bed. She kisses me again, and I feel a tremor of nervousness. I try to dismiss it, but anxiety is there, lurking beneath the surface, threatening a moment that an older gentleman, such as myself, might dream of. Perhaps I just need to slow things down a bit.

"Um, would you like a drink?"

"I don't think so. I had some wine at Aunt Shirley's."

"Well that's not fair. I haven't had anything to drink."

"You taste like you have."

"Really, I do? Oh, that's probably the new toothpaste I've been using. Herbal Whitewash it's called."

"Duane, you're lying. What have you been drinking?"

"The usual, vodka."

"Ugh."

"Ugh is right. It's disgusting. I'm going to quit drinking, uh, tomorrow."

"Do you think you can?"

"No."

"Can I help?"

"No."

"Duane, are you an alcoholic?"

"Of course. At some level, everyone who likes to drink is an alcoholic."

"What level are you at?"

"Not at the very top, but I'm inching my way up there."

"Are you worried?"

"Sometimes I worry that I drink too much. Other times, when I consider the sad state of the world, I worry that I don't drink enough."

"Okay, I'll have a drink."

"Now, Brittany, I don't want to contribute to your corruption."

"Too late to turn back now. Do you just drink it straight?"

"Well, uh, yes, sort of. I prefer to chase it with beer when one's handy. I have some Coal Country in the fridge."

"I don't think that will do for me. There's a soda machine around the corner. I'll be right back."

Brittany grabs the ice bucket from atop the refrigerator and disappears as suddenly as she appeared. I act quickly. Retrieving the vodka bottle from beside the bed, I pour myself a shot, throw it back, and pour another. I finish that and set the glass down just as the door opens.

"My God, Duane, do you have a big enough bottle? What is it half a gallon?"

"One point seven five liters to be exact. I know it looks bad, but I only buy this size to conserve natural resources. One big bottle is better than a bunch of little ones."

"I *guess*. Do you think you can spare a milliliter or two?"

"Coming right up."

I half fill a glass with ice, add a generous dose of vodka, and top it off with the lemon soda that Brittany bought. She takes a sip and her eyes open wide.

"Wow, Duane, you certainly don't scrimp on vodka."

"Life's too short for weak drinks, my dear."

"How profound; I'll remember that."

She takes another sip and then another. Brittany smiles at me; I smile back. She tilts her head back and takes a healthy swallow. Brittany grins at me; I grin back. Then she sets her glass down and converges on me. Kneeling on the bed and facing me, she straddles my lap, her knees against my hips. She sits down, and makes herself comfortable. Brittany encircles my neck with her arms and moves her face to within an inch of mine.

"You're trapped, Duane Ryan. You got me drunk and now you have to face the consequences."

"What are the consequences?"

"I'm going to tear your clothes off and we're going to have wild and crazy sex the rest of the afternoon."

Brittany kisses me lightly on the lips. She kisses me again with more force and her tongue probes inside my mouth. I knew this moment might come and yet I'm still surprised now that it's upon me. I sense a certain duality in my nature in that I'm participating and, at the same time, observing with unease.

I'm certainly not going to balk again, but I can't help but wish that I had a little more time to gather my wits. The participant is following his instincts while the observer is thinking the situation over in a practical way. I need time to bring these two psychological entities to terms with each other.

Brittany solves the dilemma for me.

"Duane, I have to take my contacts out. They're killing me, and I have to pee, too. Warm up the bed and I'll be right back."

Brittany kisses me, dismounts, and moves toward the bathroom. When she's around the corner, I lunge for the vodka bottle and the shot glass. I have a shot, and then another. The alcohol pulses through my bloodstream and surges into my brain, shutting down uncooperative synapses. My thinking becomes more basic; participant and observer become as one. I'm whole again. I undress faster than I have in decades and climb under the sheet.

I'm still nervous though. What if I can't get it up? Or worse, what if I can't keep it down?

I consider making another dive for the vodka bottle, but Brittany reappears. She sits on the edge of the bed, starts to unbutton her shirt, and smiles at me.

"Duane, could you help me?"

I sit up and reach around her. I nuzzle behind Brittany's ear as I slowly undo the buttons. She smells wonderful, like she's been wandering in an autumn meadow for hours. I wonder how I smell, having wallowed about in my motel room for hours. Brittany caught me off guard, popping in like she did and I didn't have time to make basic preparations. Now I wish I had reached for the stick deodorant instead of the vodka bottle. What can I do? I could say I have to go to the bathroom, grab my suitcase on the way and . . .

Stop, forget it, you idiot; it's too late now. For God's sake man, focus!

I help Brittany take her shirt off and then unhook her bra. She guides my hands to her breasts, and I gently cup them. Like many human males, I'm a breast man. How is it that this mass of glandular, fatty, tissue, positioned over the female pectoral muscles feels so good to the touch of the hands? I could touch all day, but Brittany has more extensive plans for the afternoon.

Soon we are under the sheets, our bodies pressed together in harmony, moving in synchrony, awash in a warm sea of desire. I forget who I am or where I am, and for one of those rare moments in life, all that matters is here and now.

I open my eyes. I'm lying on my back and Brittany's head is on my chest. She's breathing heavily and her eyes are closed. How could I ever have imagined a development such as this when I decided to come to the Saint Mathew's reunion? Here I am in a swanky hotel (by my standards), lying naked in bed, with a beautiful, mysterious women who I've just made love to. What a fool I've been for avoiding my high school reunion all these years.

Whatever comes next between Brittany and me, I'm relieved that the opening love scene in this affair is behind us and I have one less thing to worry about. On a scale of one to ten, I rate myself somewhere between a six and a seven. Not great, but not too shabby for a fifty-five year old who has been out of commission for years.

My situation reminds me of something I heard years ago, back when I worked for my father at the coal business. I was eighteen then, and a grizzled old hard hat, a bachelor of many years named Tom Drew, was sharing some of his insights on life and love.

"I figure I'm only going to get it up one or two more times in my life," he said with a roguish grin, "and by God, I'm saving it for the right occasion."

The words seemed silly to me at the time, but they've stuck with me all these years. Perhaps now I better appreciate what he was talking about.

Tom also said, "there's not much to sex; most of it's thinking about it before and talking about it afterwards."

In time, I did come to understand what he meant by that, but at this moment, I would have to disagree with old Tom. Thinking about it before was not fun—I was too nervous—and I have no need to talk about it with anyone. The experience itself was wonderful; Brittany was wonderful. I hold her a little tighter and savor the moment, one that may never come around again.

Ten minutes flip by on the clock. Brittany is still asleep and I'm wide awake, contemplating the future. *Why not pull up stakes and move to New Mexico?* Brittany planted that seed in my head with her intriguing description of the art scene there. I'll go underground in Santa Fe for a few years until I get my act back together. People will wonder where I went, and then I'll reappear with a new style and a new attitude. I'll show them that . . .

"Hmm, what; what is it Duane?"

"Just the phone. Go back to sleep. I got it."

"Duane Ryan speaking."

"Hey Duane, Bob here."

"Bob, what's up?"

"Picked up some interesting information, concerning your old nemesis, the Bishop."

"Duke?"

"Yes, that Bishop. We've got some time before the dance; let's meet at Mutt's Place for a beer and I'll fill you in."

"Why there?"

"Because the bartender is who we want to talk to.

116

17

When I pull up to Mutt's Place, Bob's Mercedes is the only vehicle parked outside. Mutt's Place, or simply *Mutt's*, as it's most often referred to, was established in 1925 by Michael Knutt, and although the history isn't altogether clear, many say that the appellation is an abbreviation of the founder's name. While that's plausible enough, others argue that Michael named the establishment after his mongrel dog who slept behind the bar during the first decade the tavern was in business. However the name came about, it's a cool bar. Not always prosperous, but cool: an old fashioned, all American type bar.

Both Michael Knutt and his dog are long gone; only the name remains. For many years, the Knutt family owned the building and lived in an the apartment above, but after Michael died, his wife sold the property and moved away. Fortunately, throughout the tenure of the next two owners Mutt's Place persevered and retained most of its original character.

As I enter the bar, my eyes need time to adjust to the dim interior, but by the process of elimination, I deduce that the human form, seated at the bar, conversing with a man who is obviously the bartender, must be Robert Macy.

"Duane, I was just telling Chris here about you."

"Don't believe him Chris, I'm not like that anymore."

"Bob was telling me that you're an artist; that's what you do for a living."

The bartender is half my age and he says this with a tone of admiration that leaves me flattered and momentarily lost for speech. Such appreciation must have been elicited by some flattering remarks from Bob. I clear my throat and am about to reciprocate with some kind words of my own when Bob interrupts.

"Of course I left out the ugly details: the failed marriages, the drugs, the Satan worship."

"Ah, that's the Bob I know and love. You had me off balance there for a while. Don't mind him, Chris, Bob's always teasing me. He's my favorite uncle."

"You jerk, you're older than me."

"When you reach our age, Robert, a few months are nothing."

"I'd rather have them then not."

"Ahem, whatever you say, Uncle Bob. Chris, would you pour me a Coal Country and put it on this gentleman's tab. He's one of those dot-com millionaires; he can afford to buy a poor philosopher like me a drink.

So Chris, are you from Homewood?"

"Yeah, I am, Mr., uh, Ryan is it?

"Ruin, it's Duane Ruin."

"Quiet Bob. Just call me Duane, okay Chris."

"Okay, Duane. I grew up across town on Pennsylvania Avenue."

"Oh, you're right up the road from Saint Mathew's. Did you go to school there?"

"No, I went to the public school, but my family's Catholic. We go to church there."

"Chris goes to Penn State now, Duane, and he's working here part-time for his uncle."

"What, are you kidding me? You go to Penn State with all the hip bars right there in State College and you're working at Mutt's Place in Homewood?"

"Uh, I like coming home. Homewood's getting to be a pretty hip place, too, and Uncle Larry pays well. He's hoping that having

118

bartenders like me in here will start to pull in a younger crowd."

"Well, best of luck with that, Chris, but you sure struck out this afternoon with just us two dinosaurs in here."

"Hey, speak for yourself, Cro-Magnon man. Let's cut the small talk and get down to business here. Chris, tell Duane what you told me about Carmen Vincenzi."

"Sure, well, Carmen never said a lot. Come to think of it, he just said the same things a lot. There's no doubt that he drank too much, but he traveled on foot, so I figured he wasn't hurting anyone. Carmen was usually complaining for one reason or other, sometimes with other customers or just to himself. He never seemed mad though; it was just the way he talked. But the night Bob and his friend were here, it was different."

"Chris was bartending the night that Nick and I stopped in and had our little exchange with Carmen about the boiler room. I do some work for Chris's father and bumped into him at his Dad's office. We recognized each other and talked about what happened that night."

"Ah, I see. This should be interesting. Go on, Chris."

"Well, after Bob and his friend got him going about the boiler room, Carmen kept muttering to himself, stuff like, 'I should never have done it. Father McGee told me it was for the best. But it was a damn sin; I shouldn't have done it'."

"Whoa, has he ever said anything like that before?"

"Not that I've ever heard. Well, he does talk about other people, but that was the first time I heard him going off on Bishop McGee. He kept going on even after Bob and his friend left the bar."

"What do you figure, Bob? Why was Carmen so hung up on this? It's weird."

"I agree, but it gets weirder. Tell him the rest, Chris."

"Well, at the end of the evening, Carmen was the last person here. He was really loaded too. I was a little buzzed myself because I'd been sneaking beers, and I was trying to be friendly with him. Nobody else was here, so it was like Carmen was talking to me, anyway. So the next time he said something about Father McGee, I asked him what was wrong with closing up a room in the basement of the school and why was it a sin.

His head bobbed up and he stared at me for a while as if he'd just noticed I was there. He started to say something, then stopped and kept staring at me. Then he spoke in a low voice, almost a whisper, and he said, 'It's not the god damn room, you little shit head; it's what's *in* the room'."

"What, he *said* that?"

"Yah Duane, that's what he said: 'it's what's in the room'. Then he got off his stool and headed for the back door. He opened the door and just before he left, he turned and stood there looking at me for a few seconds, bobbing his head. It was creepy. Then he said, 'Why do you think the good father is so anxious to cover it all up with a parking lot.' Then he walked out."

"Told you, Duane. Pretty heavy stuff, eh?"

"Sure is, Bob. What do you think?"

"Well everything Carmen says has to be taken with a grain of salt—that's always the way it's been with him—but this *is* weird. There was no reason for him to say that unless something about that room was really bothering him."

"Well what about the last thing he said, do you think that Duke might be hiding something? Do you get the impression that he's overly anxious to turn the school into a parking lot? Dale seems to think he's just being practical. He said that the cost of restoring and maintaining the building is way too high."

"I never saw him as *overly* anxious, but he definitely championed the idea, and so far hasn't wavered in the face of criticism."

"You know, Bob, the thought had crossed my mind that it would be fun to see the old boiler room again, but after hearing this, I'd *really* like to have a look inside."

"Why not just break in? What the heck, if they're going to tear the building down anyway, why not?"

"Maybe back in my wild and crazy youth, Chris, but not

today in my tame and sensible old age. I might get in trouble or hurt myself."

"I got it, Duane. We should just approach the Bishop and ask him if we could knock down part of the wall to see the old room again. That's not an unreasonable request. After all, like Chris said, the building is going to be torn down anyway."

"He'll never go along with it."

"Probably not, but he might. Duke's a lot more mellow than he used to be, and after all, this weekend isn't just another reunion. We're saying good bye to our alma mater forever. If we get a little momentum behind the idea, like a group of upstanding alumni who make the request, I think he'd have a hard time saying no."

"He'll still say no."

"Well if he does, it'll be interesting to see what his reason is. Even the way he reacts will tell us something, especially in light of what Carmen said."

"Hmm, now that you put it that way, it's not a bad idea, Bob. In fact, it crosses the line into the category of a good idea."

"Thanks Duane."

"When would you do the asking?"

"Bishop McGee's part in the show starts tomorrow. He's saying Mass and then he'll be at the grand banquet tomorrow afternoon. We could try to catch him before mass."

"Who's we?"

"Don't worry, Duane, I'll muster a crew. You know me."

"One thing for sure, I can't be on the asking committee."

"No, that's why I specified, *upstanding* alumni."

"I see, you're implying that I'm among the low-standing alumni. I'll show you then. After Duke slams the door in your upstanding faces, I'll gather a group of low-standers to break in and we'll find out what he's hiding in that room."

18

"How far is it to the Grand View Hotel, Duane?" "About eight miles. We go east out of Homewood on Route Forty and then up Pine Knob Mountain a few miles."

"Oh, we'll pass that nice little tavern, won't we?"

"The East Side Tap, yes, we'll go right by it. Are you sure you wouldn't rather skip the formalities and hang out there tonight?"

"Yes, I'm sure. I'm decked out and you look too cute in your suit and tie. I want to go to the formal."

Brittany insisted that we take her car to the formal and that I drive. As I shut the passenger door, I tell her through the open window, how nice she looks. Brittany *is* decked out. She's wearing a black dress with a V neckline and a pleated skirt that falls just below her knees. A silver pendant at her neck and auburn hair, brushing her shoulders, add just the right accents to a lovely portrait.

The day was warm, but now as the sun goes down, the air is beginning to cool to just the right degree for my liking. I like weather that is just cool enough so that I feel comfortable in a jacket, preferably my tweed jacket, although I must admit, this suit does go better with a Windsor-knotted neckerchief.

As we leave the city and enter the wooded countryside, I open the window a few inches so that Brittany and I can enjoy the wonderful autumn fragrances that permeate the air. Homewood is situated only a few miles from the Allegheny Mountain Range and the change in scenery is dramatic as one leaves the relative flatness of the valley and begins the ascent of Pine Knob Mountain.

"Are you okay, Duane? You seem distracted about something."

"I'm sorry, but I am a little. Some things I heard at the bar this afternoon, I can't seem to get them out of my mind."

"What is it? I want to know."

"Okay, maybe that's what I need, a fresh perspective on this."

With a brief preamble to introduce Brittany to the character that was Carmen Vincenzi and to familiarize her with the entity that is the boiler room, I relate Chris's information.

"What a strange story; it has the makings of a novel, and Carmen would make an interesting character. In fact, Carmen sounds like a character out of a Charles Dickens novel. Come to think of it, Carmen and the boiler room would fit into the story I'm working on, and now I agree with what you said before: Bishop McGee *would* make a good villain."

"How so?"

"Well, you remember my story line, about the priest who murders the young, nun?"

"How could I forget? I wake up at night thinking about it."

"Good, that means my story's getting to you. Think about it then, what a convenient way to get rid of the body."

"What?"

"Sure, I've been struggling with that part: what the priest does with the body. Not that I want him to get away with it, but this could be how he attempts to get away with it. The more I think about it, the more I like it, and Father McGee and Carmen would make great characters."

"So you're suggesting that Duke and Carmen hid a body in our smoking room?"

"No, it doesn't matter what actually happened with the room; all I need is the idea. That's how novels are written, Duane, with bits of information and real life events woven around a *novel* idea. It's my job to tie it all together into an interesting story."

"Ah, I see. Well, back in real life, what would you guess happened here?"

"Given what you've told me about Carmen, my guess is that it's probably something less dramatic than it sounds."

"Like what?"

"Hmm, like say asbestos."

"Asbestos, why asbestos?"

"Last year in Santa Fe, they were building an apartment complex on a site that had an old factory on it, and during the demolition, they uncovered a basement room that was filled with asbestos. The authorities figured that the asbestos once covered the original furnace and heating pipes. Rather than pay the high cost of having it removed, someone did it themselves and buried it.

It might not be asbestos in the boiler room, but it could be something like that, something that was easier and cheaper to hide than to deal with on the surface. Maybe old bibles that couldn't be thrown away because it was against church law. From what you've told me, Bishop McGee seems like the type of person who would do that. He seems like somebody who plays by his own rules."

"Those are boring theories, Brittany, but you're probably right. Considering that Carmen is the source, it would be wise to not get carried away here. But tell me, have you remembered anything more that your mother said about Father McGee? You told me that you remember her saying his name, but was it just that one time?"

"You know, I've been asking myself that same question since we first talked and I think she did, but I'm still not sure. And you know what's really creepy, for some reason I think I may have even seen him once."

"What, are you kidding me? Where would you have seen him, at your house?"

"Yes, that's where I think it was, but I can't say for sure. I never would have remembered any of this if you hadn't mentioned his name. I think I know what he looks like, or at least what he did look like. Will he be here this weekend?"

"Oh yes, count on it. He's the grand pooh-bah of the show."

"Well, I'll see if I recognize him then. But as far as the boiler room goes, I think that's a smart idea your friend Bob has, to go right up to Bishop McGee and ask permission to open the room. It's a harmless request unless there's something to hide. How the bishop reacts will say a lot."

"I agree, and that gives me an idea. Why don't you approach Bishop McGee and ask him about Sally?"

"I thought about that."

"Sure, why not? He obviously was involved with Sally, in some way at least. I mean, if nothing else, she was at Saint Mathew's at the same time he was a priest there, and if your memory serves you well, you may have already met him. Somehow he's involved in the story, and as a writer, you owe it to your novel to speak to Father McGee."

"Maybe you're right. Will you introduce me to him?"

"Um, I don't think that would set you off on the right foot, Brittany. You see, he and I have some history that's kind of hard to explain. Well, when I was in high school, he . . ."

"That's okay, Duane; I was just teasing. I already got the impression that you didn't get along with him."

"Was I that obvious? You see, Father McGee was always breathing down my neck back then. In some ways, I asked for it, but there was something more going on. Other people had worse behavior issues than I ever had, and they certainly got their share of reprimands, but Father McGee always got over it with them. He never did with me. I discussed this very point with your sister once and you know what she told me?"

"You talked to Sally about this?"

"Yes and she said that the reason Father McGee was on my case was because he thought I had great potential; he didn't think I tried like I should."

"Sally said that?"

"Yes, She used those exact words."

"Sounds like Sally knew him fairly well."

"That's what I thought even back then and I . . . What?"

"What yourself; you're the one who's talking."

"What are you grinning about?"

"I'm not grinning; I'm smiling. I was just thinking that it sounds like Sally knew you fairly well, too."

"Well yes, we were friends, I guess. I went to the library a lot. I, uh, wouldn't say she knew me *well*."

My face grows warm. We're only a mile from the Grand View Hotel but it seems like a long distance all of a sudden. Silence ensues, which is unusual for us, and I get the feeling that Brittany knows more than she's told me thus far.

As we navigate the final, sweeping curve leading to the summit of the mountain, the Grand View Hotel comes into view and serves as a welcome distraction. Lit by oblique rays of sunlight from the low country behind us, the monumental, stone edifice on the pinnacle of Pine Knob Mountain, is particularly striking.

"What a beautiful building!"

"Isn't it? I've been impressed ever since I first saw it as a kid."

When I pull into the parking area, it's nearly full and I only find parking space at the end of the lot. As we walk the distance to the front entrance, I'm determined to keep the conversation on the hotel and not let it drift back to Sally.

"The Grand View Hotel was built in the early 1900's. Some wealthy residents of Homewood decided to invest in a mountain resort to serve the new class of travelers that came with the automobile age. The place has gone through some ups and downs over the years, but it's been mostly successful. Some famous people have stayed here: Henry Ford, Thomas Edison, a president or two. President Truman stayed here, I think."

I decide to quit with the history lesson; I'm already in over my head. As we walk toward the entrance, Brittany takes my right arm in hers. I can imagine the buzz that will run through the crowd when we walk in the door, and I can't wait to hear it. If I ever imagined that I would one day attend one of these formals, I never would have guessed that I'd make a grand entrance such as this.

The temperature is cool and refreshing at the higher altitude.

The air holds the pungent aroma of autumn foliage, laced with the scent of wood smoke, drifting down from the massive chimney of the hotel. A spectacular, oversized sun is poised on the horizon, which leads me to suggest that we step down to the terrace on the west side of the hotel to watch it set.

In the dying light, Brittany and I behold a panorama of undulating hills to the west, the legendary *grand view* for which the hotel is named. Eight miles in the distance, the city of Homewood is centered in this magnificent landscape. Lights are coming on as we watch, and this patch of civilization in the western Pennsylvania countryside is revealing itself to we observers on the mountain.

As I gaze down at this familiar scene, I recall another time I took in the view from this terrace. I was in high school then and my family had come to the Grand View Hotel to attend a wedding reception for my aunt Patricia. My Father allowed Will and me to have a beer in honor of the occasion and brought us to this terrace to drink it with him. I can still picture Dad as he stood here that day, and I remember how proud he was as he pointed out the salient features of the landscape to his sons.

The image that I conjure up, of the three of us standing here on that brilliant spring afternoon, saddens me on this autumn evening as I gaze down at points of light amid the gathering darkness. I could never have imagined at such a carefree moment, when life seemed so full of promise, that my father had only one more year to live.

19

1973

I'm leaving for college. The jeep is packed and Will is waiting to take me across the state line to West Virginia University. This is a role my father would relish under normal circumstances, but his condition is bad again; he can't even get out of bed today. Will is anxious to go, and I need to go upstairs and say goodbye. I don't want to; I don't know what to say.

Dad's been sick for over a year with a strange illness that I've never quite understood. I think sometimes that the doctors who treat him don't quite understand it either, because nobody seems to have an answer. The trouble came out of nowhere: a physical exam, high blood pressure, and premature hardening of the arteries. That doesn't seem possible for someone so young, and maybe for that reason we try not to believe it.

But then there's the pain, agonizing pain in his stomach, especially when he eats. Some suggest an artery transplant; others argue that it's too risky. So we all wait and watch as the pain gets worse and Dad grows thinner. We try to look ahead, I to my first year of college, Will to his sophomore year, our siblings to the upcoming school year at Saint Mathew's, but it's impossible not to see the dark cloud on the horizon.

I'm eager to go to school; I've been looking forward to getting away. I'll finally be free of Saint Mathew's and Father McGee, and as much as I hate to admit it, I'm anxious to get away from this house and the gloom that blankets it now.

Will opens the door, glances at me, and shuts it again. He's impatient; he has other things he wants to do today. I walk up the stairs to say good bye.

My father is resting against the headboard, propped up with pillows, an ashen hue to his face. He's an inch shorter than me and only a year ago, outweighed me by ten pounds. He was stout and strong then, a man who believed in hard work and who had worked hard his entire life. Now he weighs twenty pounds less than me, his features are thin and drawn, and his body is so weak and wracked with pain that he's confined to bed.

"Hey Dad, how are you feeling today?"

"Oh, Duane, hi. I was dozing off. This medicine makes me so drowsy. I don't feel too bad today. As long as I sit up like this, it doesn't hurt too much. I'm anxious to get to the Cleveland Clinic now. I never thought I'd wish that."

"You've decided to go, then?"

"Yes, something's got to be done. I'm scheduled for surgery at seven o'clock, Monday morning."

"Well, I guess that's good news, Dad. I hope everything works out well."

"Thanks, Duane, I think it will. I probably should have had this done a year ago. So are you ready to hit the books? You are heading to school today, aren't you?"

"Yes, right now in fact. Will's waiting outside. He's going to take me down to WVU in the jeep."

"I wish I could go with you guys; have a beer somewhere."

"I wish you could, too. Maybe at Christmas."

"Yes, maybe at Christmas. Are you planning to work at the river over Christmas break?"

"I was hoping to. I already talked to Uncle Martin about it."

"Good, I'm glad to hear that. Tom will be happy to have you back, too. Well anyway, have fun at school, but first and foremost, stick to the books. That's what you're there for. College may not be what you want in the end, but you'll never know unless you give it a try."

"Well, I plan on working hard, and I'm pretty sure this is what I want to do."

"That's good; I'm glad to hear that. But you know, if you decide college isn't right for you and want to try something else, your own business maybe, I'll help you out, however I can."

"Oh, okay, Dad. I never really thought about it, but thanks."

We shake hands and I can't help but notice how weak his grip is. We wish each other good luck on our respective paths, mine to West Virginia University and a new life, his to the Cleveland Clinic and a desperate operation. I feel disingenuous for my words; I know too well that the path before him is precarious and doubtful.

"You better get going, Duane. Don't keep Will waiting. Take care of yourself."

"Good bye, Dad."

Andrew Ryan, and his brother, Martin, owned and operated a small coal business at the confluence of the Monongahela and Cheat Rivers, ten miles south of Homewood. Ryan Coal Company was situated on the north side of the Cheat and consisted of several small buildings, a front end loader, some machinery built into the riverbank, and a conveyor belt that extended out over the water. Coal was purchased from strip mines in the area, crushed into small uniform chunks, loaded onto barges, and shipped downstream to the steel mills in Pittsburgh.

I worked for my father the summer after I graduated from high school and I loved my job at Ryan Coal Company. I met some amazing and zany characters, including Tom Drew, a seasoned barge hand who had worked on the river since before I was born. Another, younger man, Ronny, was always friendly and joking with me, and was one of the hardest workers I've ever known. Years later, I learned that he had ascended to the position of grand dragon in the Ku Klux Klan. And there was Jim with his long brown hair and crooked teeth, not much older than I was. If Jim didn't show up for work on a Monday, he was probably in jail for some incident that occurred over the weekend. For some reason, I fit in with these men, and worked well with them.

Toward the end of summer, Dad was often too ill to go to work, and my Uncle Martin would pick me up in the morning. I would pack my lunch, and then stand in the hallway just as it was getting light, watching for his headlights. Some mornings my father would be sitting across the hall in the living room, and we would talk.

We mostly talked about how things were going with the business. He might ask me how many barges would be filled by the end of the week, or he wanted to know how the coal looked. Dad talked with Uncle Martin on a daily basis, but from me he learned what was happening on the barges.

There was much to talk about those days. After struggling to maintain the business during the waning years of the great coal era in southwestern Pennsylvania, Ryan Coal Company was doing well—for political reasons. Instability in the Mideast, led to greater pressure on the United States to utilize its own natural resources, and as a result, the demand for coal grew. My father and his brother had a stockpile of good quality coal at the time and their little company prospered as a result.

Sadly, as the number of barges going downriver to Pittsburgh increased, and the financial future of Ryan Coal Company brightened, my father's health declined and his personal prospects grew dim. The pain was often so great that he couldn't sleep at night, and that's why he was sitting in the living room on those August mornings. Dad's health deteriorated rapidly, and in early September, four days after I left for college, he died during surgery.

To this day, I remember the tolling of the steeple bell as his casket was removed from the hearse and carried up the steps into Saint Mathew's Church. The bell sounded solemn and final, it's melancholic tones reverberating across the Saint Mathew's campus, an institution that my father had been associated with since he was born.

When my father died, I came to realize how final death is. There were no more comments from Andrew Ryan, no more words of advice, and no more discussions of the coal business. Everything that Dad had done and everything that he said, began to drift back in time that day, never again to be updated or to intertwine with the lives of his family and friends. Sadness, anguish, and guilt, were what remained for us to deal with.

But time heals, as they say, and time kept moving. Four years later, I graduated from West Virginia University and for the next six years, I lived in Madison, Wisconsin, where among other activities, I took up woodcarving. I got married and tried to settle into a normal life; I got divorced and have never tried to be normal since. For a number of years, I lived alone in an old log house in the Allegheny mountains, eking out a living as a woodcarver. One year, I lived with a women in West Virginia, another year with a women named Vera, and then alone again.

I moved south to the mountains of North Carolina, where I met and married a pretty divorcee named Elaine Caldwell. Elaine was, witty, intelligent, impulsive, and last but not least, she had wealthy parents. At the age of thirty-eight, she had everything she needed to begin the next phase of her life except a bohemian artist husband, and that's when I rolled into town in my pickup truck.

At her insistence, and with Mom and Dad's blessing, we bought a building on Main Street in Janesville so that I could have my own galley and she could manage it (and me), while tying it all into the home decorating business she was developing. From early on, it was obvious that my work, as it was, could not be the focus of her business if she was to have any hope of success, and I flatly refused to change my style to cater to the tastes of her clientele.

Elaine and I got along in spite of this friction. After all, we had both been married before and knew that compromise is a part of marriage. Of course I still attended the lavish Thanksgiving party her parents held each year before they flew to Key West for the winter, and Mr. and Mrs. Caldwell continued to smile and introduce me as Elaine's husband, *the artist*. I began to sense, however, that

Duane Ryan and his Gallery were a disappointment in the eyes of the Caldwell family.

Elaine was out of town when I celebrated my forty-fourth birthday; I was alone in my studio, sipping vodka. I had only recently acquired a taste for vodka, having come to appreciate the quicker, cleaner buzz it had to offer relative to beer or wine.

I thought about my father that evening and not by chance, but by association: forty-four was the age he was when he died. Twenty-six years had gone by since then, and for most of that time, the number stood out in my mind because it seemed like such a young age for a person to die. In more recent times, it served as a reminder that it could happen to me.

I thought back to the last conversations I had with my father, the discussions we had about the coal business, while I waited for Uncle Martin to pick me up. I wondered what he was thinking on those mornings, sitting alone in the dark, and on impulse I picked up a sketch pad and drew a picture from the image in my head. I depicted the entry way to the living room with a simple rectangle and sketched a seated human figure to represent my father. I didn't draw anything else, just my father, sitting in space within the rectangle. I didn't retouch the drawing or dwell on it, instead, I closed the sketch pad, finished my vodka and went home.

Some years later, I came upon this curious drawing and scarcely remembered doing it, yet I was so intrigued that I decided to translate it into wood. From a board, I cut out a rectangular section and inset a piece of walnut to represent the darkened living room. The human figure, I carved out of cherry, keeping as true to the sketch as possible, and then mounted it on the walnut panel.

There was so much I didn't know about my father when I talked to him on those August mornings in 1973, that in a sense, I didn't really know him. For that reason, I titled the carving *The Man In The Room*.

Typically, I prefer not to tell the story behind a particular carving because I don't want to influence what people see in it. It's not unusual for the same piece to receive very different interpretations, and that's fine by me.

Such has been the case with *The Man in The Room*. Most people feel that the man represents someone who is isolated and alone, but the piece has received a variety of interpretations over the years. Some assume it was created as a self portrait, which at some subconscious level, it may have been. Perhaps I put myself in my father's place and tried to imagine being faced with such an overwhelming dilemma.

While many have been intrigued by the carving and it has elicited numerous comments, *The Man in The Room* has hung in my gallery ever since.

20

As Brittany and I walk into the entrance hall of the Grand View Hotel, my heart is palpitating. And why wouldn't it be? Here I am after forty years, Duane Ryan, the long lost, wayward son, finally appearing at a Saint Mathew's High School reunion. Brittany is nonchalant in the spotlight and her company helps me to relax somewhat. I'm relieved to see a bar in the entrance hall with people milling about and sitting at tables in conversation. I wasn't quite ready for the grand ballroom and this transition area will suit my purposes well.

I escort my date to a table that is situated against a wall and close to the bar. When in public, I prefer to have my back against a wall whenever possible, and when I need a refill, I don't like to weave and bob through a crowd to advertise where I'm going, or worse, get hung up in a conversation that might slow my passage to the bar. This table must have been placed here just for me.

"Brittany, would you like a glass of wine?"

"Yes, I'd love one, a white wine, please."

"I need to detour to the gentleman's room and I'll hit the bar on my way back."

"I'll be here, handsome."

The rest rooms are down a hall to the right just inside the hotel entrance. I nod and wave to a few people as I move in that direction, and grin at Bob who is standing in a corner within a small crowd, but I keep moving. I don't want to socialize until it's on my terms.

Alone in the restroom, I peer at my reflection in the mirror.

God, I get older and uglier by the day. There are too many lights in here. I look best by the light of a single bulb, shining from somewhere behind me. Does Brittany really think I'm handsome or is she humoring me?

I pull the flask from my pocket and ponder that question with a purposeful swallow. Such a classy restroom, nicer than some places I've lived in over the years. I know it seems decadent, hanging out in the restroom, drinking vodka, but I only do it to deal with my phobia of public situations. For now, vodka is cheaper than a psychiatrist.

However, I mustn't linger here; I must go back out. *You can do this, Duane.* Besides, it's just a matter of time before someone comes in and kills the mood. A few stray hairs smoothed into place, a few more healthy swallows, shoulders back, and I'm ready to face the world.

Just as I reenter the social milieu, I see this familiar hulk of a man, walking in my direction, while talking over his shoulder to someone. I recognize him as an old acquaintance, one that I never expected to see here, and who I know will be even more surprised to see me. I nonchalantly step into his path such that he nearly walks into me.

"Sorry there, buddy, I should watch where I'm . . . Jesus Christ, I don't believe it. Is it really you?"

"No, not Jesus. I know there's a resemblance, but the name's Ryan, Duane Ryan."

"Ha, hah, now I know it's you—same old Ryan."

"Hey Booker, it's been a while."

"It sure has been a while. When the hell did I see you last?"

"Long time ago; I seem to remember a late night at Corky's Bar."

"That's right. Ten, fifteen years ago? I can't remember. We got kind of drunk, if I remember, right."

"Booker, that would describe every time we were at Corky's."

"I know; we sure tipped a few back at that fine establishment."

"They don't make bars like that anymore. Is it still in business?"

"It sure is. In fact I bought Corky's a few years back just to make sure it stays that way ."

"No kidding? So drinks are on the house then."

"You bet."

Mike Prizza, or *Booker*, as he was known in high school, transferred from Homewood High to Saint Mathew's before his junior year. Exactly why he switched schools at that stage of his academic career was a bit of a mystery. His mother was an alumna of Saint Mathew's School and the story went that she wanted at least one of her sons get a Catholic education. His father was never in the picture at Saint Mathew's and Booker didn't talk about him often. All I knew about the man was that he had a wholesaling business in Pittsburgh and wasn't around town much.

Booker appears much as I remember him, an imposing figure, six foot four, large-framed and strong-looking. He has much thicker hair than I do, and combs it straight back to frame his swarthy features. When he was in high school, Mike Prizza actually booked bets on sports events, hence the nickname, *Booker*.

Booker and I didn't hit it off so well when he first arrived on the scene at Saint Mathew's. To be more specific, he didn't really like me and I hated him. A big, loud, redneck jerk is how I sized him up at first; an intellectual, sneaky, hippie-type was how he characterized me. At the same time he was intrigued by my odd personality and he wouldn't leave me alone, often teasing me in a playful, mocking way, while I mostly ignored him.

One day, when I wasn't in the mood for his antics, the Ryan temper kicked in, and I told him where to go and how to get there, employing some of my favorite profanity. Booker was taken aback, but instead of responding in kind, he grinned from ear to ear. I think when he realized that along with being the intellectual, sneaky, hippie-type, I was a bit of a hard ass too, he thought I was alright, and we hit it off from then on.

"So what are you doing back in these parts? I figured that after your family all moved away, we'd never see you around here again."

"I'm still not entirely sure myself, but I'm glad I came now. Good to see you again."

"Likewise. I wasn't planning to attend this thing, but decided just to blow through and see who was here. I never thought I'd bump into you. Are you here with someone; you married?"

"Nah, I was, but not anymore. I do have a date. Brittany Shuster is her name and she's over there at the table by the bar."

"Whoa, you son of a bitch, she's gorgeous, and she's staring right at us."

"That's because I was supposed to bring her a glass of wine ten minutes ago."

"Why you cad. There's the damn bar; get the lady a drink. I'm going over to introduce myself and try to steal her from you."

"Okay, what do you want?"

"Ah, get me a Scotch on the rocks, I guess. Hey, this is on me, Duane. I got a tab running."

"Nah, come on now, Book, it's on me."

"No way, this is my town, therefore, my treat."

Booker shouts toward the bar.

"Hey, Billy."

The bartender looks up as he pours a pina colada into a glass. Booker tilts his head toward me; Billy nods and returns his attention to the pina colada.

I wend my way toward Billy and lean on the bar while he works his way down the line. Billy is a classic bartender in dress and demeanor, like a character in an old movie. He's wearing a red vest over a brilliant, white shirt with a neat, black bowtie at the collar, and he's the master of doing several things at once with his hands, all the while making witty, verbal exchanges with the crowd. I had only been at the bar a minute when he spun in my direction and smiled.

"Hey, I know Mike said to put it on his tab, but I . . ."

"You might as well enjoy your drink, because nobody wins this argument with Mr. Prizza. Besides, he loves to buy drinks for people. I don't know how well you know him, but believe me, he can afford it. Mr. Prizza can afford to buy everybody in here drinks all night, and knowing him, he just might."

"Wow, what's he do?"

"Lot's of things, building supply, real estate; family has some sort of wholesaling business in Pittsburgh. You from around here?"

"I grew up here, but I've been away for a while."

"Well, take my word on it, and enjoy your drink. I'd tell you more, but your party is waiting."

Billy nods in the direction of my table. When I turn, Brittany and Booker are looking my way and Booker is demonstrating his impatience by gesturing with an imaginary glass. Billy fills my order quickly and is attending to another patron before I leave the bar. As I approach the table, Booker and Brittany are deep in conversation.

"So you say this priest kills the nun to keep her quiet about their affair."

"Yes, that's the story line I'm working with now."

"Hey, stuff like that *does* happen. Are you a Catholic, Brittany?"

"No. My mother used to be a Catholic but became a Baptist when she married my father, so I was raised Baptist. I haven't been to church in years, though. I'm an agnostic now."

"Agnostic, what does that mean? I forget."

"Agnostics believe that it's impossible to prove the existence of God, so I don't really follow any organized religion."

"It's not the same as an atheist?'

"No, I believe there's some spirit or force behind everything; I can't believe that life is all by chance. But what that force or spirit might be is what I wonder about. Are you a Catholic?"

"Oh yah, sure, I'm Catholic. I've been a member of Saint Mathew's Church all my life. I don't go to Mass every Sunday like

I should, but I'm a Catholic all the way."

"I heard that. You know well from the instruction we received at Saint Mathew's that every time you skip mass, it's a mortal sin, and all it takes is one to seal your fate, brother."

"Well look who's finally back from his great journey to the bar. And don't tell me about mortal sins, mister atheist, I know I got some and I'll deal with them. Yours must number in the thousands by now."

"What are mortal sins to an atheist? It's you believers that have to worry about them. Better hit the confessional Booker. You're toying with eternal damnation here: do not pass go, do not collect two hundred, go straight to Hell."

"Hey, I'll save you a place when I get there. Let's change the subject; I don't want to argue with you about religion now.

So, Mr. Ryan, I have to know, what finally brings you back to this part of the world? Surely you're not here just because of the reunion."

"Actually, it *is* the reason. Dale prodded me about coming this year because the school is slated for demolition, and believe it or not, the fact that the old place is going to be torn down, struck a chord in me."

"Yah, doesn't that suck? Some of us are working to keep the building standing, but it won't be easy. The Duke is the Duke, and he usually gets his way. He did back when we were in high school and he does now.

Do you know who Duke is, Brittany?"

"Yes, Bishop McGee."

"Right, and the man wields a lot of power as the Bishop, in the church and in local politics. He seems to want Saint Mathew's High School leveled and unless we mount an overwhelming case against it, that's probably what's going to happen."

"Dale mentioned that a group of alumni are making an effort to stop the demolition, but I never guessed you were one of them, Booker."

"Yah well, I've been watching this situation develop from the sidelines, and only recently jumped into the fight. I probably would have stayed out of it except that my mother went to Saint Mathew's, too, and she's a mess over this. She asked me to try to do something about it and she doesn't ask stuff like that often."

"Well, tell me, Booker, do you think there's some personal reason why Duke would want the building torn down? There are plenty of practical reasons, and they're hard to argue against, but do you think he might have an ulterior motive?"

"Nah, I think he's just a jerk who always has to have things his way. He looked at the books and made up his mind. Why, do *you* think there's more to it than that?"

"Well, I didn't, but in the last twenty-four hours, I've heard some things that make me suspicious. I think there's a chance he might have something that he wants to cover up."

"Are you serious? Hey, I'm all ears. I'd love to get something on Duke."

"Why do you want to get something on Bishop McGee?"

"Leverage, Brittany; leverage is everything in life—better than money. We need something to convince him that it's in his best interest to leave the school alone. So, let's hear it, Duane."

"Well Booker, why don't we save it for now. It's kind of a long story and I see Dale and Jen headed this way."

"Okay, I want to hear it though."

"Right. Maybe later we can belly up to the bar and I'll fill you in."

"I won't be here later. I'm picking up Maureen at the Pittsburgh airport at eleven, so I should be cutting out of here after this drink. How about breakfast in the morning? Are you staying a while?"

"Yah, until Monday. I was up in the air about how long I would stay, but things are getting interesting around here."

"Where are you staying, anyway?"

"Expresso Inn."

"I should have guessed that."

"Why?"

"Cause I know you, that's why. But hey, let's hit Duval's for breakfast. How about I pick you up in the morning, say eight, eight-thirty? You can drink your espresso on the way."

"Breakfast at Duval's, that sounds good. I don't think I have anything in my planner for then."

"A planner eh, that's a laugh. You probably scribble your appointments on the back of a bar napkin. Brittany, are you up for breakfast?"

"I don't think so; I'm planning to sleep in."

"Well, then it's nice to meet you, and I look forward to seeing you again."

Booker stands and bows.

"You two have fun tonight. I have to run."

21

The Allegheny Room isn't as large as I remember it, but just as grand as the picture I have carried in my head over the years. The first time I saw this majestic ballroom, it seemed huge, like the inside of Saint Mathew's Church. No doubt that's because I was small at the time. My father took Will and me on a tour of the hotel one day when we were here for a family reunion, and his reason for showing us this particular room was because the wedding reception for him and my mother had been held here.

The Allegheny Room is a beaux-arts treasure and a part of Homewood history. Whatever American president it was who stayed at the Grand View Hotel (Truman, I think), he and his wife are said to have danced here. The room features white oak floors, thirty foot high ceilings, gold leafed, egg and dart molding, and turn of the century, teardrop chandeliers. Ten foot high double hung windows add stunning mountain vistas to the general air of opulence. Even an unrefined figure such as myself appreciates a little opulence from time to time.

As we enter the room, the band is playing a mellow, jazzy tune that appeals to my higher senses and beckons me to the dance floor. I haven't danced in years and would be uneasy, strutting my stuff at such an event, except that I have vodka-induced boldness to keep me in step. I wasn't a bad dancer in my day, and while my day is long past, to such compelling music, I think I can still shake a leg.

Decorated tables, each lit with a solitary candle lantern, are clustered at one end of the oval room. Most alumni and guests are sitting there or hovering about the perimeter of the room, staying clear of the dance floor for now, but there are couples dancing. Not surprisingly, Dale and Jen are front and center. They took dance lessons when still in high school and have been dazzling audiences ever since. What I do know about dancing, I learned from them.

"This room is wonderful, Duane, classy and formal, but not overdone, and everybody looks so nice. I haven't been to a formal since I was in high school and nothing ever as nice as this. Thanks for bringing me."

"My pleasure Ms. Schuster. Shall we dance?"

"I'd love too."

Brittany and I join the dancers and all around us heads turn. Does it get any better than this? I appear after all these years, me, the bohemian alumnus, the renegade artist, the Great Sphinx, twirling about the dance floor with a beautiful, mysterious women in my arms.

Let them wonder about my good fortune, my mysterious life of art and romance. They need not know that I'm a financial wreck, dealing with depression, and alcoholism, a man who in recent years has questioned the life that he's chosen, and in some dark moments, even if life is worth choosing. In spite of that, or maybe because of it, I deserve to enjoy this moment. Let them watch me now, living a life that they will never know and can only imagine.

"May I cut in here?"

"What? We just got started."

"Too bad, hippie. Mind your dance etiquette."

Dale grins as he steps away with my date, and I turn to see his wife, Jenifer, smiling at me.

"I know I'm not so young and sexy, but I'll try to hold my own."

"That's nonsense, Jen, you can hold your own against anyone."

I take Jen's hand in mine and we dance. She has a mischievous smile on her face that hints at what's coming.

"You have a lot of nerve bringing someone so young and pretty to the formal. Did you do it just to make all of us old girls jealous?"

"That's not really how it happened, Jen. Didn't Dale tell you? I didn't even know her until . . ."

"I know, Duane, I'm just teasing. Well she seems nice, and however you got together, you two make a nice couple."

"You think so?"

"Yes, I mean that. You seem really comfortable together."

"You know, we *are* comfortable together. I was just thinking that this morning."

"She's very pretty. Not in a glamorous way, but in a natural way, which I prefer. Did you ever notice how much Brittany looks like her sister, Sally?"

"No, I hadn't thought about it. But now that you mention it, she does in a way. It's been so long that it's hard for me to clearly picture Sally. I'm surprised that you remember her that well."

"There's a picture of her in the yearbook. We were looking at it last night with Bob and Darlene."

"I never thought of that. I wouldn't have, though, since I never bought a year book."

"Well, I'll show you the picture, but take my word for it, there's a strong resemblance. Dale thinks so too. Considering that Sally and Brittany are half-sisters and separated by twenty years in age, I think the resemblance is remarkable."

"I *have* noticed that her eyes are like Sally's: the same shade of green and with the same sparkle to them."

"You seem to have looked into Sally's eyes a time or two."

We had just made a turn, and I was looking away. When I return my gaze to Jen, the look on her face indicates that she had not made an uninformed statement.

"All right, how much do you know?"

"Everything. You can't expect a couple who has been together for as long as Dale and I have, to not know everything about everything."

"Well, what do you think?"

"I think it's a sad story, Duane. Were you in love with Sally?"

"Yes, I was, at least as much in love as an eighteen year old can be."

"Was that incident in the library the only time you held or kissed her?"

"Yes, but it had been coming on for months, and we both knew it. And it was so nice, right up until Father McGee barged in."

"He should have handled that better. After all you were only eighteen and Sally was young, too. I don't care what his feelings might have been for Sally."

"Oh, you know about what Bob told us, then?"

"Yes and I don't see that as an excuse. As far as I'm concerned it just makes his behavior all the more inexcusable."

The music stops; I thank my partner and give her a hug as Dale and Brittany come up beside us. Dale leads us to a table in a corner of the room, a location much to my liking. A couple is already seated there who I recognize as Paul and Jamie Grimm, and it's such a surprise because I haven't seen them since we were in high school together. Paul and I were classmates from first to twelfth grade, and Jamie transferred to Saint Mathew's as a freshman in high school. Along with Dale and Jen, Paul and Jamie are one of three married couples who started dating while they were students at Saint Mathew's High School.

Lenny Bryson and his wife, Pat, join us at this point and sit between Jen and Brittany. Lenny graduated from Saint Mathew's a few years after me, so I never knew him well. I do remember him as a quiet, likeable fellow and know that he's an architect who works with Dale on occasion. I had never met Pat until this evening, but learn that she and Lenny met while they both attended college in Arizona. After everyone is introduced, the Brysons and Brittany settle into a conversation about the southwest.

Paul and Jamie and I exchange highlights of our lives from the decades since high school, and Paul asks the question that seems to be on everybody's mind.

"So Duane, what brings you to a reunion after all these years?"

"Oh, a number of factors played into it, Paul. The timing was right for me, both with my work and with life in general. But I have to admit, a desire to see the old school before it was torn down was definitely a reason."

"Good, whatever it takes to get you here, only too bad it's happening. That's a crime, isn't it? You know, there are some people who are working hard to stop the demolition plans."

"I know; I just talked to one of them. Mike Prizza was here earlier. Do you think there's still a chance the demolition could be stopped?"

"A slim one, but if anyone can stop it, it's Prizza. The man has the ways and the means, if you know what I'm saying?"

"Hmm, I *think* I know what you're saying."

"But the Bishop's no pushover to anyone, and in the end, he has the final word."

"I know what you're saying there, too. Tell me Paul, do you ever wonder why Duke is so determined to tear the school down? It seems strange to me considering all the years he spent at Saint Mathew's. Do you think there could be a reason that he wants the building torn down, besides the obvious economic arguments, like some personal reason?"

"You know, Jamie and I were just talking about it the other night and we think it's strange, too that he's behind this. But does he have a personal reason? I can't imagine what it might be. Why, do *you* think he does?"

"Actually I wouldn't have given it much thought a day ago, but now I think it's a real possibility. You remember Carmen the janitor?"

"Sure, how could I forget Carmen? Someone told me that he died recently."

"Yah, he did, the day before yesterday. Did you happen to hear about the talk Bob Macy and Nick Smathers had with Carmen a few weeks ago?"

"No, Jamie and I just got into town this afternoon and really haven't had a chance to talk to either of them."

I notice that Lenny is attending to our conversation, so I tell both him and Paul the story of the encounter with Carmen at Mutt's Place. Then I augment the tale with what Bob and I learned today from the bartender.

"Well isn't that bizarre that Carmen would die shortly after saying those things?"

"Hmm, I think it's a coincidence, Paul, but why bizarre? Are you proposing that he might have killed himself, like maybe out of guilt for something he did?"

"Maybe because of guilt, or *perhaps*, he could have been killed for something that he knew, to keep him quiet."

"Uh, excuse me Paul, but are you a conspiracy theory nut or something?"

"You've hit the nail right on the head, Duane," Jamie said, laughing and pushing against her husband's shoulder.

"One of Paul's favorite websites is *The True Story.com*."

"Hey, that's alright with me. I love a good conspiracy. Tell us more, Paul. What do you think the *true* story is here?"

"Okay, how about this? Duke was up to something with the old boiler room, and Carmen obviously had a hand in it. After the passage of time, Carmen couldn't live with his conscience, took to the bottle and began to talk too much. In the end, he had to be knocked off to keep him quiet, especially with the reunion coming to town."

"Wow, I like it, Paul, but that's pretty far out there, don't you think?"

"I don't know if it's so far out there", Lenny added, obviously excited by our line of conversation. He leans closer to say something, but is interrupted by two young waiters who begin weaving in and out among us as they serve dinner. We suspend our discussion of intrigue and conspiracy to join the general conversation around the table and partake of our meal.

I focus on my shiitake mushroom fettuccine—a dish to rival chili dogs with coleslaw. If I could cook like this, vegetarianism would be easy.

While listening to the discussion around me, I'm distracted by Paul's boiler room theory. Part of me wants to reject it out of hand as too far-fetched, because for some reason, I don't really want it to be true. Yet I must admit that alongside the explanations I've come up with to explain Carmen's behavior, Paul's hypothesis is not so easy to dismiss. Apparently this is the case for Lenny as well because after dessert, when Paul and Jamie move to the dance floor, he takes the seat next to me.

"Hey Duane, I have some information that may back up what Paul said, something that I was reminded of when I heard you guys talking just now. Did you know that I'm related to the Hanlons that used to live on the corner of Shady Lane and Jefferson Street? John Hanlon was my uncle."

"Big Bad John was your uncle? I remember him well. He was the head usher in church and Monsignor Schroeder's right hand man."

"That's right, I think he was an usher for nearly fifty years, twenty years before Father McGee even arrived on the scene."

"How'd he like Duke?"

"He didn't. They locked horns from the start and he watched him like a hawk. In some ways, Uncle John was the watchman of the parish anyway, and even though he wasn't on the payroll, believe me, he took the job seriously. When Father McGee arrived on the scene, he made it his personal mission to keep an eye on him."

"Is Big John still alive?"

"No, he's dead now, but what I want to tell you about is a story he used to tell that involved Father McGee and Carmen, something he saw years ago. He said that Carmen's truck pulled into the high school parking lot late one night and Father McGee was with him. They got something out of the bed of the truck and carried it into the building."

"You're kidding me."

"No, I kid you not. Uncle John said that they were in the shadow between street lights, so he couldn't make out what it was, but he said that it was something big enough that they both had to carry it."

"Whew, I don't know what to think about that. Why those two and why at night? Whatever they were carrying, Lenny, it's weird."

"I agree. And get this, Uncle John said that after they went into the building, the basement lights came on."

"Well isn't that interesting? When exactly did your uncle see this?"

"That's the *real* interesting part of it. Uncle John told me it happened toward the end of my freshman year, which would make it . . ."

"The year I graduated, and about the time the boiler room was sealed up."

"Right, and I never thought of a connection until just now."

"Lenny, are you sure about all this?"

"I'm sure about the story; I heard it more than once, and I really can't imagine Uncle John making something like that up."

"Did he tell anyone official, like someone on the parish committee?"

"Apparently he did, but it never went too far. From what my mother has told me, Uncle John had issues with a number of people, anyone who didn't see things his way, so he had a reputation for stirring up trouble. I never thought much of the story either and pretty much forgot about it, but now with what Carmen said, I think it's worthy of note."

"Duke and Carmen hid something in the boiler room before it was closed up."

"Yes, that's the way I interpret it, Duane, but since Carmen is dead, and the room will soon be under a parking lot, we'll never know what it was."

"Well, let's not give up yet, Lenny. There's a movement afoot

150

to gain access to the boiler room. Bob came up with the idea to come right out and ask Duke if we can open the boiler room for old times sake, to see the old hangout one last time."

"What do you think the chances are of him saying yes?"

"I thought they were slim before, but considering what you just told me, I'd guess they're zero. But the real gist of the plan is to see how Duke reacts to the question. If he laughs and says yes, then all is well, and we can laugh too. If he panics and pulls out a gun, then we have a problem."

"Ha, hah, what do you thinks going to happen?"

"I don't know, Lenny. I'm really hoping it'll end with a good laugh for everybody, but I've got an uneasy feeling that there's a problem here."

22

"**B**rittany, are you awake?"

No response; she's asleep. Perhaps I went into too much detail about the people she met this evening. She asked for it, but I probably did get carried away. I'm surprised at how much pleasure I find in recalling the stories of my former classmates.

Through the open window, I hear the whirring and clicking of night insects, certainly a more soothing sound than the mechanical hum of the interstate highway outside the Expresso Inn. I was hesitant to stay at the Oak Park Motel rather than return to the security of the Expresso Inn, but lying here now in this quiet setting, next to such wonderful company, I'm glad I overcame my reticence. How have I come to grow so old and conservative? And after all, I can still swing by in the morning and pick up my espresso.

Brittany told me that she had fun at the formal and she was certainly a delight to be with. Everybody seemed to like her, even the women. I was actually expecting to see some serious eyebrow raising, but I didn't notice any. People seemed to accept the fact that we were together, young, pretty woman that she is and old, not-so-bad-looking-for-his-age man that I am.

I had fun, too, I have to admit. I never thought I would see some of those people again, let alone drink, and laugh and dance with them. Carla Daniels told me that I dance now just like I did when I was in high school, and she ought to know. We danced together often back then. Carla is another of the twenty students of our graduating class who went the entire distance, attending Saint Mathew's School from first grade to twelfth.

Carla is a few months younger than me, much prettier than me, and divorced like me. She is of fair complexion with soft features that have become more refined and dignified with age. Her brown hair is flecked with gray, a highlight that I find appealing in a woman's appearance at this stage of the game.

Throughout our school days, Carla and I always had *a thing for each other*, as they say, something that was true even when we were kids in grade school. Most of the time we were just good friends, but occasionally it got more serious. Oddly enough, the summer after our senior year a real romance began to take root. She had recently split up with a guy from Homewood High that she had been seeing for a few years and I was still in a state of confusion over what had transpired between Sally and me.

I think that Carla and I were just the company each other needed to weather that transition period. Over the next year, we got together when we were home from college. We partied together, kissed and hugged a time or two and slept together once, but there was always reluctance to allow a full-blown relationship to develop. We kept in touch, even for a while after we graduated from college, but never again after Carla married.

I was there that day, sitting among the congregation at Saint Mathew's Church, with my long hair flowing down the back of the suit jacket I had purchased at a second hand boutique only a few days before. I was all smiles and congratulations, but secretly fantasized that I was the groom, standing beside the beautiful bride that Carla was. Yet, even then while I daydreamed, I realized that such a match would never work.

I moved along on my career path as a scientist and then as an artist; Carla raised a family, and pursued a business profession. Our memories of each other remained back in a simpler, happy era, which is just as well.

But lo, I think I may have sensed a spark between Carla and me tonight on the dance floor. Could it be that the fledgling love of our youth might finally take wing after all these years? Let's see, she's a successful financial advisor in Connecticut and I'm scraping bottom, in North Carolina. It just might work; I've heard that opposites sometimes complement each other.

What an absurd notion! Time to ease off the vodka for tonight. Carla has led such a typical life: marriage, children, a successful career, divorce, grandchildren. There's been nothing typical about my life, except for the divorce part. Carla and I would never work as a couple. Regardless, it was fun seeing her again and the experience has stirred up many memories.

Carla is the youngest of six children from a traditional Saint Mathew's family, and at one point her family was represented in the school system from third grade to eleventh grade. Carla's brothers and sisters were well liked, and I knew them all, but it was with the oldest, Bill, that I became good friends.

The campus cafeteria at Saint Mathew's School was located in the basement of the grade school, and each day the high school students walked across the grade school parking lot to the cafeteria for lunch. Bill Daniels would often stop to talk with Carla as he went by our recess area, and that's how I met him.

Bill and I became friends, and sometimes he would stop and talk even when I wasn't with Carla. Bill Daniels conversed with me differently then other older people did. He listened to what I said and remembered what we talked about whenever we spoke again. And he never talked to me like I was a kid; he just talked about things, like we were buddies. I waited for him at lunch break and looked forward to talking with him.

Bill was a good basketball player and played for the Saint Mathew's Eagles varsity team, so we often talked about basketball. He urged me to get my own basketball and begin practicing so that I could play for the team one day. I lobbied my parents and received a basketball for my next birthday. I wanted to be like Bill Daniels someday.

After the school year ended, I spent many hours on the basketball court at the Crawford Street Park with my new basketball.

I had a hard time just getting the ball up over the rim of the basket and dribbling was not going well, but I kept trying because Bill had encouraged me to do it. As the next school year approached, I was anxious to show him how much better I had gotten over the summer.

1965

I stayed at the basketball court too long and I'm late for lunch again. My brothers and sisters are finishing their meals as I arrive at the table. My mother doesn't like it when I'm late for lunch, but she isn't saying anything about it today.

Mom spreads mayonnaise on a toasted bun, the beginning of a fried green tomato sandwich. In our family, we eat fried green tomato sandwiches a lot at this time of year, and it's one of my favorite meals. After she serves me, Mom watches the next batch of breaded tomato slices that are crowded into the big iron frying pan on the stove.

Mom is really quiet and my brothers and sisters have left the table, so that the sound of tomato slices popping and sizzling in hot oil is louder than I ever remember it. When the last of the crispy slices are laid on a paper towel to soak up the oil, she turns off the burner and sits down across from me at the table. I'm eating my fried green tomato sandwich when she tells me.

"Duane, I have some bad news. Your friend, Bill Daniels, drowned at Ohiopyle this morning."

I stop eating and look at my mother.

"He was with some other boys, wading up above the falls. Bill slipped and fell into fast water and was swept over the falls. He couldn't get out of the undertow."

"Bill's dead? They can't save him at the hospital or anything?"

"He drowned, Duane. It's too late to save him. Bill Daniels is dead. I'm sorry, but these things happen in life. I know it doesn't seem right when someone young dies like this, but it happens."

I'm in shock. I feel like crying, but I can't for some reason.

Could my friend Bill really be dead, forever? It seems impossible. I can picture him so well, the way he smiles, the way he talks. Am I to believe that I'll never see him smile or hear him talk again? As much as I like fried green tomato sandwiches, I only finish half of mine and ask to be excused.

We have a big yard with a thick hedge around it. In one of the back corners of the yard, where the hedge is real wide, my brother and I cut out a space inside for a secret hiding place. I take my basketball and go there after lunch. I don't feel like practicing basketball anymore. I use my basketball for a seat, instead.

Ohiopyle is a park up in the mountains, and I've been going there since I was a baby. I know it so well that I can picture it in my mind. Ohiopyle Falls are so strong and loud that I've always been afraid of them. Even the ground shakes when you stand close to the falls, so I never get too near the edge. I wonder what it was like for Bill going over. I picture him swinging his arms and screaming, because that's what I would do if I was going over Ohiopyle Falls. But no matter how hard I try, I just can't picture Bill as a dead person.

In religion class, we learned about the different places people go after they die. There are four of them: heaven, hell, purgatory, and limbo. Just a person's soul goes to one of these places and their body is buried at the cemetery. I never can imagine what a soul looks like, so I picture it as looking like the dead person it came from, but sort of white, and you can see through it.

Limbo is a place where babies go if they die but aren't baptized. Baptism washes away original sin, the sin committed by Adam and Eve that we all have on our soul when we're born. A soul with original sin can't go to heaven, so when babies die who aren't baptized, their souls have to go to limbo.

Sister Saint Hubert told us that limbo is almost like heaven and the babies will always be happy there, but because they have original sin, they can never see God. limbo doesn't sound too bad to me: just like heaven but with no one watching you. I think I would rather go there than heaven, but I never tell anyone that.

156

I know that Bill was baptized, and besides, he's sixteen years old, so I know that he's not in limbo. And Bill is such a good guy, that he can't be in hell either. A person goes to hell if they die with a mortal sin on their soul. A mortal sin is a bad sin and breaks a person's link to God's grace. Because of this, the person's soul dies, and unless they go to confession, and have the mortal sin forgiven, they go to hell.

Now, one good thing is that most mortal sins aren't that easy to get and you have to do something really bad, like murder someone, to get one. But there's one mortal sin that's fairly easy to commit, and that's missing Mass on Sunday. I think that's too big a punishment, burning in hell forever with murderers just for missing Mass, but I believe it, and I never miss Mass. I hope that Bill didn't make the mistake of skipping Mass and thought he would get to confession in time.

I really hope that Bill is in heaven, but I know that it isn't easy to get right in. Even with no mortal sins there are always small sins, or venial sins, on a persons soul. And even after sins are taken away by Confession, Sister Saint Hubert says that our soul is still stained and not holy enough to go right into heaven.

Souls with venial sins and stains must go to purgatory for a while before they can enter heaven. Sister Saint Hubert told us that purgatory isn't as bad as hell, but it isn't nice either. You still get burned. The reason is to punish us a little and clean our soul for heaven. How long we stay in purgatory depends on what's on our soul. Even though I'm only eight years old, I know that if I die, I'll have to go to purgatory for at least a little while before I get into heaven. I bet that even as good and famous as President Kennedy was, he still had to go to purgatory for a little while.

I guess that Bill is in purgatory now, but I don't think he'll be there too long: six months maybe, a year at the most. He's only sixteen and he's a good guy; his soul can't be too bad. Besides that, the time a person stays in purgatory can be shortened by prayers. Sometimes we offer our classroom prayers to the souls in purgatory to help them get out early. I think it's a neat idea: we pray to get the souls out of purgatory and into heaven, and then someday other people pray for us when we're in purgatory.

But I still can't believe that my friend, Bill, is drowned and dead. I don't want him to be dead. I want to see him when school starts and show him how much better I got at basketball over the summer. I want to hear him laugh and talk again.

I hang my head, cover my eyes, and cry. After a little while, I roll off the basketball onto my knees. I say Hail Marys and Our Fathers, the prayers I know best. I want to help my friend get out of purgatory and into heaven.

23

"You a vegetarian or something?"

"No, not really. I just like mushrooms and this sounded good. Well, actually, I *am* a vegetarian most of the time. I'm trying to be, anyway, but don't always stick to it, especially when I'm around meat eaters. Like yesterday at Sileo's Bar, I was going to just have a salad, but Dale and Bob practically forced me into eating chili dogs with them."

"Well, I'm not going to force you, but why don't you get some bacon or something. You're giving me the creeps. You need some meat on your bones. I think you're skinnier now than you were in high school."

"No thanks, not now; it's too early for me. I prefer not to gnaw on animal flesh first thing in the morning."

"There you go; same old Ryan attitude. I'm just concerned about you and trying to offer some nutrition advice and you have to get philosophical with me."

Mike Prizza and I are talking over breakfast at Duval's restaurant. Duval's is located only a few blocks from Saint Mathew's school and has been in operation for as long as I can remember. These days, I rarely eat much in the morning, but I enjoy a good old-fashioned breakfast when I'm out in the world, and I don't have to cook it. The fare at Duval's fits the bill perfectly. I'm enjoying a delicious cheese and mushroom omelet with biscuits and gravy on the side. Booker is working on pancakes and sausage links, with hash browns.

"Okay, forget it. If you're going to get touchy, I'll change the subject. Let's get down to business. What's the story you got on Duke?"

"You remember Carmen the janitor?"

"Sure, how could I forget him? How about the time he threw his mop at me?"

"Ha hah, you deserved it though."

"Oh, just because I walked across the floor he mopped?"

"It wasn't just that. It was because he told us to stop and you ignored him."

"Yah, I guess. Pretty good shot though; he got me right in the back of the leg."

"Those were the good old days, Booker, when an irate janitor could get away with throwing his mop at a kid. Well, anyway, Carmen died a couple days ago."

"No kidding. I didn't hear that. What did he die from?"

"I don't know; lots of things, I would guess."

"Well that too bad. He was an old curmudgeon, but he was alright sometimes. I'd never wish him dead."

"Neither would I, but the reason I brought Carmen up is that he imparted some interesting information about Father McGee before he departed from the world."

I tell Mike of the recent encounter with Carmen at Mutt's place, starting with Bob's first interaction with him. By the time I fill him in on Carmen's rant against the bartender, I can see that Mike is excited. After I tell him of the information I garnered from Lenny Bryson last evening and tie it all together with Paul Grimm's conspiracy theory, Mike is grinning.

"What the hell, Duane, we got some dirt on the Duke here. There's something he's hiding in the boiler room, and now he want's to cover it up with a parking lot. For him to go to that much trouble, destroying an architectural landmark and bumping off poor, old Carmen, it must be big. I wouldn't be surprised if he's hiding a body in there."

160

"C'mon Booker, I don't like the guy either, but that's jumping to conclusions, don't you think? It could be something like asbestos. Brittany said that happened once where she lived. A bunch of old asbestos was found in a buried basement when they were digging a foundation for a new building."

"I don't care if it is something like asbestos, that's still something. I just want an angle on this guy, some leverage. We got to find out what's in that room somehow."

"The bartender at Mutt's suggested that we break in."

"That's not a bad idea. After all, the school's going to be torn down anyway. It's not like we're out to steal something or vandalize the place. I'm all for it."

"I thought you'd like that approach, but there's another plan in the works. Bob and a coalition of respectable alumni are going to meet with the Bishop and ask permission to break down the wall to see the boiler room again, for old times sake."

"Hmm, I don't know what I think about that. Why show your hand when you don't have to?"

"I think it's worth a try, because whether Duke gives his permission or not, his reaction will tell a lot."

"Yah, that's true; I guess it's worth a try. But if Duke doesn't grant Bob's request, which my guess is that he won't, do you want to go ahead and break in, you and me?"

"I don't know about that. Are you serious?"

"Hell yes, why not?"

"Well, for one thing, it's a crime."

"Life's a crime, Duane. Besides, I've got a good lawyer, and if we get caught, he'll pin it all on you. I don't want the old school to come down, and I promised my mother I'd try to stop it, so I'll do whatever it takes.

And think about it, how hard would they come down on two old alumni like us, upset over the fact that our alma mater is going to be destroyed, who have a little too much to drink at their class reunion and just have to see their old hangout one last time. We would be totally vindicated in the court of public opinion and probably just get a slap on the wrist in a court of law."

"I don't know, Book, I . . ."

"C'mon, where's that old Duane Ryan insanity I used to know and love? Aren't you the guy that drove down the church steps in the jeep that night after we beat Greensburg Central Catholic for the diocese title?"

"Well, yes, I did, but . . ."

"And what about the time I went flying out Route 40 in the parents station wagon and you were on the roof, half drunk, hanging on to the luggage rack. You told the cop that you were superman."

"Phew, that's right. He didn't think that was funny, either. Well, with that resume, I'm definitely qualified for the job. Alright, I guess I'm in. When should we do it?"

"Almost has to be tonight."

"Might as well be. Nobody would expect good Catholic boys to stage a break-in on a Sunday, would they?"

"Nah, and if we aim for sometime after ten, the campus should be deserted. Hey, I think this will be fun, Duane, whether we find anything or not. I haven't done something like this in a long time. Let's hit Corky's this evening to plan it out. How about for dinner about seven? I think the cook can come up with something vegetarian for you."

"Sounds like a plan, Booker."

"I like it, and now that it's settled, let's turn the discussion to another topic that needs to be talked about."

"Like what?"

"Like your love life. Like what's with you and Brittany? God, it's like the beauty and the beast."

"Don't you think that's kind of a personal subject?"

"Yah, I know it is. That's the most interesting stuff to talk about. You can't expect to waltz into town with some pretty lady like her, half your age, and expect a decent church-going person like myself to not wonder what the story is."

"She's not half my age, she's three-fifths my age."

162

"C'mon Duane, open up. You probably need my counseling on this one."

"Well, alright, I'll tell you. Why not? It won't take long."

I give Mike an outline of my relationship with Brittany Schuster, and in doing so, remind myself of just what an unusual affair I've wandered into.

"I can't believe you just met her on Friday. You dog, you, you're a fast worker."

"Hey, believe me, this sort of thing doesn't happen to me every day. In fact it's never happened to me on any day. I'm just as surprised as anyone."

"So let me get this straight. Brittany is the half sister of the mysterious Sister Sally and she's trying to find out where Sally disappeared to after she left Saint Mathew's. Then Brittany bumps into you, who just happens to show up at a class reunion for the first time in a hundred years, and you two pair up."

"That just about sums it up, Booker."

"Hmm, maybe, but something doesn't quite add up for me. What about after the weekend?"

"No discussion of that."

"Well, be careful, man."

"Oh I don't think Brittany has any ulterior motive here, although I have to admit, there is something that makes me uneasy about it. I guess our age difference is the main thing, but then, I can't think of any relationship I was ever in that I didn't feel uneasy about something."

"Hey, I don't blame you one bit for going along, but just keep your eyes open. The older I get the more I'm convinced that you need to know as much about a person as possible before you get too friendly. You want me to have her checked out?"

"Like a background check, you can do that?"

"Yah, I can do that. You'll just get the basics on her, to see if her story's straight. No dirt, unless you want dirt."

"No, no dirt, I like Brittany. I want to believe her, but I have to admit that during sane and sober moments, it doesn't make sense to me that we paired up like this. I know I'm handsome and sexy, and she probably just can't help herself, but I still should be careful. Who knows, she might be after my money."

"You know Duane, I think I may have a background check run on you too, to make sure you haven't recently escaped from a psychiatric ward."

24

At Brittany's suggestion, I check out of the Espresso Inn to move across town to the Oak Park Motel with her. We're taking an alternative route to the motel so that I can resume the cultural and historical tour of Homewood. I'm surprised at how much I enjoy my unofficial post as tour guide for the greater Homewood area. Maybe when I finally hit rock bottom with the woodcarving business, this is an occupation I can fall back on.

I must confess, however, imparting local culture and history to my sole client is proving to be a bit of a challenge this morning. I presumed that a circuitous route to the east of town that rode the crest of Chestnut Ridge would be the pièce de résistance of the tour itinerary, but Brittany is too distracted by religion to appreciate the scenery.

"Why are you so interested in communion now?"

"I'm not *so* interested in communion, but it's something that Baptists practice too, so I'm curious."

"You have sacraments too, eh?"

"We call them ordinances, but I think they're basically the same thing. There are two of them: communion and baptism."

"Only two? I'm so sorry. I don't like to brag, but we have seven. But you know, if I had to guess which sacraments Baptists might have, baptism would be at the top of the list."

"Yes, how about that? Although I'm sure that our baptism is a lot different than yours, and I'm guessing that communion is too. For Baptists, communion is simply a remembrance of the Last Supper and anyone can receive it at any time."

"Not so simple with us. You have to be in a state of grace to receive communion. You *do* have grace in your religion, don't you?"

"Yes."

"Good. Well, to receive communion you have to be in a state of grace and even though I can't clearly explain what that means, I'm certain that I'm an example of someone who isn't."

"So, you can never go to communion?"

"Oh, yes, I could go again, if I wanted to, but I would have to return to good standings with the church and get some grace. I don't know what all would be required of me at this point, but at the least, I would have to go to confession and get my backlog of sins absolved."

"I've heard of confession, but I don't know much about it."

"Confession is basically a method by which a person has their sins forgiven by a priest. It's a fairly handy tool to have; you Baptists might want to think of picking up on it. As far as I know it's the same procedure as it always was: you have to be sorry for your sins, confess them to a priest, do some penance, and then the sins are removed from your soul."

"It's that simple?"

"It's not as simple as it sounds. Have you ever done anything like that, tell your sins to somebody, let alone a holy person?"

"No, I can't say I have and I don't think I'd like it. But, does a Catholic *have* to go to confession?"

"Uh, no, I don't think so. At least you wouldn't automatically go to hell for not going. Well, unless of course you had a mortal sin on your soul. If you died without confessing a mortal sin, then you *would* go to hell."

"What's a mortal sin?"

"A bad one, a deadly one, a sin that leads to death of the soul. In the Catholic religion, there are two types of sins, mortal sins and venial sins. Venial sins are bad too, but they won't keep you out of heaven. They're sins like cursing, lying, stealing, talking about Bishop McGee behind his back, or drinking vodka first thing in the morning. At the most, they can slow down your passage to heaven. But a mortal sin such as killing someone, missing Mass, or having sex out of wedlock with a young woman you've just met, that's a ticket to hell."

"You better go to confession then."

"Brittany, if a priest were to hear my confession at this point, they would probably have to carry him out of the church afterwards."

"You tell your sins directly to a priest?"

"Yes, well not face to face, you tell them in a confessional. There are different types of confessionals but basically it's some sort of partition between you and the priest. He can hear you but not see you."

"What's it like to tell your sins to a priest like that?"

"Brittany, what were we talking about before we got sidetracked into this exhaustive liturgical discussion? Did you happen to notice the magnificent view of Homewood to your right? Why are you so interested in this?"

"Because of Sally. Growing up, I wouldn't have known there was a religion such as Catholicism if my mother had anything to do with it. When I learned that Sally wanted to be a Catholic nun, I began to ask questions.

Many years ago, I found a picture of Sally dressed in a gray uniform and I asked Mom about it. I don't think she wanted to tell me; she just felt like she had to. But she also let me know that the Catholic Church had been bad for Sally and that's what made her go away."

"And you're turning to me, renegade and heathen that I am, to educate you about Catholicism?"

"Not just you; I've learned some on my own over the years, but there's nothing like hearing it from someone who's been there. And you're a good one to hear it from because even though you're no longer a Catholic, you don't hold a grudge against the church.

Your answers are objective."

"I guess I understand."

"Okay, good. What was it like confessing your sins to a priest?"

"Hmm, where do I begin? I first went to confession when I was in second grade, and I last went to confession when I was eighteen. Believe me, there was a world of difference between the first time and the last. When I first started going, my sins were so innocent that a person might have thought I was kidding, and by the time I last went to confession, I routinely left some of them out so the priest wouldn't yell at me.

But it was always a little weird, from the first confession to the last. In the beginning, I took it seriously and tried to remember every sin I'd committed. There really weren't many back then: a lie here and there, disobeying my parents a few times, but certainly no mortal sins. The priests were nice and rarely questioned me about them; they just listened and then gave a light penance."

"What was the penance?"

"Prayers, usually Hail Marys or Our Fathers. Once in a while a priest would make it a decade of the Rosary, especially as I got older and the sins got more serious. You learned early on to avoid Monsignor Schroeder. He was a strict one that would give you some grief while you were in the confessional and then a stiff penance, like maybe an entire rosary or going to Mass every day for a week."

"And what do you think your penance would be now?"

"Whew, I hate to think about it; it wouldn't be nice. Probably something like being suspended with my head downward over flames, or standing on one leg on top of a pillar in the middle of the desert."

"What are you talking about? You're not serious."

"No, I'm not serious. Those are some penances I read about in the Bible or some old book. In those days, they didn't mess around with sinners. It's no wonder people decided to become Southern Baptists."

"Duane, what do you really know about Southern Baptists?"

"Nothing, other than they're from the south and they only have two sacraments."

"Well there's a little more to it than that, but we certainly don't have anything like confession. Baptists believe that only Jesus has the power to forgive sins, not a priest, and we believe that any sin, not just a mortal sin, is enough to send a person to hell. So all sins should be confessed immediately and directly to God."

"I like that approach; it's much simpler. The Catholic church does have a tendency to make the solution more complicated than the problem. It's funny to me now, I can remember a time when I believed it all, everything I was taught about the church."

"Sally must have believed it all if she wanted to be a nun and was willing to give her life to the Catholic church. Tell me, Duane, back when you *did* believe, did you ever think about being a priest?"

"Yeah, I guess the thought crossed my mind back in those early years at Saint Mathew's. Actually the idea of being a monk was more appealing to me. In fact, I think I could be a monk now except for the religious part of it."

"Would your parents have been supportive of you if you had chosen a religious life?"

"Ah, yes, probably supportive, but they wouldn't necessarily have encouraged it. I'm certain that my parents believed in God and Catholicism, but they were Catholics almost like they were Democrats, because their parents were.

It's interesting to me now that I can't recall ever seeing my father pray or make any religious references outside of church, and yet he went to Mass every Sunday and insisted that we do the same."

"That *is* interesting. Speaking of which, how much time do we have before Mass?"

"A couple hours. Why?"

"When we get back to the motel, I want to do a little research. I've never been to a Catholic Mass and I want to make the most of it."

"I've only been to Mass a handful of times since graduating from Saint Mathew's and then it was for either a funeral or a wedding, so I'm looking forward to it, too. In fact, when we get back to the motel, I'm going to trim my beard, just for the occasion."

"Didn't you just trim it yesterday?"

"That was a rush job. First you surprised me, then Bob lured me to Mutt's, so I didn't have time to do it right."

"Sorry we cramped your style. I'll tell you what, if you let me borrow your laptop, the bathroom is yours."

"It's a deal."

25

Some people think that growing a beard is taking the easy way out for a guy, but that's not necessarily true. Starting a beard is certainly easy: you just have to stop shaving, anybody can do that. But it's the issue of shaping and trimming that is of concern once a person moves beyond that first step. To cultivate a decent looking beard takes more time and experience than most people realize.

I've never been an extremist about facial hair neatness, and in fact my opinion of a beard that is too prim and proper is that it's creepy, like a human French poodle, clipped for a dog show. But I'm not keen on long, scraggly beards either, unless of course, you're Liver-eating Johnson, roaming the Rocky Mountains with the Crow tribe in hot pursuit, or the legendary moonshiner, Popcorn Sutton, back in the hills of Tennessee, plying his noble craft. No matter what I think of ZZ Top's music, their beards are a turnoff for me.

Moreover, I aim for a look somewhere in between the extremes and then fine tune the whiskers to fit whatever the particular occasion might call for. Today, for a Catholic Mass, I want my beard to be on the trim and neat end of the spectrum, with just a hint of unruliness to offset the formality of a suit and tie.

While I am thus employed, Brittany is on the bed, propped up with pillows, researching the Catholic Mass on my laptop. I hope she learns a lot so that she doesn't rely on me so much for information. My knowledge is a bit dated and I'm not sure if half of what I've said thus far is true anymore. Through a slight opening in the bathroom door, I can see her peering intently at the computer screen.

I reach into my pocket and take out a slim, fashionable, silver flask. One December day, a clerk at the liquor store I frequent most often, slipped it into the bag alongside the vodka I was purchasing, and then wished me a Merry Christmas. At the time, I assumed it was a gift from the state of North Carolina, and the employees were instructed to give one to regular customers. However, I wouldn't have been surprised to learn, instead, that it was a gift from the employees of that particular liquor store, presented to me because I helped to pay a substantial part of their salaries.

The flask is stainless steel, holds two hundred milliliters of vodka, and has served me well on many occasions since its reception. The design is perfect: thin and narrow with a slight curve from one side to the other, such that the flasks fits comfortably and inconspicuously in any pocket. Such a nice gift; it was just what I needed. How did they know?

I spy into the other room again and then take a measured swallow from the flask. I trim my beard for a minute, focusing on the area under the chin, a challenging region to get shaped right. I check out the side profile, and it looks good. I take another long, cool swallow. It's funny how a person can acquire a taste for a beverage such as vodka while another will gag at the mere mention of drinking it straight. And I don't just tolerate it; I truly enjoy the taste of vodka, in all its raw, burning, bitterness—an acquired taste to the extreme.

One more drink and I know that about half the contents of the flask have been consumed, which is enough for now. One hundred milliliters is the proper dose when I'm with good company, two hundred for most other occasions. When Brittany is taking her shower, I can refill for the road.

I don't know exactly why I feel a need to hide my drinking

from Brittany. I guess for the same reason I hide it from Hannah and the rest of the world. It's my secret and why should anyone else know? After all, I'm not hurting anyone except myself. I'm not disruptive or mean; in fact, I think I'm a pleasant and friendly drunk. I don't want anyone's criticism, or advice, or pity. This is my choice: my problem and my pleasure.

Besides, the element of cunning somehow adds to the experience for me, and in a sense, the fact that I can keep it a secret assures me that I'm not too far gone yet. It's like that age-old philosophical question: Can a thing exist if it can't be perceived? If a man can drink all day long and no one knows it, is he really a drunk? I say no. In fact, I'll take the last drink to that sound bit of wisdom.

One more look in the mirror, a few more wayward hairs snipped off and I'm ready to face the rest of my life. I open the door to a vision of beauty, young Brittany Schuster, engrossed in her research. As I was checking out of the Expresso Inn, I allowed the old Ryan paranoia level to elevate such that I began to question the wisdom of such an involvement, a young, pretty woman such as her and a codger such as me, but now that we are settled in at this wonderful little motel, I feel that this domestic arrangement could go on forever.

"Well, what do you think?"

"About what?"

"My beard."

"Oh, I'm sorry. Yes, it looks good. I was wondering what was taking you so long in there.

I've found some really interesting information. Listen to this.

The Catholic Mass is the most sacred act of worship a person can participate in upon earth. At the Last Supper, Jesus Christ, sat down with his Apostles for what He knew would be their last meal together. At that supper, Jesus did something never done before, and yet something which will continue until the end of time."

"Wow, that's pretty deep, Brittany. Where did you find that?"

"On this website named *Inside the Catholic Mass*. It has a complete outline of the Mass with details about each section. This is just what I was looking for. I want to be as familiar as possible with the Catholic Church as I work on my book, and the Mass is really the center of the Catholic religion."

"That's interesting to hear it put that way. We went to Mass so often when I was in school that I never really thought about it that way. For me Saint Mathew's was the center of the Catholic religion."

"As an insider, you took the Mass for granted."

"Yes, and especially so after I became an atheist."

"Well I wonder why. Do you think that not believing in God might have taken something away from the Mass experience?"

"That just might be it. But the funny thing is, I didn't mind going to Mass and actually found it relaxing in a way. I especially liked the big Masses at Christmas and Easter, complete with bells and incense; and the costumes and processions."

"Will this be a big one?"

"I would think so, especially with the Bishop saying it."

"Oh good. Okay, let's see here, where was I?

Mass is an audience with God Himself. Our whole life should be a preparation for Mass. At Mass we offer ourselves to God, and in return, we receive him.

Wow, so if a person truly believes, they believe that God is there and part of the service."

"That's right."

"So does the priest become God for the moment or something like that."

"Uh, sort of, I think, but communion is where God really comes in. Skip ahead to communion."

"Communion, holy communion, here we go.

When God delivered the people of Israel out of bondage in Egypt, he ordered that they sacrifice a lamb and sprinkle its blood on their door post. This would be a sign that the angel of death should pass over their houses. Hence was instituted the feast of

Passover."

"Hmm, I can't remember what that has to do with it. I thought communion was all about the Last Supper. Keep reading, Brittany, maybe it'll come back to me."

"Come on, Duane, you went to a Catholic School for twelve years."

"I know, but religion was never one of my strong subjects. Skip ahead a little."

"Okay, how about this?

Holy communion is a sharing in the same meal that Jesus shared with his disciples at the last supper. We all consume the same lamb who is Christ himself . . ."

"Ah, there you go. Do you get what the meal is?"

"It's holy communion, right?"

"Yes, but do you understand what the communion actually is, what it is that is being consumed?"

"I guess not."

"Here, move over."

I sit beside Brittany on the bed, and we place the computer between us.

"This is rather nice, studying in bed, side by side. I might have done better in religion if these had been the study conditions. Let me see here. Okay, here it is, the mystery of the Eucharist, that's what I want you to know about.

The priest consecrates the bread and the wine by saying, 'this is my body, and this is my blood do this in remembrance of Me'. As these words are spoken, the Holy Spirit changes the bread and wine into the body and blood of Jesus Christ. Through communion, we receive Christ in his body and blood, and He becomes the food of our souls."

"Are you kidding me?"

"Not this time. That's the mystery of the Eucharist. If you can't swallow that, so to speak, then you can't accept the core of the Catholic Mass."

"Sorry I can't. Are you sure it means literally the body and the blood of Jesus?"

"Yes, I'm sure. That's something I remember from religion class. It always kind of gave me the creeps, too."

"I don't think I'll go to communion."

"You better not; Catholics only."

"Well are you going, Mr. Catholic?"

"No way. I've only been to Mass a handful of times in the last thirty years. So I've missed fifty-two Masses a year times thirty, uh, let's see, that's roughly sixteen hundred and some mortal sins on my soul."

"What would happen if you received communion anyway?"

"My tongue would probably burn off."

"I'd like to see that."

"You would. More likely though, if Duke saw me up there, trying to partake of the sacrament, he would hit me on the head with the chalice."

"He would not."

"I know, probably not, but I don't want to tempt him. We should both just skip communion."

"I agree, but I must say that I'm surprised at the central role of communion in the Mass and I never would have guessed that it's actually supposed to be the body and blood of Jesus. We don't even have communion every Sunday, and when we do it's on special occasions, like Christmas or Easter. "

"No kidding. That *is* a big difference. In the Catholic Church, communion is offered at every mass, and for many people it *is* the Mass. In fact, the rule of thumb used to be that if you skipped out on Mass early, it still counted and you weren't tagged with a mortal sin, if you at least stayed through communion."

"That's useful to know. See, that's the sort of information you can't get out of books."

"Maybe you've given me an idea here, Brittany. I should write a book: *The Drunken Heathen's Guide to the Catholic Church*."

"That's a catchy title, Duane. Put me down for the first copy."

26

"I think it's sad that your high school is going to be torn down."

"You know Brittany, I have to admit, so do I. There must be some trace of sentiment in me after all. I'm not ready to stand in front of a bulldozer, but I'm willing to do what I can to save it now."

"What can you do at this point that hasn't already been done?"

"Break into the boiler room to see what Father McGee's hiding in there."

"Break in, why?"

"Leverage, Brittany; leverage is everything in life."

"What happened to the plan to ask permission?"

"That was plan A, but because of the history between the Bishop and me, I have no part in plan A. Plan B was agreed to this morning over breakfast with Booker and will be set in motion if Plan A fails, as it most likely will.

I have to admit, I'm hoping that Bob and crew got the go ahead from the Bishop to knock the wall down, because I'm not real comfortable with what I've committed to here. If Duke stands firm, it seems Booker I will be breaking and entering. Do you want to come along?"

"No thanks; not my kind of thing."

"Come on, think of the potential material for your book."

"That's true, but you can give me that information after the fact. Besides, if you get into trouble, someone has to get you out of jail."

"Good point. I don't think I would last long in jail."

Brittany and I have a little time before Mass starts so we're walking around Saint Mathew's High School, inspecting the old building from various angles. We complete a circuit of the school by walking up a narrow alley of broken asphalt and gravel on the side of the building opposite the parking lot.

Saint Mathew's Church comes into full frontal view as we approach Jefferson Street, and then as if on cue, the steeple bells begin to peal a joyful, welcoming melody. The faithful are converging on the church from all directions, as Brittany and I cross the street to become part of the congregation.

As we enter the vestibule, an elderly, white-haired man, greets us and hands each of us a copy of the Saint Mathew's Sunday Bulletin. The Bulletin is a booklet that contains an agenda for Mass and a weekly church newsletter. I glance at the cover and tuck it under my arm for future reading, perhaps during the sermon.

In the latter years of high school, when Will and I had the jeep at our service, we began to attend Mass separate from the rest of the family. Our justification was that we could go at a more convenient time, which was typically at whatever time the rest of the family wasn't going. The truth was that we often skipped Mass and went to Duval's for breakfast.

To cover for ourselves, we would drive by the church and one of us would run in and get a copy of the Bulletin as proof that we had been present at Mass. I can't recall that this was ever necessary, but I do remember once when we came home from our Sunday outing, Bulletin in hand, Dad casually asked us what the sermon was about and then listened with an amused look on his face as we stumbled over an answer.

Brittany is paging through the Bulletin when she pauses and focuses on something on an inside page. When she catches up with me, she tugs at my sleeve and speaks in a whisper to ask if we can sit toward the rear of the church.

I select a pew that is a few rows from the last, in the same area where my father preferred to sit. I favor sitting in the back as well, but I have to wonder why Brittany would choose to do so. I would think that with her desire to gain the full Mass experience, she would want to be front and center.

Once seated, she reopens the Bulletin and focuses on an image at the top of the second page. I open my copy of the booklet to see that she's viewing a picture of His Excellency, Bishop Thomas McGee. I start to ask her if something is bothering her when I see Booker in the aisle beside me, looking very formal and reverent in a long gray topcoat.

"Hey, hippie, I had some cancellations at my table for the banquet this afternoon and I need two mortal beings to fill it up again. You're a mortal, aren't you?"

"Uh, well, actually I wasn't really planning to . . ."

"Well why not do me a favor and plan on it? You and Brittany, okay?"

"I guess, thanks for the offer."

"Don't mention it. Hey, say a prayer for me today."

Booker taps my shoulder with the back of his hand and walks toward the front of the church where his family is seated. I turn to speak to Brittany, but the organ begins to play, drowning out any hope of conversation.

How familiar all this is to me, a scene that is among my earliest memories: the inside of this grand old church, filled with hundreds of people, and the sound of the pipe organ, heralding the start of Mass. I gaze up at the vaulted ceiling and marvel at this small architectural wonder that is Saint Mathew's Church. Even a cynic like me can't help but be moved by the grandeur of the setting.

Two boys dressed in cassock and surplice hustle about the altar, making final preparations for Mass. When I was their age, I sometimes regretted that I joined the choir rather than becoming an altar boy. We dressed in the same uniform and attended all the same Masses, but altar boys somehow seemed to have more prestige than choir boys. They were up front at the altar, near Jesus and the priest, and got to give all the pretty girls communion, while we choir boys were hidden in the choir loft, with grumpy sister Marguerite.

A bell rings, the organ music becomes louder, and heads turn as a procession moves slowly up the center aisle. Four altar boys lead, followed by a middle-aged priest who I recognize from a picture in the Bulletin as Father Walsh, and last comes Bishop Thomas McGee in all his glory. I have to admit, the man looks impressive. He's decked out in a long, white garment adorned along the hem with elaborate embroidery and with a purple cross centered on the front. A large, white, pointed hat that I remember is called a miter, renders him a tall and imposing figure, while the ornate, golden staff in his right hand adds a positively regal touch to the man.

Thomas McGee looks to be in good shape for a man who must be in his late seventies by now. He turns his head from side to side, smiling benevolently as he makes his way to the altar.

The main altar area of Saint Mathew's Church is a striking space, defined by a marble canopy resting on four fluted, marble pillars. The long wooden altar, itself, is quite simple by comparison, but its significance is exemplified when the Bishop and Father Walsh make their way behind, bow, and then solemnly kiss it.

"In the name of the Father, and of the Son, and of the Holy Spirit," the Bishop proclaims in a loud voice.

All around us, people are making the sign of the cross. Brittany looks at me and, in an exaggerated manner, I demonstrate how it's done. She doesn't smile though, instead she wears a serious, thoughtful expression.

"The Lord be with you," says Bishop McGee.

The audience responds, "and also with you."

At first I'm confused at what the Bishop and his assistants are doing, but when I recognize the elaborate, silver container that holy water is stored in, I know what's next. One of the altar boys pours some of its contents into a smaller vessel, which is basically a hand held, metal wand, perforated on one end and designed for the

180

distribution of holy water. We are about to participate in a ceremony of the Roman Catholic Church in which holy water is sprinkled over the altar and the congregation, a rite that is performed at the start of an elaborate, or *High* Mass such as this one.

In the Catholic Church, holy water is water that has been sanctified by a priest for the purpose of baptism and for the blessing of persons and places. At Saint Mathew's we were introduced to holy water in first grade by Sister Timothy, and like most of my classmates, I was fascinated with this mysterious, sacred liquid that, up close, seemed just like any other water. A large supply of holy water is contained in an elaborate marble Baptismal font located in a niche at the back of the church. That's where baptisms are performed, and where, for the record, I was baptized.

Smaller containers of holy water are mounted on the vestibule wall at each entrance to the church to serve as a reminder of baptism, but also so that a Catholic can dip their fingers and bless themselves with the sign of the cross before entering the church. In grade school, we thought this was really a cool thing. Imagine that, holy water at our disposal, and we were just kids. In fact some of us thought it was so cool that even though we weren't permitted to enter the church without supervision, we couldn't resist sneaking in to make the sign of the cross a time or two during recess.

One winter day, when I was in fourth grade, Carla Daniels coaxed me into the church vestibule to show me something that she said was really serious. The vestibule wasn't heated well, and it was so cold that the holy water had frozen. Now this would have been shocking enough, but even worse, the bowl-shaped chunk of holy water (or holy ice as it would be more aptly described), was out of its bowl and lying on the floor, upside down. The ice was melting slightly so that a trickle of water trailed to one side and formed a small puddle.

I stared in disbelief; it didn't seem possible for holy water to meet such a fate. And what were we to do about it? When we were taught about holy water they never told us what to do in a situation like this. Should we run for a priest? At that suggestion,

Carla shook her head and warned that the priest would think that we did it since we weren't allowed in the church anyway.

I then suggested that we might pick up the ice and put it back in the bowl, but neither of us could bring ourselves to touch it. In the end, we just stared a while longer at the melting ice, incredulous that such a thing could happen to holy water, and then left the scene.

Forty years later, the memory haunts me still: the dark and cold vestibule, the look of distress on Carla's face, the frozen holy water, lying helpless on its back, bleeding.

"Dear friends, this water will be used to remind us of our baptism. Let us ask God to bless it, and to keep us faithful to the Spirit he has given us. We ask this through Christ our Lord."

The congregation responds in unison to the Bishop, "Amen". I forget myself and respond with them.

Bishop McGee moves down the aisle, blessing the audience and sprinkling them with holy water. The organ begins to play, and to my delight, the boy choir begins to sing. I turn and look up toward the choir loft, and there they are in cassock and surplice, the Saint Mathew's Boy Choir, positioned in elevated rows behind the organ. It's hard for me to imagine that I was once up there, looking so holy and singing like that.

Wouldn't it be nice to be in that place again, young and innocent, committed to the cause, believing in the Church and all its teaching, confident about life and eternity? I remember the feeling, oddly enough, and it was wonderful to have the great mysteries of life and death explained in one magnificent story. And there I was, holy and important, singing God's praises, a part of His glorious plan.

I feel drops of water on my cheek and even though I'm getting sentimental here, I know they aren't tears. I turn to see Bishop McGee across from me in the aisle, the holy water wand pointed in my direction. Just as I make eye contact, he turns, raises the wand, and proceeds to sprinkle and bless his way back to the altar.

I'm stunned; I never expected him to come so far down the

aisle. From what I remember of this ceremony, the blessing of the congregation was more a symbolic thing and usually only the audience near the altar got sprinkled. For that reason, my guard was down and Duke was able to sneak up on me. And what a shot! I was fifteen paces away and he got me right in the head.

I turn toward Brittany for support, but she doesn't seem to have noticed that I was assaulted and doesn't even acknowledge my gaze. Instead she keeps her eyes fixed on the procession as it returns to the front of the church.

Upon reaching the altar, Bishop McGee turns and in a deep baritone voice sings, "Kyrie eleison." The audience responds in turn.

Kyrie Eleison, Lord have mercy, how nice it is to hear that grand old tune again, reverberating up to the high, vaulted ceiling, filling this cavernous space with the sound of hundreds of voices, old and young, high and low.

The *Kyrie* ends; the choir launches into the *Gloria,* accompanied by the lush tones of the pipe organ. What *A Day in the Life* is to rock music, the Gloria is to sacred music. Hearing it again stirs up memories of singing the Gloria, myself, with Sister Marguerite playing the organ, looking over her shoulder at us and nodding to help keep time. I remember every word, every note. I feel like singing again: *Glory to God in the highest and peace to his people on earth.*

But I don't sing; the *Gloria* isn't really a song for unbelievers. I better stick to *A Day in the Life*, lyrics I can better relate to. Who knows, but many centuries from now, *A Day in the Life* might be the *Gloria* of the times and could be sung in some great galactic church by an android boy choir under the direction of Sister Unum Crypto: *I'd love to turn you on.*

Meanwhile back on earth, the music ends, and a profound silence ensues, setting a dramatic tone for the reading of the gospel. In my youth, I was taught that the gospels describe the life, death and resurrection of Jesus Christ, and I believed it. Now of course, I view the gospel accounts of His life as mythical in nature, and

183

don't believe that anything about Jesus, including His existence, can really be determined from them.

That notwithstanding, I have to wonder what Jesus would think of all this if He walked up the aisle right now. Would He approve of the gospel reading? Would He be impressed with the Mass or would He drive us all from the temple? He'll do that sometimes, you know.

An interesting reading from the gospel ensues, one that is easy to attend to: Luke chapter six, verses twenty seven to thirty eight. Bishop McGee looks down from the pulpit and hardly glances at the Bible as he recites lines he knows well.

"But I say to you that hear, love your enemies, do good to those who hate you, bless those who curse you, pray for those who abuse you. To him who strikes you on the cheek, offer the other also."

What a radical idea: to love ones enemy and to not strike back after you've been struck. Jesus was truly one of the first nonviolent revolutionaries. It's unfortunate for humankind that these words, like so many of His teachings, aren't adhered to, or worse, they're reinterpreted over and over until they're shaped to support the popular trend of society.

Didn't Jesus condemn materialism, that great hallmark of modern civilization? As I remember it, He called on His followers to forsake material needs. From my vantage point of frugality, the hypocrisy of many Christians on this matter is particularly obvious. They devote the bulk of their days to the accumulation of wealth, and then each Sunday, dutifully sit up front in church and have the gospel read to them as assurance that they're on track to get into heaven.

"Judge not, and you will not be judged; condemn not, and you will not be condemned; forgive, and you will be forgiven."

I look up at the pulpit as Bishop McGee finishes his reading, and it seems that he's looking directly at me as he recites this line.

The church is filled with the sound of the congregation shuffling and settling into their seats for the sermon. Father McGee is actually a good speaker and as I might have assumed, he is at his best for an occasion such as this. He talks of getting older, which is appropriate since we alumni of Saint Mathew's School *are* getting older now. I particularly like his suggestion that we reduce our possessions, simplifying our lives in preparation for the later years and allowing for a peaceful departure from this world. I wonder if Bishop McGee has been reading Thoreau along with the Bible.

Inevitably, the discussion turns to God and heaven, and I drift away as I often did in the past. Brittany seems to have no problem following the sermon. I'm surprised at how intently she stares at the Bishop, but even more so when she suddenly turns to me and asks if we can leave.

"Leave Mass; right now?"

"Yes."

"Well, we can, but you know, the rule of thumb: it doesn't officially count as a Mass unless you stay through communion. It's coming up next."

"I'd really like to go."

"Okay, let's go. I think the sermon's almost over; we'll leave then."

When Bishop McGee finishes his talk, he asks the congregation to rise. As the organ begins to play, and people are opening their missals to the proper hymn, I escort Brittany from the pew. It's a strategy that I like to employ in social situations, that is to slip away at just the right moment, in a transition such as this, so that one's departure is noticed by the least number of people.

27

"So what's up, Brittany?"

"I'm sorry, Duane, but something really bothers me about Bishop McGee. I know I've seen him before. When I was a little girl, he came to our house."

"Brittany, are you sure of this?"

"Yes, I remember him. He wasn't a priest though; he just had a regular shirt on. He was talking with my mother in the kitchen; I even remember his voice. They were sort of arguing and my mother kept asking me to stay in my room. And yet, it doesn't make sense because that would have been well after Sally left here. Why would he still have contact with my mother? Duane, how well did Bishop McGee know Sally?"

"Oh, uh, let's just say, he knew her pretty well."

"What do you mean by that?"

"Well, I mean that he knew her, he must have. He was here at the same time she was here, so . . ."

"Duane, that's not what you meant. By the way you said that, I know there's more to it. Please tell me. I have to figure this out."

"Uh, well, okay, you're right, there is more, and I might as well tell you. Brittany, there are some who feel that Father McGee and Sally were romantically involved."

"Oh my God, do you?"

"I, I didn't until this weekend. I don't want to think it's true, believe me, but I've heard some things that pretty much made a believer out of me."

I tell Brittany of the interactions between Father McGee and Sally that Agnes Reuben observed in the rectory. She's shocked but comes to the same conclusion that I did.

"Oh, Duane, that's about the last thing I would have guessed and I hate to think it's true. It really changes the image I have of Sally."

"It did for me, too, and it changed my opinion of Father McGee, from bad to worse. In fact I wanted to kill him. How about him, so pompous and self righteous, when all the while he was, uh, well, it seems like he was having an affair with Sally. He had a lot of nerve to . . ."

"Duane, was there something between you and Sally?"

"Huh, why would you think that?"

"Because my mother told me there was."

"Your mother said there was?"

"Yes, Sally told her a long time ago, and Mom told me about ten years ago. We were sitting up and talking one night and she was in one of those strange moods when she seemed like she had to talk about Sally. Mom couldn't remember your name anymore; just remembered that you were a senior then and that later you became an artist.

Mom said that Sally really liked you and talked about you a lot. The thought of it always intrigued me. I even imagined that you and Sally had taken off back then and were still together."

"And you took it from there and tracked me down? So our getting together wasn't just about art and literature?"

"No, not really."

"How did you know I would be at the reunion?"

"I called your gallery a couple weeks ago and said I was coming to Janesville this weekend. I asked if there was a chance I could meet with you. The person I spoke to said you were going out of town for the weekend, so I assumed you were coming here. You're not mad are you?"

"No, I'm not mad. That was a sneaky thing to do, but clever, too, and I like that. I don't know what I think, so let's drive. Mass has ended, and I don't want to get caught in the after church crunch. They may all look happy and full of grace, but believe me, they'll run you down in the rush to get out first."

I take back roads, meandering about Homewood with no destination in mind. Brittany is silent, and I know she's waiting to hear more about Sally and me. The thought of Sister Sally and I, wandering out into the world together, young, naïve, and happy, has hung in my imagination for decades. On a realistic plain, the notion has been easy to dismiss for the crazy, youthful fantasy that it seems to have been.

Yet when I look back on the other relationships I've been involved in, which range from failures to disasters, who's to say what would have happened with Sally and me? Was the notion any crazier then the year I spent in West Virginia with Haven, the hippie woman, and her ten dogs? And Sally and I certainly had a more solid basis for a relationship than I ever had with Vera, the nymphomaniac. Even at the less extreme end of the spectrum, was Sally and I, making it as a couple any more naïve an idea than marriage working out with Cathy or with Elaine?

So I tell Brittany about Sally and me, both to answer her questions and to garner her opinion. She listens quietly until I'm finished and then speaks in a sympathetic tone.

"That's so sad, Duane. You and Sally loved each other and maybe you should have ended up together."

"I've thought that very thing many times over the years. I wanted to go for it then, but Sally disappeared after the incident in the library, and I never saw her again."

"Didn't you ask what happened to her?"

"No, who would I ask, anyway? I didn't know who knew what at that point and I was walking on egg shells all the time, expecting Duke to lower the boom any day. I just wanted to graduate and get out of there, and that's what I did."

"So now, looking back, with all you learned this weekend,

what do you think happened to Sally? Do you think Father McGee could have done something to her, out of jealousy, maybe?"

"Are you asking me if I think that Duke might have physically harmed Sally?"

"Yes, I told you, something about him bothers me, and the way he was so angry and violent with you, a person would have to wonder. Maybe he was afraid Sally would tell people about what was going on between them and did something to her, like the priest in the novel that I'm writing."

"Like maybe he killed her?"

"Yes, it's possible."

"Uh, Brittany, I'm definitely not a member of the Bishop McGee fan club, but do I think he's a murderer, let alone a nun-in-training murderer? No, I don't think so."

"What about the boiler room? What do you think he's hiding in there?"

"I don't think it's a body, not Sally. What happened to your asbestos theory? I thought the hidden nun body was just for literary purposes. That's an interesting idea for a novel, but let's not jump to real life conclusions here."

"Things like this happen in real life. I told you, while I was doing research for the novel, I found several cases in which a priest murdered a nun."

In Ohio, a priest who didn't get along with a certain nun he worked with, strangled her, and stabbed her. And get this, he wasn't convicted until thirty years after the murder. How long has it been since Sally disappeared?"

"Okay, I get the point: it happens. But if you're asking me if I think that our own Father McGee, jerk that he was at times, did something like that, the answer is no, I just don't think so."

"Why are you sticking up for him all of a sudden?"

"I'm not sticking up for him, but I knew the man back then and I can't imagine him doing anything to Sally. Personally, I don't think there's anything in that old room, anymore. I think Duke just closed it up to keep us out of there and to be a jerk."

"Wait a minute, Duane, what about what your friend Lenny told you last night at dinner, about Father McGee and Carmen carrying something into the basement of the school late at night?"

"That's right. I admit that *is* suspicious."

"And what about what Carmen said? 'I should never have done it. Father McGee told me to do it. It was a damn sin. It's not the room, it's what's in the room.' Isn't that what he said?"

"Yes, he did say those things, didn't he? Brittany, you have a good memory."

"Not good enough. I'm going back to Pittsburgh."

"What, why?"

"To talk to Aunt Shirley again. I want to find out what she knows about Sally and Bishop McGee."

"Why do you think she knows anything?"

"Because my father and her have always been close and he would have told her."

"But why hasn't she told you by now? She knows you're at the reunion this weekend, doesn't she?"

"Yes, I told her, and she was already familiar with Saint Mathew's because she came to visit while Sally was here. Now that I think about it, she even mentioned Father McGee and asked me if he was here this weekend."

"No kidding? Did you tell her he was?"

"I did, and I told her about you and your relationship with Father McGee, since that's really how I know about him. Now that I think of it, I wonder why Aunt Shirley didn't ask me more about you; she seemed interested, but really didn't say much. *Unless,* she already knows about you. That settles it; I've got to talk to her about what happened back then."

"Which comes back to my question: If your aunt knows anything about Father McGee and Sally, why didn't she tell you by now?"

"It might be because she doesn't want to talk about it, like it's something she's protecting me from, or has been asked not to tell, but I know if I ask her face to face, she'll tell me. I'm going to call

190

Aunt Shirley right now."

Brittany pulls out her cell phone and makes the call, while I cruise the back roads and eavesdrop on the conversation. We turn into the parking lot of the Oak Park Motel just as she signs off.

"Aunt Shirley is delighted to get together again. She wants to take me out to eat."

"Then you won't be attending the banquet this afternoon?"

"I wasn't going to be attending anyway. I didn't think you were either."

"I wasn't planning on it, but right before Mass, Booker told me that he has empty seats at his table and would like us to fill them. He'll be disappointed that you're not attending. Why not invite your aunt to come and you two can talk over dinner while I stay here at the motel and meditate?"

"No, I need to talk to Aunt Shirley alone, without distraction."

"Will you be back tonight?"

"I plan to be back, but if not, I'll call. What are you going to do this afternoon? Are you still going to tour the high school?"

"Yes, I think so. You know, it's funny, but I'm really looking forward to walking the old halls again. Maybe I'll call Dale and see if he can get free for an hour or so. I'm also anxious to hear about the meeting with Father McGee this morning, although I think it's safe to assume that the boiler room won't be part of the tour."

"I hope it is, I really do. That would settle at least part of the mystery. I don't want to avoid the truth, but I really hope that Father McGee didn't do anything to Sally. Oh, which reminds me, if Bob's plan didn't work out, be careful, tonight."

"Careful? Oh yes, Plan B, the break-in; I almost forgot. Well, if something goes wrong and I don't make it, tell the world that in the end, I gave it all for my alma mater, Saint Mathew's High School."

28

"You know, Dale, it smells good in here."

"It does, doesn't it. That's the aroma of old wood. Older buildings often smell like this, particularly after they've been closed up for a while."

"I like the smell; it reminds me of my grandmother's house. How kind of His Excellency the Bishop to open up the school so that we old timers can take a few whiffs."

"Speaking of the Bishop, let me finish telling you about Bob's meeting with him."

"Oh yeah, give me the details on that. I can't say I'm too surprised with what you told me over the phone. I think we all knew that the chance of Duke letting them tear his wall down was slim."

"Yep, no surprise there, but his reaction is what's interesting. Apparently Bob coached his team ahead of time and it sounds as if they played it well. He said that they had a pleasant chat about the school in general and then brought up the boiler room almost in passing. Once they had Duke talking about it and even laughing a little about how we used to hang out in there, Bob asked about the possibility of opening the room up as part of the tour, almost as if the idea had just come to him."

"That Bob, I think he may have missed his true calling as an FBI interrogator."

"Isn't he good? Anyway, Bob said that Duke got nervous from

the moment he realized what was being asked."

"Really?"

"Yah, he said it was like somebody flipped a switch. Duke immediately insisted that opening up the boiler room was out of the question, and then seemed to struggle to come up with a definite reason why that should be. He finally claimed that it was because of insurance issues."

"Ah, the old insurance issues thing. I've used that one a number of times to keep people out of my workshop. Nobody wants to mess with the insurance company.

So how nervous was he? What was Bob's opinion of the way Duke behaved?"

"He really felt that the Bishop was acting like he had something to hide."

"Ah, just the response we were hoping for—I think. You know, Dale, the more the evidence seems to suggest that Duke is hiding something in that room, the more uneasy I get. What if it's Sister Sally?"

"Sister Sally? What in the heck are you talking about?"

"You may be sorry you asked. To make a long story short, Brittany has postulated that Father McGee murdered Sally Schuster to keep her quiet about their love affair, and then, with Carmen's help, hid her body in the boiler room."

"Wow, what an imagination she has. Come on now, Duane, what do you think? That's pretty far-fetched."

"At first hearing, yes, but consider the facts: the things Carmen said at Mutt's, Mrs. Rueben's observations of the goings on at the rectory, and what Lenny's uncle saw that night with Duke and Carmen. Then think of the timing: Sally's disappearance, the mysterious object being carried into the basement of the school, and the closing off of the boiler room, all happened about the same time."

"Those things did all happen right at the end of our senior year, didn't they? Now that you've spelled it out, it's not such a far-fetched idea, but I sure hope it's not true. Odds are there's nothing in that room, but I wish Father McGee would have just opened it up and settled the matter. Now I guess we'll never know, will we?"

"Ahem, well, I uh, I guess not. What's wrong; why are you looking at me like that?"

"You and Mike are going to break into the boiler room aren't you?"

"Uh, as a matter of fact, yes, but how did you know? That's top secret information."

"Because Bob told me about the suggestion the bartender made when you were at Mutt's, and I know you. I also know what happens when you and Prizza get together. When?"

"Oh, if all goes according to plan, tonight. Actually, come to think of it, we don't have a plan yet. We're meeting at Corky's this evening to draw one up."

"Well good luck. Don't get caught."

"You're not going to try to talk me out of it?"

"No, I know it wouldn't do any good."

"Want to come along?"

"Can't, old man. You know that."

I nod; Dale smiles and looks the other way. I'm just teasing and probably shouldn't have asked the question because I know well that he wouldn't risk such a caper. Even when we were young and crazy, he was reluctant to cross that line, which is really to his credit. At the present time, considering his career and social status in Homewood, such an escapade is entirely out of the question.

If I get caught, it'll be embarrassing for the moment, but it won't affect my career as an artist or my life in general to any great extent. Beyond the legal consequences, which would probably be minimal, it would be laughed off here and even more so in Janesville, should the news reach that far. The public almost expects that sort of anarchic behavior from counterculture types like me.

On the other hand, if Dale were caught breaking into the school, there would be immediate repercussions with regards to his career, his status in the church and his position in the community. This principle manifests itself in many aspects of Dale's life: the way

194

he dresses, how long he wears his hair, what drugs he uses, and even who he socializes with. It's not just a personality difference that has kept my association with Booker separate from my friendship with Dale.

All such social parameters are very foreign to me who inhabits the fringes of society and follows my own course in life. On the other hand, equally foreign are the concepts of domestic tranquility, financial security, and a sense of place in a community. I better stop here. Whatever the point is I'm trying to make, it seems to be turning on me.

Dale and I stroll down the first floor hall of Saint Mathew's High School, something we did decades before on a daily basis. The old place is stripped bare; the rooms are empty and forlorn. Gone are the desks, crucifixes and portraits of John Fitzgerald Kennedy. The sound of shuffling feet and muted speech remind me more of a museum than a high school.

I stop midway down the hall and stare at a rectangular outline on the wall that is much lighter than the surrounding area. I'm puzzled for a few seconds but then realize that the contour defines a spot where the base of a statue once rested against the wall.

"Saint Francis of Assisi used to be there, Duane. You always liked that statue."

"Yes, I looked at it so often that I can still picture it today. In fact, I bet I could draw it right now, exactly as it was. It was made of wood, too, which was different than the other statues on campus. I remember once, Sister Mary Agatha chided me in a teasing way for looking at the statue so much, but she didn't move me along. About ten years ago, I . . ."

"The way she liked you, I'm surprised she didn't just give it to you."

"Don't start on that again. I'm trying to be serious here."

"*You*, serious? Then this is a rare occasion. Continue by all means."

"Thank you. I did a carving some years ago of an elderly woman, sitting on steps feeding pigeons. I based much of the piece on the Saint Francis statue, especially the woman's features and her pose. I titled it *Woman Feeding Birds*, and I think it's one of the best pieces I've ever done. I often wish I would have kept it."

"Where did it go?"

"Oh, a wealthy lady from Durham bought it. *Woman Feeding Birds* probably sits in a commodious living room now, and fancy people rest their cocktails on it while they chat ever so merrily."

"Don't be so cynical, Duane. Your carving could well be someplace where it's seen by many people, people who are moved by it just like you were by the Saint Francis statue."

"I can only hope that's true. In the end, that's really what it's all about for me. I wonder what ever happened to the Saint Francis statue. Do you know?"

"Nope, can't help you there. Who knows where the old statues go?"

Dale and I reach the end of the hallway and I motion toward the stairs that lead to the second floor. Dale glances at his watch and shakes his head.

"Got to run here, old man. It's my father's eightieth birthday, and we're heading over to his place this afternoon to celebrate. You go ahead. I've toured the building many times. Hey, be careful tonight and good luck. Call me if you need me."

"Will do."

Dale walks down the back stairs and out the door. As much as I enjoy talking with my friend, it's nice to be alone in the old school building without the distraction of conversation. For the same reason I hope I won't run into someone else I know. I switch into anonymous mode: head low, no eye contact and no sudden moves that might attract attention. Most people toured the building earlier in the day, so I'm able to slink about the halls unnoticed.

I wander upstairs and into the first room on the left. Room 201 was my homeroom when I was a freshman and my teacher was Sister Charles. She was such a ditz in a way, but a very nice person in every other way. I still remember remarks Sister Charles made when she welcomed our class to the high school. She asked us to

196

look out the window at the leaves on the maple trees, surrounding the rectory, and to realize that we would see the leaves fall and reappear only four times before the high school era of our lives would be over.

That didn't seem like the most appropriate remark for our first day here, but that was Sister Charles. I think her point was that the years would go quickly and that we should make the most of our time at Saint Mathew's High School. She was right about the years going quickly. Those four years went by, then four more for college, six in Madison, five years here, eight years there, fifteen in Janesville, and now as I look out at the trees, the leaves have fallen and reappeared forty times since Sister Charles drew our attention to them.

Because Saint Mathew's was such a small school, I have memories of time spent in every room along this hall. I wander in and out of each of them, but linger longest in Room 210, the homeroom of my senior year. Located in the front of the building, the room is at eye level with Saint Mathew's Church, which is directly across the street.

I stand with my back to the blackboard, trying to visualize what it was like to face a classroom of students back then. I can still picture Sister Mary Agatha and recall how enthused she seemed to be when she was up here every day. Could she really have loved her job that much? I wonder how I would have handled it, or how I would have dealt with a character like me.

As I enter the front stairwell, I stop to look at the barricade on the stairs leading to the condemned third floor. Dale wasn't kidding when he said the floor was shut down as inexpensively as possible. The barrier consists of a locked door built into a framework constructed of two by fours and wire fencing.

How I would like to see the old stage again, lit up and decorated as it was for the high school's production of the musical, *Brigadoon*. I didn't act in the play, but I helped with the background art, and was a stage hand during rehearsals and performances. To this day, I remember most of the scenes and many of the lines from the Saint

Mathew's High School production of *Brigadoon*.

I have often thought of that final scene when Tommy Albright returns to Scotland with his companion, Jeff Douglas, only to find that the mythical city, Brigadoon, and his beloved Fiona have vanished into the mists of time.

Tommy laments, "why do people have to lose things to find out what they really mean?"

Brigadoon was the final play produced by Saint Mathew's High School, because the school, itself, was soon to fade into the mists of time.

In the play, just as they turn to leave, Tommy and Jeff hear voices that are singing the theme song, *Brigadoon*, and then Mr. Lundie, the schoolmaster, appears. Tommy walks toward him in a daze.

Mr. Lundie says, "Oh it's you Tommy, lad. You woke me up. You must really love her."

Tommy, still dazed, stammers "Wha' how....?"

Mr. Lundie replies "You shouldna be too surprised, lad. I told ye when ye love someone deeply enough, anythin' is possible. Even miracles."

Tommy waves goodbye to Jeff, and disappears with Mr. Lundie into the highland mist to be reunited with Fiona and live happily ever after in Brigadoon.

Can an analogy be drawn between *Brigadoon* and the loss of Saint Mathew's School? If we love this old building enough is anything possible, even miracles?

Nah, I'm just being theatrical here, but at the least, I want to see the old stage one last time.

Upon closer inspection of the barrier I guess that with my long nimble fingers, I can probably reach the deadbolt release on the other side of the door. I listen carefully for the sound of footsteps in the stairwell as I sip from my silver confidant and partner in crime. When I'm convinced that the coast is clear, I go for the lock with both hands. The knob turns, the door opens, and I creep up dusty, timeworn stairs toward Brigadoon.

I'm coming Fiona.

Upon reaching the top step, the music in my head stops, and I'm crestfallen at what I see. The scene is lit by the afternoon sun, forcing its way through clouded windows and generations of spider webs. The auditorium is not empty as I had expected because it obviously became the repository for unwanted equipment and furniture from the floors below. These objects are loosely organized in colonies of somewhat related items as if there was hope they might one day be called back into service.

The stage is not just a scene of abandonment, but of ruin, thick with dust and littered with chunks of plaster that have fallen from the ceiling. As I wend my way towards it, I recognize various stage props, and other relics of the old days, interspersed among the debris. It's a disheartening scene and I begin to wish I hadn't added it to my memories of this place. Did I really expect to find Brigadoon after all theses years? Does anybody ever really find Brigadoon again?

With a heavy heart, I turn to leave, and as do, I see graffiti on the wall to the right of the entrance way, evidence that I'm not the first to penetrate the barricade on the stairs. At first I wonder who would sneak up here to write words that few people would ever see, but as I move closer, the answer is obvious: someone in love. This is no hasty script but delicate lettering, painted in a burgundy color and highlighted in white. It reads *James D. Loves Pamela H. 1998.* James created this masterpiece twelve years ago, and so the question comes to mind: Did it work out for those two? Did Jim's love for Pamela persevere through the years as well as his artwork did?

Hmm, my guess is that it didn't. *Aren't I awful?*

As I ponder *the writing on the wall*, a similar work of art comes to mind. With renewed motivation, I circle behind the stage to a narrow staircase and ascend amid the cracking and groaning of ancient boards. At the top of the stairs, I enter a narrow room with a balcony that hangs over the stage and look down from a vantage point I often assumed during the production of *Brigadoon.*

How nice it would be to see the stage alive with colorful,

costumed characters once more; how wonderful it would be to immerse myself in such a grand artistic endeavor again. What would it take to make that possible: some repair here and there, a little paint, another stairway, an elevator or two? Why not?"

My mother once performed on this very stage. As a sophomore, she played the part of Titania in Shakespeare's *A Midsummer Night's Dream*. My father who, like me, was not the dramatic type, participated from the sidelines as a stage hand. There is no doubt that he leaned against this same railing and watched from this very spot at times.

Above my head, a wall separates the loft room from the stage area. It extends down about three feet from the ceiling, but is still eight feet above me. I follow it to the middle of the room and position some shelves beneath it to serve as a ladder. The shelves quiver and creak under my weight until I relieve their burden by placing my right foot atop the railing. Slowly, I raise myself, firmly clutching the frame of the overhang from both sides. I don't want my final performance in life to be a plunge to the death onto the Saint Mathew's High School stage.

Squinting into the dimly lit corner above me and coughing as I brush away dust from old pine boards, I uncover a small relief carving that I first learned about many years ago. I had just begun carving then, and my parents were looking over some small pieces I had completed for my Boy Scout merit badge. Mom was teasing Dad by telling about a carving he had done while in high school.

I first saw my father's artwork some years later, and last viewed it shortly before I graduated. Although it's been painted over a number of times, the inscription is still distinct. I blow away more dust and trace the characters with my index finger.

Andrew R.
Loves
Adele W.
1950

29

W hen I see Booker and his wife coming up the drive, I
stop near the entrance to the Old Stone Inn and wait
for them. As they walk toward me, I note that he's wearing a dark
blue pinstripe suit and appears unusually stylish and debonair for
such a big lug. Maureen is stunning in a low-cut, black gown that
for all it's formality makes her look comfortable and informal. She's
a beautiful woman, with a fair complexion, luxurious, dark hair that
dances in curls along her shoulders, and who possesses a mysterious
smile that causes a person to wonder what she's thinking.

Maureen is Booker's second wife and while they might seem
like an unlikely couple, they've been happily married for over
ten years now. I don't know much about her except that she's a
professional photographer and is from the Republic of Trinidad and
Tobago, which I know are islands and also a country. Now wouldn't
that be cool to say that you're from someplace like Trinidad and
Tobago? Not that I'm knocking the name of my town, but let's be
honest, 'Homewood' just doesn't have the same exotic ring.

The daughter of academics who teach at the University of
Trinidad and Tobago, Maureen is actually British, and so along
with her other charms, she speaks with a captivating accent: British
with a touch of Trinidadian. On impulse, I bow and kiss her hand
to which she responds by laughing and giving me a hug.

A man and woman walk up behind us, and Booker introduces
Maureen and me to Tim and Jeanette Haliday, a couple who will

be joining us at the table. I learn that Tim Haliday is a county commissioner and his wife, Jeanette is a trial lawyer who is currently running for the office of district attorney. Soon the Halidays are chatting with Maureen about Trinidad and Tobago, and since they aren't nearly as interested that I'm from Homewood and Pennsylvania, Booker takes me aside to talk.

"Say look, this is what I've got so far: Brittany Schuster has no sisters, half or whole."

"She doesn't?"

"No, not by blood. She was adopted."

"Adopted, what does that mean? That changes things, or does it? It's strange, that's for sure. I'm fairly certain that Brittany doesn't know she's adopted; she really thinks she's Sally's sister. What do you make of it?"

"How would I know; I just met her. Where is she now?"

"Pittsburgh, talking with an aunt. Something about Duke freaked her out today at Mass. It's the strangest thing, Brittany feels certain that she's seen him before. In fact she thinks he was at her house when she was a child."

"Are you kidding me?"

"No, I kid you not. That's why she went to Pittsburgh, to see if her aunt knows anything about how that might be possible."

"Man, this is getting weirder by the hour."

"That's for certain. What about Sally, did you find anything out about her?"

"No, the family moved around a lot. They were in one place in California for a few years and that's where they left some records behind, but that's it so far."

"Well, Brittany came up with a theory about what might have happened to Sally and believe it or not, it has to do with the boiler room. Speaking of which, are you still up for tonight?"

"The break in? Hell yes, let's do it. I take it Duke turned down Bob's request."

"Yes, as expected, and Bob's opinion is that he definitely was uneasy about being asked and acted like he had something to hide."

"There's no doubt something suspicious went down here, Duane. We've got to see what's in that room, but let's not talk about it anymore. For now, I think we should mingle with our fellow alumni and not mention another word about it. We can continue this conversation at Corky's."

The Old Stone Inn is located at the top of a hill on the west side of Homewood, although it's hard to imagine a hill in any pastoral sense of the word in this landscape of concrete and commerce. The restaurant is on Main Street and at a busy, five-corner intersection with heavy traffic converging from all directions. When I was a boy, I could easily recognize a hill where I now stand because then there were many trees covering a spacious lawn that sloped downward away from the Inn in all directions.

The first time I dined at the Old Stone Inn was with two hundred people; the occasion was a celebration following my Grandfather's funeral. Granddad Wiley had requested that such a banquet be served so that his friends and family could have a good time to mark his passing. I can still picture Grandma Wiley at the head table, flanked by her children and their spouses, my aunts and uncles. Father Hanlon, who had served the requiem mass for granddad, sat next to grandma, and they all seemed to be having fun, laughing and talking; and smoking and drinking.

I was nine years old at the time, and seated at a large, round table with a collection of my cousins, I thoroughly enjoyed the festivities. My grandparents had six children and all of their offspring had at least three children at this point in time, so the next generation was well represented.

The only person missing was Grandfather Wiley, or Pa, as we grandchildren called him, and he would be missing forever now. That was hard for me to comprehend at that age when there was still so much living ahead of me.

One night before my grandfather's death, I was awake in bed and I heard my parents talking in hushed tones about how ill he was. When I sensed from their words that he was so bad that he might die, I got out of bed, knelt down, and prayed, asking God to let Pa live. No immediate family member had died thus far in my life and this was the first time I made such a personal plea to God. In the dark, at my bedside, I prayed more fervently than I ever had before and like I never would again.

Grandfather Wiley died in spite of my prayers, just like President Kennedy died, in spite of all the prayers from me and my classmates and even Sister Mary Sean.

"You look like you've drifted to some far off place, Duane. Please come back and escort me to dinner. Michael is campaigning to save the school building again, and once he starts, there's never an end in sight. I want to sit down."

"Your wise to shed yourself of that neglectful man, Maureen. I would be honored to escort you to the dinner table."

I don't know Maureen Prizza well, having only talked to her on a few occasions, but conversation came easily each time, as if we had been friends for years. Perhaps it's understandable since we're both involved in the arts, but while I'm sure that's where the attraction begins, I sense there's something more. If I wanted to explain it in poetic terms, I might say that Maureen and I are kindred spirits, walking along different paths in life, while in essence, we are forever in step.

I know my poetry stinks, so let's just say that I like her. Now that's in a platonic way, of course—not that I haven't imagined it otherwise. Now don't get me wrong, I'm all for platonic relationships. After all that's one of the attributes of civilized humans that separates us from the savage beast: the ability to experience friendship, affection, or even love for another person without having sexual relations with them. I *do* believe that it's possible to be involved in a platonic relationship, but what I don't believe is that it's possible not to at least imagine it otherwise.

Oops, what commandment have I broken this time? It's the ninth: *Thou shall not covet thy neighbors wife*. Ah, just a venial sin;

no big deal. Nonetheless, the fact that God had to issue a specific commandment for coveting shows that it's been a concern for a long time, a problem of biblical proportions.

However, I'm in platonic mode as I escort Maureen into the banquet room, her arm on mine. Mike's table is in the middle of the room and two couples are already seated there. I'm introduced to Bill Humphries, owner of Mountain Laurel Energy Company and his wife, Michelle, who attended Saint Mathew's school several grades behind me.

To their right are Dr. Paul Cummings, a heart surgeon and his wife, Amy Cummings, the former Amy Boyd, a noted socialite about town these days, whose exploits as a young woman were so wild that the gossip would sometimes even reach me in North Carolina. Her family is so wealthy that even wealthy people refer to them as *people with money*.

I know who these people are by name and hearsay, but I don't really know them, and I would never choose to dine in their company. To say that they're not *my crowd* is an obvious understatement, but then who is my crowd? On the other hand, Booker moves in many circles. He rubs shoulders with a bartender in a dimly lit tavern one night and dines with a state representative at a gala fundraiser the next. One thing I am certain of is that he has assembled this group of people around the table for a reason.

After introductions and a round of small talk, I begin to feel uncomfortable and wish that Booker would get in here. It's just my luck that Michelle Humphries has actually been to Trinidad and Tobago, thus prompting an engaging conversation between her and Maureen, and thwarting my hope for continued platonic association with my kindred spirit.

Amy wanders off as she is still likely to do on such occasions, and I'm stuck here with Paul and Bill, who after feeling me out with a few questions about my occupation and no doubt sizing me up for the eccentric and indigent that I am, commence to discuss their investment portfolios. I'm starting to wish I hadn't come to this and nervously finger the flask in my pocket, wishing we could go somewhere more fun, like the Oak Park Motel.

Since I was a kid, it's been like this in social situations. All around me, other humans seem to comfortably settle into conversation while I watch, squirming in my skin, caught between a longing to fit in and an urge to scream and run away.

How can I join in a conversation about travel when in my fifty-five years, I've never even left the United States? While the summer I wandered around the country in a pick up truck with my dog, Emma, might be a charming tale to some, it's hardly the story to follow that of a luxury cruise vacation to an exotic island in the Caribbean.

And the fact that I recently paid off my credit cards and started a savings account as a buffer against old age would hardly add to the high stakes conversation about stocks and investments. I doubt these wise financiers would be interested in the long term investment I've made in wood and the returns I've accumulated in experience and personal satisfaction. Of course they wouldn't; that's not something that can be measured in the marketplace.

The seconds tick by, and I remember well why I avoid this sort of situation. I grow warm in my coat and tie; the Windsor knot tightens against my long neck. I look from side to side to see other tables of laughing and talking heads, discussing their illustrious travels and measuring each others worth through seemingly innocent chatter and narrative.

I don't fit in here, and I have a feeling that they think so, too. In fact, I wouldn't be surprised if some of them are talking about me right now, as I sit here alone with my long hair and cheap suit. They're probably laughing about my eccentric ways and unrefined manners, expecting me to do something unorthodox or stupid.

Why disappoint them? Perhaps I should give them something to talk about. How about if I leap out of my chair with a maniacal howl and tear my clothes off. Then run amok through the crowd with a fork in each hand, stabbing and . . .

"Excuse me sir, is this seat taken?"

"Uh, no, I . . . Oh, Carla, hi. No, as far as I know this seat's open. Please, sit down."

I scramble to my feet and pull out the chair beside me.

"I never expected to see you here. I thought you would be halfway to Connecticut by now."

"I thought I would be too, but I got sidetracked and didn't take off when I planned to; and then Mike called me up and said he had a place left at his table. I was a little surprised at the invitation, since I don't really know Mike that well. I don't even know how he knew I was still in town or how he got my cell number. But I had already decided to stay another day anyway, and when Mike told me you were going to be at the table, I took him up on it. Otherwise, I would have been nervous about this."

"I know how you feel; I was getting a little edgy here myself. The weekend's been fun, but I'm about at my social threshold. How about you?"

"I think my tolerance for society is a little higher than yours, Duane. In fact another reason I took up Mike's offer was to meet some new people in the area. To be honest with you, I'm still in town because I'm planning to move back to Homewood."

"Really? What a surprise. Is this something you've been thinking about for a while?"

"Yes, I've been thinking about it for over a year now."

"I guess I shouldn't be surprised at this point. You're the third classmate I know of who has made that decision. I'm really glad to hear that people are moving back to the area."

Just then, Booker arrives and the mood of the table changes. Conversations end and Booker brings the table to order with more formal and comprehensive introductions. He then thanks us for joining him and proposes a toast, to affirm our common interest in saving Saint Mathew's High School from the wrecking ball. I raise my glass, now with a better sense of why we are dining with millionaires and politicians.

No sooner do we lower our glasses when the master of ceremonies approaches the lectern at the head table. Carla leans toward me and whispers that she'll tell me about her plans to move back to Homewood later. I'm anxious to hear about her decision because I had always presumed that Carla was the type of person who would never look back once she ventured out of town.

I wasn't paying attention as the head table was seated, so now I study the occupants to see who I might recognize. Other than Bishop McGee, I'm not having much luck until I conclude that an elderly woman, seated in a wheel chair to his right, must be Sister Mary Agatha. She's being attended to by a young woman who sits beside her.

As I watch the two women, I get the distinct feeling that Sister Mary Agatha is looking at me. She says something to the young woman, who turns in my direction, stands, and walks toward me. The woman smiles as she approaches our table and acknowledges the other occupants, but she comes around next to me, bends down and speaks in a soft voice.

"I'm Sister Charlotte, Sister Mary Agatha's personal assistant. Sister Mary Agatha's would like to meet with you sometime before you leave, if that's agreeable to you."

"Well, of course, I would like to see her too. Do you mean after the banquet?"

"No that isn't possible. Sister Mary Agatha is very weak and she will probably not be staying for the entire program, but she will be seeing people tomorrow morning in the convent sitting room. Is it possible for you to come there about ten o' clock tomorrow morning?"

"Ten o' clock, sure, that's fine with me."

"Good, I'll let Sister Mary Agatha know."

Sister Charlotte smiles and makes her way back to the head table as I contemplate this pleasant surprise. I had hoped to see Sister Mary Agatha this weekend, but never expected a private audience with her. Sister Charlotte didn't approach anyone else in the room, so I have to wonder why I've been singled out by Sister Mary Agatha. I can't imagine what she might have to say to me after all these years.

For now, however, I focus my attention on the master of

ceremonies, determined to get my money's worth, or rather, Booker's money's worth, out of this event. While I recognize the speaker's name, William Hayden, and remember that he was a few years ahead of me in high school, I would never have known who this thin, bald man was if we had run into each other on the street.

William is a congenial host and after some well chosen introductory remarks, which allude to the high school, but never mention its imminent destruction, he introduces the head table and then other noteworthy persons who are scattered throughout the room. This proves to be an entertaining exercise, connecting names and memories from the past with older faces of the present. Some of the changes in people are so dramatic that I can hardly believe it's the same person, but then, I would probably be fooled by my own appearance if I hadn't gradually gotten used to it.

Immediately after the introductions, the waiters and waitresses are weaving in and out among us and I take the opportunity to inquire as to where the rest rooms are located. With such a mixed crowd of people at the table, I suspect that dinner conversation will be one of those trying social experiences that requires a vodka state of mind.

Besides, when I picked up my water glass, my right hand shook so badly that I had to steady the glass with my left hand to keep from spilling its contents. These tremors are something that I've noticed of late and while certainly of concern, I need to deal with the symptoms for now and worry about the disease another day.

I excuse myself with an innocent smile and make my way to the restroom. It's empty as I had hoped and I'm able to enjoy a few quick drinks with my haggard looking friend in the mirror.

My God, it's Duane Ryan, after all these years. He looks older, but he's still the same, still an oddball.

With that thought, and another hearty swallow for the journey back to the table I rejoin society. I must admit that I take great comfort in the fact that Carla will be at my side. We were very close once, and although many years have passed, I know that the bond between us is still there. Carla understands my insanity.

Moments later, I'm laughing and talking, surprised at my own gregariousness. I had nothing to fear except fear itself because conversation over dinner is actually enjoyable. Everybody at the table is a member of Saint Mathew's Parish and most had either attended Saint Mathew's School or at least went to summer catechism classes under the tutelage of the Sister's of Saint Francis.

We go around the table, telling of our more memorable experiences, and when Booker points out that Carla and I attended Saint Mathew's School from first grade through twelfth, we are elevated to an esteemed position in the discussion.

Carla prods me into telling the story of my departure from the boy choir, and then I insist that she relate the tragic tale of the frozen holy water. Perhaps because Carla and I seem to know each other so well and in light of our history together at Saint Mathew's, Jeanette Haliday assumes we are husband and wife. I place my hand on Carla's and explain that she was too smart and would never have me, but for a moment there with her hand in mine, I wish it were true, that I had once asked and she had said yes.

I've wondered sometimes in these latter years what it would have been like to have lived a normal life. That is, got married in a traditional fashion to someone like Carla, raised children together, and pursued a conventional occupation. I could smile and respond to Jeanette that Carla and I were indeed married, and add perhaps that we just celebrated our thirty-fifth wedding anniversary.

Our reminiscences are interrupted when William Hayden returns to the lectern to introduce the keynote speaker, the valedictorian of my senior class, Donald Hassan. A huge, white-haired man who now walks with the aid of a cane, Donald is hard to recognize as my former classmate. Obviously his tendency to put on weight hasn't abated since he left high school, but the smile on his face when he turns toward us and the eloquence in his words are familiar and contradict his sluggish appearance.

In fact, Donald is a gushing fountain of enthusiasm and optimism to an even greater extent than I remember from high school days, and his public speaking ability has clearly expanded to befit his large size. He opens with generalities about the passage of time, of friendship and memories, of aspiration and hope, and I'm drawn in, lulled to believe that his words might touch on my own life.

When he becomes more specific and talks glowingly of the value of family and career, drawing freely from his own circumstances for shining models of each, my attention begins to wane. When I realize that he's tying the whole picture together with a nice white Catholic bow, accrediting our successes and especially his own exalted position in life to an education at Saint Mathew's School, my attention runs for an exit.

While the other occupants of the table exhibit greater tolerance for this sort of oration and politely attend to the speaker, I take the opportunity to study them more closely. While we are certainly a diverse group, I am the most diverse, which is the case in most gatherings.

A void opened between me and people with normal lives soon after I began carving for a living. In the early days when we were all relatively poor and free, the gap between us was bridgeable, and we could still communicate with each other. Now, decades later, the gap has widened into a chasm, a distance that we must shout across in conversation, straining to hear, and never quite understanding each other.

My eyes stop wandering when I look at Carla. I'm thinking how pretty she looks in profile when she suddenly turns and catches me staring at her.

She smiles and asks if I would like to go for a walk.

30

"I can't believe how big these trees are, Duane. Do you remember when they were first planted?"

"Yes I do, right at the beginning of our senior year. Turning this lot into a park seemed like a lost cause then, but now these pines looks like they've always been here."

"Do you ever use pine?"

"No, too soft. I love the trees though. Do you know that pine trees are hermaphrodites?"

"No, I didn't know that."

"Yes, a pine tree possesses both male and female cones."

"That's interesting. Is that why you love them?"

"Funny, Carla. But you have to admit, it would be much simpler that way."

"Tell me about it. So where was I, anyway? Ah yes, well, I was so naive, Duane. I've been kicking myself for years for being so blind. I kept believing Scott, practically right up until he moved in with her. I never saw it coming."

"Nobody sees it coming, Carla."

"Hah ha, I guess you're right. I have to tell myself that."

"Uh, I just said that off the top of my head because I felt like I should say something. Don't listen to me. I think I got that line from a Clint Eastwood movie."

"That's okay; I like it. In fact, I think I'll just turn it around and use it on you. So you didn't see it coming with Elaine?"

"Hmm, I sure didn't see this question coming. Did I see it coming with Elaine? Let's see. Well, yes and no. We got along fairly well after ten years of marriage. I thought that was doing pretty good, but, looking back . . . What's so funny?"

"Typical guy remark, that's all."

"Well thank you. I don't often get called a typical guy, so I take that as a compliment. Ahem, as I was saying, Elaine and I got along *well enough*, but I have to admit, we weren't really around each other a lot in the end. We both worked all the time: me at the building and her, all over the place. If Elaine ever came to the studio during the day, she just breezed through on the way to an appointment with another client. She'd talk a little, freshen up and rush off again. I used to call it her pit stop."

"Elaine's an interior decorator, right?"

"Yes, and her career definitely took off. All the rich people with their so-called cabins in the mountains that are actually mini-mansions, wanted her to decorate them. 'Contemporary rustic' was the term she used to describe the look she was trying to achieve. To me it was elegance and extravagance with a country veneer."

"Is that how you described her work around her?"

"Uh, yes, now and then. That's the way I felt about it. Why?"

"I wouldn't have, even if I felt that way."

"Hey, whose side are you on?"

"I'm not taking sides; I'm just being objective. So when did you realize something was wrong?"

"What have I gotten myself into here? Let's see, when *did* I realize something was wrong. I guess my first real clue was when Elaine told me she had met somebody else and wanted a divorce."

"But I thought you saw it coming to some extent."

"In hindsight, I feel like I knew it was coming, if that makes sense. Our relationship was stagnant. She went to bed early; I stayed up late. We made love on occasion, almost on a schedule. We got along, coexisted; we were like roommates. I knew our relationship wasn't good, but I didn't care as long as I could keep working and

213

the gallery was surviving. It was like I had already accepted that it was over and just played along because it was convenient."

"So you didn't care when she asked for a divorce?"

"No, I *did* care; I was shocked. I didn't really love Elaine anymore, but it bothered me that she wanted to leave me and especially that she had already met someone else. I needed a more dramatic ending. 'Closure' is the word they use now. I needed some closure, like a big fight, a dish or two thrown at me, not 'I met somebody else and I would like a divorce, please'."

"So you blame Elaine?"

"I don't blame her for falling in love with someone else or wanting to get away from me—I can relate to that. The way she sprang it on me is what hurt. She made up her mind about what she wanted to do and *then* let me in on it. And it was more than that; it was her attitude. She was almost boasting about her new plans, she and this old college professor."

"How old?"

"Sixty something, I think."

"That's not that old anymore, Duane."

"I guess you're right. Anyway it's over now; we never see each other and I don't think about her too much. Is it over for you?"

"Uh, yes and no. It's a little more complicated with kids. They keep Scott and me in touch, whether we like it or not. Julie's wedding was last spring and we were all there, including Scott's new wife."

"Yikes."

"Yikes is right. But, I got through it. You know what's strange to me, is how Julie and Philip still like Scott. The fact that he cheated on me and abandoned us for his little love fantasy seems to have been forgotten. He's still their dad. That bothered me for a while, but now I accept it. In fact, I make my decisions with that knowledge in mind."

"You do, like your decision to move back here?"

"Sure, why not? At first I felt I should maintain the house in Hartford for them. I needed to keep the place together so that they would have a home to come to for the holidays, a place where we could take pictures with the grandchildren one day. Now my attitude is different; I'm looking out for number one."

"Really?"

"Well, not a hundred percent. I'll always be their mother and will help them when I can. I would say about seventy five percent for number one though."

"But why move back here? You never struck me as a home town girl."

"Actually I didn't plan on moving here at first. I wanted away from the cold weather, and at first, considered someplace in Florida. But I decided it would be too hot for me in the summer and having two homes was definitely out. Then I though about your area, the Carolinas, where the weather is somewhere in between, but it seems like everybody's moving there.

Anyway, while I was considering my options, a great aunt of mine died, my Aunt Eleanor, who lived here in Homewood. She was ninety-seven years old and died in the house she was born in."

"Wow, that's incredible."

"Yes, isn't it hard to imagine in this day and age? Anyway, Aunt Eleanor died last April and I came through for the funeral. There was no real grieving because everyone, including Aunt Eleanor, knew that her time had come. Instead, the funeral became the motivation for a small family reunion. That's when the idea of moving back came to me. I still went back and forth on it for a few months, but then finally made up my mind to move back to Homewood. I want to be part of the family again. Besides, this is where my parents are buried, and it's where Billy's buried."

"I think it's a really cool idea, Carla; I mean that. Do you have a place yet?"

"Yes, I do. The old family home no longer exits or that would have been my first choice. It was torn down ten years ago, and now there's a convenience store there. Did you know that?"

"Yes, I went by there yesterday morning, and I nearly drove off the road when I saw how much your street has changed."

"I know, isn't it awful? Well, fortunately, my Aunt Eleanor's place was being put on the market, so I moved in quick."

"Is it a done deal, then?"

"Yes it is. I haven't told anyone yet, but it's a done deal. I'm moving back to Homewood this year, hopefully before Christmas."

"How neat. How old fashioned. I'm jealous."

"Really, or are just saying that?"

"No, I wouldn't make something like that up."

"Good. I feel better about my decision then. What are you going to do?"

"Me, with my life you mean?"

"Yes, with your life."

"I really haven't given it much thought lately. Since Elaine left, I've been devoting a large portion of my life to drinking with a little art spattered in from time to time. The gallery is still . . . Why are you looking at me like that? That's the way Hannah, my gallery manager, looks at me."

"Then maybe she cares about you, too, Duane. I noticed your hand shaking at dinner when you picked up your water. How bad is it?"

"Oh, I rate myself about an eight out of ten."

"That's not good."

"No, it's not good, but that's where it stands. I'm only hurting myself, Carla. I'm not a mean or annoying drunk, and no one depends on me for support."

"But I hate to see you go down this way. You went out on a limb with your career, and I know you've struggled and had some problems, but you created some wonderful art over the years, art that touches many people's lives. You deserve a better ending."

"Do I? And who says it's such a bad ending? Life's full of worse endings. I read about them in the news sometimes to cheer myself up."

Carla looks at me with a blank expression, which gives way to a pretty smile. We're sitting on a bench, facing each other, and she rests her hand on mine before she speaks.

"You know something, Duane, in some ways, you're the same as you always were."

"I know; I was just thinking that the other day. It's scary, isn't it?"

"Do you still smoke pot?"

"No, I haven't in years. See I'm not a total derelict."

"I know you're not; that's not why I ask. I think you *should* start smoking again."

"You do?"

"Yes, start smoking pot and ease up on the drinking. A good friend of mine did that and it worked. She was drinking heavily and now she rarely has a drink. Karen swears by the pot treatment and she knows other people who do, too."

"Hmm, I haven't really considered treatment yet, but that certainly sounds like the direction I might go if and when the time comes."

"Duane, consider this a one person intervention. The time *has* come."

What Carla meant by that was just sinking in when she glances at her wrist watch.

"I've got to head back. I really need to leave for Connecticut this afternoon. I wish I didn't. It's so pretty here, and relaxing. I'm glad we did this, Duane; it's nice to talk to you again."

Carla and I turn to a new line of conversation as we walk back to the Old Stone Inn. We talk about the twelve years we spent together at Saint Mathew's School, which seems a more appropriate subject to part on.

At her car, we hold each other for a moment and promise to keep in touch. Carla kisses me lightly on the lips, and we let each other go.

31

As my eyes adjust to the dim light, I look toward the bar for Booker. I half expect to see him there, shoulder to shoulder with bikers, drunks, loud women, smokers, and jokers—the serious partiers—because that's where we always sat in the old days, Booker and me, the hippie-redneck, Saturday night, outlaw duo. Alas, these aren't the old days and to make matters worse, it's not Saturday night, it's Sunday afternoon.

The bar would be empty, except for one extremely thin man, munching nachos over a beer, and a young waitress, talking to an even younger bartender. All three of them look up as I come in and the bartender welcomes me with the information that Mr. Prizza is in the last booth.

Corky's is an unusually narrow and long space for a tavern or any business for that matter. There's only enough width to accommodate the bar and the kitchen on the left side, an aisle down the middle, and a row of ten, enclosed booths on the right. Two of the booths are occupied: one, halfway down the line, by a man and woman who are concentrating on their sandwiches and don't look up as I pass, and the last by a large man sitting stoically beside a plate of food and a pint of beer.

"I bought some quesadillas to munch on. What do you want to drink? We got Coal Country on tap, frosted mugs."

"That sounds good. Say, how did the bartender know who I was?"

"I just told him that Duane Ryan, the famous woodcarver, was coming."

"Yah right."

"Nah, I told him to look for some old hippie dude in a tweed jacket. Actually, as slow as it is tonight, I could have just had him watch for a male human."

"Well, it is Sunday evening."

"To be honest with you, it's not much better on lots of other days. I'm happy if this place breaks even in a year."

"No kidding. What are you going to do?"

"Nothing, breaking even is good enough. There are changes that could be made, like ripping out these old booths and getting more seats in here, but I like it the way it is, the way it's always been. If I needed the money, it would be a different story, but I don't. Besides, Duane, you can't let money always be your guide in life. There are some things worth doing just for the sake of doing them."

"I'll remember that, Booker."

"So how did it go with Carla today?"

"Good, we had a nice talk, just like old times in some ways. Was that your plan, to get us together?"

"No, Dale thought of it. I asked him to sit at the table first, but he couldn't swing it. I had politicians and money, but I thought it might help to have an architect there to talk nuts and bolts."

"I figured out that your guest selection was about the school, that's why I wondered why I was there."

"Hey you did good. You and Carla added just the right touch to the story. Too bad you aren't married, though, because that would have been even better."

"So what's the deal with those people?"

"The idea was actually Tim Haliday's, the commissioner. We go back a ways and I asked his advice on this one. He suggested making a move to bypass the diocese and buy the school outright."

"And do what with it?"

"Fix it up big time. Have Dale and company give it the primo treatment. Then set it up as a nonprofit, or some kind of foundation. What it's called is for the accountants to decide, but the idea is to make it something that would benefit the whole community."

"How does it look?"

"It looks real good. And you know who really loved the idea? Ms. Amy."

"Really?"

"Yah, she suddenly tuned in to what we were saying and is all for it. She's an only child, you know, and her family, they're . . ."

"*People with money.*"

"You better believe it—beaucoup bucks."

"Well that's that; I'm glad we had this talk. There's no sense breaking into the newly formed Saint Mathew's High School Foundation. Might as well have a few more beers and call it a night."

"I don't think so. It may sound good over dinner and drinks, but talk is cheap and time is short. Rumor has it that demolition on the high school could start by the end of the month."

"Then the break-in is still a go?"

"Uh-huh. Let's face it, no matter how much money we have behind us, we still have the Duke in front of us. But if we can get an angle on him to make him more receptive to our plans, and have the cash in hand to see them through, *then* it's a done deal."

"All right, I guess there's no getting out of this. Do you have a plan?"

"Of course; it's simple, really. At twenty-two hundred hours, we meet on Shady Lane with flashlight and pickax in hand and proceed down Tuesday Alley to the school. We enter the building by the left rear window, which I unlocked when Maureen and I toured the building today. Once inside, we proceed down the stairs to the wall that covers the boiler room. There you'll hold the flashlight, while I commence to pick a hole in the wall. Once the wall is breached, you climb through with the flashlight and see what's inside."

"Why me?"

"Because I'm the demolition expert and you're the investigative specialist. Another reason is, you're skinny and the hole won't have to be as big. Last but not least, there might be asbestos in there or worse."

"Oh, I understand now. But all kidding aside, Booker, do you think we'll really find anything in there? I hope if we do, it *is* something like asbestos, not the worst case, like finding Sally Schuster's body."

"Sally Schuster, why in the hell would you think that?"

"Well there's a fun little theory circulating around that the boiler room is where Sally may have disappeared to."

"Wow, I never thought of that."

"I didn't either; Brittany did. At first hearing, it seems pretty far-fetched, but if you think about . . ."

"No, I can see it now. Sure, from what we've found out, it all adds up. Wow, I hate to believe it, but I'd say there is a chance. Weird things like that *do* happen."

"Oh I know, when Brittany was doing research for her novel, she found a number of instances where a priest killed a nun. In one case, a nun at a hospital was strangled and then stabbed to death."

"Oh man, a priest did that?"

"Yes, the hospital chaplain, someone that worked with her."

"Whoa, that's creepy, and that settles it; you're definitely going through the wall."

"Okay, I'll go in."

"That's the old Ryan spirit. Look, if there's nothing in there, we'll come back here and laugh about it over a few more beers. If there *is* something in there, we'll, uh, well, depending on what it is, I guess we'll just have to play it by ear."

By the tone of his voice, I can tell that Booker is now somewhat anxious about what we might find in the boiler room, which is unlike him and adds to my own unease. I reach for the flask in my coat pocket and then withdraw my hand when I realize what I'm doing. Booker glances away in the direction of the bar for a few seconds and then looks directly at me.

"How long you been carrying a flask?"

"What flask?"

"The one in your coat pocket."

"Oh, that one. Um, how long? Uh let's see. This flask, it was a gift, actually, and I guess I've been carrying it around for about two years now."

"Well, you better be careful, Duane. From my experience, when a man starts carrying a flask, he's on a slippery slope."

"Life's a slippery slope, Booker."

"I'm serious, when you start carrying it with you, the booze isn't just a reward in life anymore, it's a way of life."

"Hey, I know I drink too much, but I think I keep things under . . ."

"I'm not going to lecture you, but I can tell you this, I've seen many a good man go under over the years. They don't necessarily end up on the street, but their lives are a shell of what they were. They live and work for the booze. Anyway, that's all I'm going to say about it.

Hey, I don't know about you, but I want another plate of quesadillas. I'm going to go back and order it myself and give my compliments to the cook. You want another beer?"

"Uh, yah sure Book, thanks."

Booker makes his way to the kitchen, and I stare at my glass, trying to decide if I'm embarrassed or irritated at his admonition. Regardless, as soon as he's out of sight, I reach for the flask, take a long, resolute toke and follow it with the last of my Coal Country. I do find it disconcerting that within the span of a few hours, he and Carla, two people who I haven't interacted with in years, feel a need to caution me about my drinking. Is it that obvious now?

During a recent attempt to assess my condition, I did some research on alcoholism and read that a person passes through different phases on the way to full addiction. The first is the *alert phase*, during which alcohol actually enhances one's behavior and facilitates performance. That's something I was already aware of in practice and in fact can be somewhat scientific about it, adjusting the dosage to the situation at hand. What I read about the alert phase only verified what I already suspected, and in a sense, told me what I wanted to hear.

Unfortunately, the experts report that next comes the *sloppy phase,* during which a person's performance and social skills are compromised by alcohol. The lesson seems simple enough: to drink just enough to maintain the alert phase but never cross the line into the sloppy phase. The problem is that there's no clear line, and typically a drinking person believes they are still alert and in control, confident and witty, when they have in fact become sloppy and reckless. Have I crossed the line?

Booker interrupts my thoughts on alcoholism by plopping a frosty mug of beer in front of me—just the distraction I needed. He mustn't be *too* concerned. My honest assessment is that I'm still somewhere in the alert phase with just a tad of sloppiness showing through. Probably just have to tone it down a little, that's all.

Booker and I order a third round of beers when our quesadillas arrive and forget about our upcoming caper for the time being. We fill each other in on what we've been doing over the years and by the fourth round, we're laughing out loud about old times.

Ours is an odd friendship that I know surprises my other friends, especially Dale, and I'm sure that Booker's crowd wonders why he consorts with the likes of me. One thing that I never thought about over the years, which is obvious now, is that we really have no mutual friends. Somewhere on the fringes of each other's personality we find common ground, but no one else from either side ever seems willing or able to join us there.

Why a friendship develops between two very different people is a mysterious thing, perhaps some deep-rooted genetic compatibility that overrides surface differences. Or maybe in our case, it was something more simple: we were two odd ducks that didn't fit into the Saint Mathew's system for our own particular reasons and so naturally gravitated toward each other. Whatever, the friendship has endured through the years. We can make fun of each other, but beneath the surface is a mutual respect and most important of all, trust.

Booker finishes his beer with an animated swallow, slides his mug to the end of the table, and stands.

"As the walrus said, 'the time has come'. I'll swing by the plant and grab a pick."

"I have a flashlight in my truck."

"Alright, good. Meet you in half an hour on Shady Lane. Do you have any final words of wisdom to inspire us, oh bearded one?"

"Uh, let's see, yes, of course: *for duty and humanity*."

"I like that. I can't remember who said it, but it sums it all up."

"That would be The Three Stooges."

"Great, my heroes. We're in good company then."

32

I take a left off Fayette street and drift slowly down Shady Lane. Small, elegant, homes nestle shoulder to shoulder along both sides of the road, many of which have been inhabited by members of Saint Mathew's parish for generations. Huge maple trees have lined each side of the road for as long as I can remember and shade out almost all sunlight during the day.

Shady Lane runs perpendicular to Jefferson Street for about two hundred yards and ends where the two streets intersect. I park about midway along the road, turn off the headlights and let the shadows close in around me. When I switch on my flashlight, I'm dismayed to see a weak and unsteady beam shine on the truck floor. I meant to test it, but forgot in the rush to swing by the motel and refill my flask. After rapping it on the floor a couple times, the beam brightens. It will have to do.

It's not surprising that Booker would choose Shady Lane as the launching point for this clandestine operation. Despite its proximity to the school, the road is still around the corner on the next block and separated from the Saint Mathew's campus by long backyards and dense foliage. Twenty yards away from where I'm parked, is Tuesday Alley, a narrow, gravel passageway that connects Shady Lane to the high school parking lot.

I step from the truck, pull the flask from my coat pocket and take a few sips. The autumn air is cool, but I'm comfortable enough in my tweed jacket. I bought the garment many years ago in a second hand store and have often marveled at how well it's served me over the years, especially on those numerous occasions when I don't know what else to wear. This is my first break-in, so naturally I was at a loss over how to dress. I admit the old jacket is a little shabby these days for a dinner party, but will still make for a classy mug shot.

A couple more swallows from my flask and I feel boldness coming over me, such that I'm ready to perform this great service for Saint Mathew's School. In spite of the risk, the chance of injury or incarceration, I will solve the mystery of the boiler room. This isn't about me, it's about justice, about school spirit, about duty and . . .

Eh, what the, what was that? A strange noise comes out of the darkness from somewhere behind me. There it is again! It sounds like the call of an owl, but not quite–almost like an owl that has laryngitis. The sound comes from close behind me this time, and I return the flask to my coat pocket as I peer into the darkness. I see movement and start when Booker walks out from the shadows, carrying some sort of tool.

"Man, Ryan, you look like a suspicious character."

"I am a suspicious character. What was that noise?"

"That was the secret owl call to let you know that I was approaching."

"How was I supposed to know that? You never told me about a secret owl call."

"I couldn't tell you because it wouldn't have been a secret then. Actually, I made that up; there's no secret owl call. I just wanted to see if you were ready."

"Am I?"

"Ready as you'll ever be. Are you sure you haven't been followed?"

"Even if I told someone else of our plans, they wouldn't have followed."

"That's good. The less people involved, the better. I figured from the start that it would be best if it were just you and me."

"Why is that?"

"Because those other guys, they got to toe the line; they don't have a choice. They're not like you and me."

"What do you mean like you and me? I never though we were much alike."

"We're not; we're opposites. You're a hippie, derelict artist and I'm a rich, redneck asshole. What I mean is that you and I are in a better position to do something like this. If we get caught, I can pay my way out of it, you'll get a slap on the wrist because you're a crazy artist, and neither of us cares what shows up in the papers."

"We don't?"

"Hell no. In fact it would probably help our careers more then hurt. I'm the maverick businessman, that's always doing off the wall stuff. I never play by the rules and my clients know that. I do whatever it takes to get them the best deals—even if it might not be entirely above the table. Most of the people I do business with would laugh about something like this and probably place another order with me."

"What about your friends in higher places?"

"Ah, they'd think it's funny too. Of course they couldn't say that in public. They'll have to talk around the issue, but in the end they'll stick with me. It's always a matter of who's got the money with politicos—sad but true."

"But how would it help *my* career?"

"Exposure, my man. Your name is out there in the media in an unusual way. Not some boring art opening that always draws the same boring crowd. You'll attract a whole new audience that can relate to a bit of lawlessness like this, people who deep down would like to join us but can't step out of their little world. They'll admire you for doing this and will show their support by investing in your work."

"I have to admit, that's a marketing strategy that I never considered before."

"Trust me. I don't know a lot about art, but I know business and I know people. So let's go for it. You have the flashlight? Good.

This is my handy sawed-off pickaxe. I think it's a felony to possess one of these, but it's served me well on many a job."

I smile as Booker holds up a short-handled pick that looks like it's designed for a job such as we have planned, and it probably was.

Tuesday Alley is lined with thick shrubbery and overhanging tree limbs, making this little used avenue even shadier than Shady Lane. Booker and I have to rely on the feel of loose gravel beneath our feet for guidance.

When we emerge from the tunnel of foliage, the vision of the old high school on the opposite side of the parking lot is somewhat surreal. The glow of lights from Jefferson Street make it look like a huge, grainy, black and white photograph, as if the building is already gone and I'm looking at an image in a picture book. That could very well be the case in a few short months.

As we make our way around the back edge of the parking lot, I look up at the rectory and see a light in the upper floor of the building. I tell myself that it's probably just a nightlight, but for some reason the glow makes me uneasy. Booker is careful to stay in the shadows as we circle the lot, but I still feel more at ease when we're behind the school and the rectory is blocked from view.

The unlocked window is located about six feet from the ground, and it might prove too great a height for us old timers to overcome if not for the decorative ledge that runs along the base of the building. This step affords me the altitude I need to raise the window sash and pull myself through the opening. Mike's size is to his disadvantage at this stage of the operation, but driven by a belief in our cause and spurred on by taunts from me, he follows through the window.

Once inside, we take a moment to catch our breath as we gaze into the shadows of what had once been a science lab. The room is empty and ghostly in the dim light, and hard to imagine as the same space where tireless Sister Margaret paced up and down the aisles between lab benches, working hard to instill the fundamentals of biology and chemistry.

"Get your flashlight ready, but don't turn it on until we're in the basement. And as always, Mr. Phelps, if you are caught or killed, the secretary will disavow any knowledge of your actions. Good luck, Jim."

"Good luck to you, too, chief. Now I know this never happened on Mission Impossible, but I've got to hit the men's room before the action starts."

"Why didn't you just go outside?"

"Because I didn't *have* to go outside. It's my blood pressure medicine that does this too me: any exertion, any sudden moves, and I've got to go. In the old days, I could hold it for a week. Here, take the light and go on down. Clear out any booby traps and I'll be right behind you."

The restroom is conveniently located next to the science lab so as Booker feels his way down to the basement, I swing open the heavy wooden door, just as I did hundreds of times in the past. Inside the room, I reach to my right and switch on the lights. Florescent bulbs click and buzz along the ceiling, and sudden brightness startles me to an awareness of what I've done. *How stupid can I be?* I immediately switch the lights back off and stand still in the darkness, feeling like a dope.

Only one small window faces the world from the restroom and I move toward it to look for any sign that our mission has been compromised. All is still in the gray light of the parking lot and beyond that is shadow, but to my dismay, if I look to the extreme right, I can just catch sight of the light in the upper floor of the rectory. I try to control my paranoia, reasoning that the bathroom was lit for only a second and even if someone is up there, the chances are slim that they would have noticed such a brief illumination.

I relieve myself in the same urinal that I used when I was in high school, the one on the far right, in the corner of the room. Many were partial to this particular urinal as evidenced by the fact that it had been christened *Old Faithful* before I even arrived at the high school.

A urinal is one of the most practical devices ever invented for human males. By comparison, a toilet is a poor compromise for a man since no matter how accurate the trajectory, there's always the splashing to contend with. When I first learned to use a toilet that wasn't a problem, because I was short and the surface of the water was near, but as I grew taller, gravity became more of a factor, and splashing developed into an issue.

Some years back, a certain female suggested that I could eliminate the problem by *sitting* on the toilet to urinate. Not surprisingly, that relationship didn't last long. Who knows, but if we had simply installed a urinal in our bathroom, we might still be together today.

With this absurd thought in my head, I exit the restroom, and grope my way down the stairs to the basement. I move toward a faint glow, halfway down the hall, turn left into the custodial room, and join Booker at the block wall that seals the boiler room.

"What the hell's wrong with this flashlight?"

"It's a little temperamental this evening, but it's never let me down before. I just used it about a year ago and it worked fine. Watch, just a few taps on the wall and . . ."

"Well, that's a little better. Shine it here a few feet from the floor. There that's good. Now I'm going to demonstrate the fine art of tearing down a concrete wall while making as little noise as possible."

I keep the beam of my flashlight focused as Mike picks at mortar joints between concrete blocks that Carmen Vincenzi set in place four decades ago. The sound of mortar fragments hitting the floor signals that the demolition is progressing, but grunts and expletives from the man who wields the pick, hint that the wall is not yielding easily.

I don't sympathize with him much. After all, when a hole of sufficient size is created, his work will be done, and then it is I who will go to work, facing unknown risk and perhaps unspeakable horror. I smile at the prospect, cool and confident, exhibiting that late night bravery that only heroes and drunks can imagine.

The dim light that illuminates our operation renders the rest of the surroundings all the more dark and mysterious. I peer into the gloom toward the end of the hall to where the school library was once located. The room is abandoned now with not a book to be found and only empty shelves to suggest what the space stood for. Earlier in the day, when Dale and I made our way through the room, I realized that it was the first time I had seen the library since the incident with Sally and me.

How could I have known in that wonderful moment when Sally and I were in each others arms, young and carefree, that we would never see each other again? And how could I have ever guessed that one day, I would be back here, old and careworn, perhaps to uncover evidence of her murder?

I turn back to the excavation as a sizeable chunk of cinder block hits the floor. The barricade has been perforated and a pungent, earthy aroma wafts through the hallway. Booker widens the hole to the extent that a number of blocks in the row above are loosened. These come down and others soon follow to create an aperture of sufficient size for me to crawl through. Then Booker turns to me and whispers.

"Duane, I'll go in with you, if you want me to. After all this was my idea."

"Nah, let me go in Booker and you wait here. That was the deal. If something does go wrong, at least you can go for help."

"What could go wrong?"

"I don't know: poison gas, ceiling collapse, you never know."

"Good point; I'll wait here. I got your back."

The opening is large enough for me to manage if I stay low and steady myself with one hand. The weak beam from my errant flashlight scarcely cuts through the gloom, making it necessary to explore each wall and corner up close. The room is about ten feet wide and twice as long with a small alcove at the rear that juts to the left for about four feet. We called this niche the *luxury suite*, and this was where we would sit on wooden boxes that Carmen gave us, smoking cigarettes and pondering the foibles of life.

"So what do we have in there, Duane?"

"Nothing so far chief, just like we left it, but I haven't checked the luxury suite yet."

"Well check it out and let's go. We've been in the building too long."

The main room is empty and cold and I'm relieved to find it so, but I grow anxious as I approach the luxury suite. Perhaps it's because I know that if something is hidden in here, especially something like a body this is where it will be. This is where I would have placed a body if I had chosen to hide one in the boiler room.

I try to dismiss my fear, but it envelops me like a thick blanket, a primordial fear, of darkness, of enclosed spaces, and of hidden bodies. My delinquent flashlight adds to the tension, as it flickers and threatens to fail and leave me blind in a black catacomb.

"Duane, let's do it and move out of here, man."

"Alright, I, I'm almost done. So far, I don't see anything in here. I just have to check . . . Oh no, Jesus Christ."

"What happened? Where'd you go? Are you coming out?"

"You're damn right I'm coming out. I can't believe it."

"Can't believe what? Here's the opening; follow the light. Where's your flashlight?"

"I dropped it. Mike, there's a body in here."

I scramble to the break in the wall drawn by Mike's voice and a faint light that emanates from his cell phone. When I stand up, Mike is holding the phone near my face and is looking into my eyes.

"Did I hear you right? You saw a body?"

"Yes, I saw one alright, propped up in the corner, just where I was afraid it would be."

"Propped up in the corner, how could it be propped up in the corner after all these years? If there's a body in there, it should be nothing but bones and dust by now. Are you sure it wasn't something else, leaning in the corner?"

"No, it was a body, a human body. We should call the police. It must be Sally. I saw her face. I saw teeth, sticking out, like from a skull, and eyes, staring straight ahead."

"You saw eyes? That's impossible. It's been forty years. This doesn't make sense. We can't call the police yet, not until we're sure."

"Then we'll need another flashlight. Mine is probably finished after hitting the floor and even if it isn't, I'm not going back in there to feel around for it."

"We can't risk leaving and coming back again. Let's both go in; we'll find your flashlight quicker that way, and hopefully it still . . ."

The fluorescent lights along the hallway ceiling flicker on, and we hear the sound of slow, measured footsteps moving down the hall toward us. A figure steps into the doorway of the custodial room, a silhouette defined by the light from behind. I'm not surprised that it's Father McGee, but what does surprise me is the shotgun he cradles under his left arm. He switches on a flashlight and shines the beam in our faces.

"Well, well, what a surprise. Couldn't leave well enough alone could you?"

I'm speechless, while Mike seems undaunted, even by the gun pointed at us.

"It's over man; you won't get away with this."

"I suppose I won't, Michael, but I'll take my chances."

"Last I heard, there's no statute of limitations on murder."

"Murder, what are you talking about?"

"We've been inside. Well, Duane has. He's seen what you and Carmen did to Sister Sally."

"Who? Sister Sally? Are you talking about Sally Shuster? I never did anything to Sally; she's not in there. That's outrageous! Why would you ever think something like that? Duane, is this some kind of cruel joke you're playing on me after all these years?"

"Father, or, uh, Bishop McGee, I saw something. I dropped my flashlight, so I'm not really sure . . ."

"I know what you saw. Let's go in and I'll show you. I'll leave the gun here; it's not loaded anyway."

Bishop McGee stoops down and crawls through the opening;

Booker and I follow. We come up behind him as he turns into the luxury suite and directs his light on the object in the corner.

The Bishop's flashlight is more reliable than mine and many times brighter, so that the object in the corner is well illuminated. I hear Mike draw in his breath when he sees what startled me moments before: teeth and eyes, nested in macabre fashion within decades of cobwebs and dust.

As Mike and I stare in bewilderment, struggling to interpret the bizarre scene, Bishop McGee walks up to the figure and wipes away the sediment of years with his hand. This time both Mike and I take a deep breath.

"I don't believe it. It's that statue of Jesus that used to be in the back of the church. You remember it, don't you Duane?"

"Yah, I remember it. How could I forget. What's it doing in here, Father? Did you put this in here?"

The priest turns toward us and sighs.

"Yes, I put it in here. Carmen Vincenzi and I are the ones who stole it, or as I preferred to think about it over the years, we *relocated* it."

"But why?"

"Why? Because everyone hated it. The statue scared children and even made adults uneasy. It would never have made its way into the church in the first place except for the politics and the money behind it. Monsignor Schroeder was caught in the middle of an uncomfortable situation and the compromise he came up with was to have it installed in the church vestibule so that at least it wasn't a distraction during Mass."

"But why did you deal with it?"

"I took that on myself. I was a new, and I saw my appointment at Saint Mathew's as a mandate for change in the parish. I had no patience for the politics of the past and once I learned the inside story, this statue symbolized that to me. Amid all the closed door discussion of what might be done, I came up with a plan to settle the matter. The beauty of the plan was that I could solve two problems at the same time."

"Like shutting down our smoking lounge."

"Oh, yes, that too. The fact that you guys hung out in here *was* a problem, but there were other ways to deal with that. This room had other issues that were of more concern."

Bishop McGee turns his flashlight upward and lights a series of four pipes, that span the ceiling. Two of them are encased in a grayish, paper-like material.

"Those are pipes left over from the old heating system and that's asbestos covering two of them. At the time, health concerns over asbestos were starting to be raised, and a building inspector advised us to just seal the room up if it wasn't being used. In here, undisturbed, the asbestos wasn't a threat.

I'm not the one who came up with the idea to close the room; I'm just the one who tied everything together, including a way to deal with the statue. Don't think I haven't questioned the decision ever since. It wasn't the right thing to do, but at the time I was young and full of myself and it *seemed* like the right thing to do. An object that's been blessed shouldn't be discarded but should be buried, and in a sense, that's what I did."

"Is that why you're having the school torn down and covering it up with a parking lot, just to make sure everything stays buried here?"

"No, of course not, Michael. What's in this room was never a part of that decision. I have the entire diocese to consider when it comes to the budget and that includes many buildings. As much as I hate to do it, I have to let this building go so the expense doesn't drag others down with it."

"I can understand that, but if enough money was put up so that the school could be maintained separate from the diocese budget would that change the picture?"

"Certainly, but that's the key word, 'if'. I've been hearing talk like that for years now but never see any numbers on paper."

"But if you got those numbers, the building wouldn't come down?"

"No, it wouldn't. I don't want to see the high school torn down any more than you do. I'll be honest with you, I only pushed for demolition because I hoped that it would get some of the alumni with deep pockets to finally loosen up. Father Walsh came up with the idea to make the announcement just before the reunion."

"That was good thinking, Bishop, and it worked. You're going to have some numbers real soon."

"Really?"

"Yah, trust me. Hey, and as far as this statue goes, I think I can help here, too. A thought just came to me. I have an uncle who I'm sure would be glad to give it a home. He's a hard core Catholic of the fire and brimstone kind, if you know what I mean. Uncle Leo's got a place on the Jersey shore, gardens all around with other statues. There's one that he's had for years of the Blessed Mother, looking up to the sky, praying, and at the same time, she's crushing the head of a snake with her foot. This will fit right in there, believe me. Would you be cool with that?"

"I, I don't really know what I think about that. I *would* feel better if this statue were out of here, and even more so if it was someplace where it was appreciated. You're sure your uncle would like it?"

"Uncle Leo? He'll love it."

"Okay, well, let me think on that, Michael, but it sounds like something that could work. We'll talk about it another day, soon. Speaking of another day, I have more to do this evening and appointments start early in the morning. I didn't plan on this little rendezvous, so let's turn out the lights and lock up for the night."

Bishop McGee turns and makes his way to the opening in the wall. Booker and I follow and crawl through after him. I feel compelled to apologize for our actions and even more so for implying that he had murdered Sally Schuster, but as we reach the hallway, the Bishop speaks to Booker and me first.

"Good to see you again, Michael. Give my regards to your mother. And Duane, could I see you in Father Walsh's office tomorrow?"

"Y-yes, father. What time is convenient for you?"

"How about eleven?"

"Yes Father, that's fine. And Father, or, uh, Bishop McGee, I just want to say . . ."

"It's late Duane. We can talk about it tomorrow, after I've had time to think everything over and after you've spoken with Sister Mary Agatha."

"Oh, okay, yes Father."

33

Sitting on the bed, propped up with pillows, fatigue sets in. Fortunately a large, cheerful, bottle of vodka sits close at hand, like a faithful Saint Bernard, waiting to revive me. In spite of my weariness, I know that sleep will not come easily with thoughts of this evening's events bouncing around the inside of my brain.

I adjust the pillow behind my head, fill my glass, and settle in for some philosophical introspection. Staring at my reflection in the mirror across the room, I raise my shot glass to the tired old image, and drink its contents down in one fluid motion.

A phone message from Brittany was awaiting when I opened the door, recorded to inform me, much to my disappointment, that she's staying with her Aunt Shirley for the evening. I'm alone with my conscience tonight—not always the best company. I raise my glass again to the curious apparition, gazing at me from across the room, and to my delight, he raises his in return. Perhaps it's not a reflection at all, but my conscience that's separated from me to gain a better perspective on the creature it inhabits.

I click the play button on the telephone and listen to Brittany's message again, hoping to find some clue in the tone of her voice as to what sort of information her aunt might have imparted to her. It may just be the mood I'm in, but I detect a note of sadness.

What am I to make of the information Booker uncovered about Brittany? It could be incidental to the mystery surrounding Sally, but something tells me it's more than that. Whatever the explanation, I believe that Brittany is telling me the truth as far as she knows it. She has an honest and forthright way about her, a character trait that I've come to appreciate and wish that I could emulate.

Since I left the scene in the basement of Saint Mathew's School, I've adjusted to the fact that Father McGee didn't murder Sally Schuster and hide her body in the boiler room. In spite of my embarrassment, I'm relieved. Learning that he was behind the *relocation* of the creepy, Jesus statue, actually improves my opinion of the man. The mystery of the boiler room has been resolved, yet questions about Sally's disappearance and her involvement with Father McGee still remain.

Maybe Father McGee will answer these questions tomorrow, and maybe I'll be honest and forthright with the man and just ask him. While I'm at it, perhaps I'll tell him what was behind my poor attitude, back when I was a kid in high school and he had to deal with me, or go one step further, and tell him what's behind my poor attitude these days, even though it's not his problem anymore. I don't know who would be more surprised, him or me.

Whatever happens, it'll be strange indeed, to enter that office and face him again after so many years. In my high school days, whether a student was sent to Father McGee's office by a teacher or summoned by the priest himself, it was never for a good reason. If a student was sent to his office, it was for something that they did; if they were summoned to his office, it was for something that they didn't do. I was always *summoned* to his office.

I was never sure why I was standing there in front of him, but I came to expect that the issue stemmed from my poor attitude, poor in the sense that it wasn't the attitude he wanted me to have—whatever that was. I sometimes wonder if he even knew what he expected from me. If I would have suddenly sat up straight in class, transformed into an A student and spent all my spare time praying, would that have made him happy? Somehow I don't think so.

Whatever the issue was, it seemed unfair to me that I was called to his office for subjective reasons and had to walk the same route as people who had committed concrete offenses, like skipping class, or smoking on school grounds. Or like the time Bob Macy and Dave Marker broke Jesus' arm; you would *expect* to land in Father McGee's office for that sort of thing.

It happened one day during our sophomore year when Sister Dorthea was called from the room, and the two of them started a game of tossing an apple back and forth over the hanging fluorescent light fixture. Bob made an errant throw and the apple sailed over Dave's head and struck the crucifix that hung above the blackboard.

The crucifix bounced on its hook and hung tenaciously to the wall, but Jesus didn't fare so well. His right arm broke off just above the elbow and swung down, hanging on by the brass nail in the palm of His hand. (Poor Jesus, just when He thought things couldn't get any worse.)

Interestingly enough, even for a transgression such as this, Bob and Dave's time before Father McGee was less than my own sessions often were, and their punishment was as straightforward as the offense: a few reprimanding words, payment to have the crucifix repaired, and some time in detention.

In my case, there was never a simple reason why I was in Father McGee's office, and there never seemed to be a definite conclusion to our discussion. He never really hollered at me or overtly threatened me, and come to think of it, for all his macho show, Father McGee never really physically hurt anyone that I know of. Grabbing me by the collar in the library was as far as he went in that direction.

Now legend had it that for certain grievous offenses, Father McGee *would* resort to corporal punishment. I never knew of anyone who actually received such treatment, but back then, I didn't doubt that it happened.

When I was a freshman, an upperclassman even described to me, in a grave tone of voice, a long wooden paddle that hung on the door inside Duke's closet. He'd never really seen the paddle but heard that it was a wooden plank, two feet in length, with an extended handle that allowed for two-handed swinging. The contact end had holes drilled in it to lessen wind resistance and insure a swift, hard strike. I could only wonder what sort of crime would warrant such punishment, but it must have been something that was at least more heinous than breaking Jesus' arm.

Thomas McGee is a complicated character and someone that I've never quite understood. I wonder sometimes why he ever became a priest. He seems to be the type of person who would want to run his own business, so that he could be totally in control at all times. I think he would have thrived in such a secular arena. And the truth is, if I didn't know better, I would never presume Father McGee to be an overly religious person, let alone a priest. Yet he staunchly adheres to and defends the dictums of the church.

My God, who does that remind me of? I could be talking about my own father. Now that I think about it, he and Father McGee were alike in other ways as well: in stature, in age, and even in temperament. While I never liked to admit it, on the few occasions they met, Father McGee and Dad seemed to get along well with each other. I remember once seeing them standing together after Mass, laughing and talking, like old friends. What could they have possibly had in common? I don't remember ever laughing with my father like that.

I wonder if, like Father McGee, Dad didn't understand me either. Was he bothered by my attitude, too? Was he hoping for some potential to surface, but instead of prodding like Duke did, he remained silent and waited? I can only hope that my brief tenure at Ryan Coal Company gave him some reason to believe before he died.

Enough, it's late now, and I'm wandering out into a psychological quagmire that could bog down even a sober man. Besides, I want to look and feel my best for tomorrow's meetings. I'm certainly glad that the first is with Sister Mary Agatha and not Father McGee. Isn't it interesting that he was aware that I was speaking with Sister Mary Agatha and even knew when?

I can't imagine what he wants to talk about tomorrow. Surely he's not going to holler at me, even though I deserve it after the fiasco of this evening. All I know is he better not try to paddle me with the two foot long board with the holes in the end. I'll sue if he does.

I'm thinking nonsense now. My blood vodka content is just right to induce a mild coma to get me through the night. Time to screw the cap on my big plastic companion.

Now don't rush to judgment about my drinking. I've certainly taken to heart, the admonitions I received today from my good friends. I just don't want to consider them now. And why? Because that's what tomorrow is for. Tomorrow, the new dawn, the first day of the rest of my life. That's when I begin again, turn over a new leaf, get back to the way I used to be, and so on and so forth, forever and ever, amen.

34

I'm greeted at the convent door by Sister Charlotte who informs me that Sister Mary Agatha isn't quite ready. She asks if I would care to wait in the parlor, but since the weather is so nice I opt to sit on the porch. What sleep I did get last night has not rendered me as sharp as I would like to be, and I think the fresh air will do me good.

Seated in an old wicker chair that is smooth with many coats of white paint, I gaze beyond the convent lawn to Saint Mathew's Grade School and the grass covered recreation area beside the building. All is quiet now, but I know that in a short while, the air will be filled with the whoops and hollers of children playing. I was one of them once, running about in my blue, uniform shirt with the school insignia, SMS, on the pocket, and with my blue tie, flapping in the breeze. That is, until third grade when I got recruited for the boy choir.

With that thought, I look to my left at the little brick building known as the Music Room. That's where I served my time in the choir and where I performed my infamous, career-ending rendition of *Old Folks at Home.*

The building was originally a carriage house, and along with the mansion that is now the convent, and the land upon which the grade school is built, was once part of the estate of Pennsylvania Congressman James Snyder. I didn't know that until ten minutes ago when I read a plaque affixed to the wall at the entrance to the convent grounds.

I doubt Congressman Snyder ever imagined that one day, a century after his passing, his estate would still be thriving as part of this little Catholic School campus. Could I have ever imagined as I ran and played in the recess area, that one day, half a century later, I would be sitting on the Congressman's back porch, contemplating my own history on these grounds?

Time and change are relentless. When I was young, I embraced both as advantageous to the fulfillment of my dreams, but now, time and change threaten me with the possibility that I've missed my chance to make a difference in the world.

"Mister Ryan, Sister Mary Agatha can see you now."

"Oh, Sister Charlotte, you woke me from my daydreams. You see, I went to school here a long time ago."

"I know; Sister Mary Agatha told me. She's really looking forward to talking to you."

In all my years at Saint Mathew's School, I only entered the convent twice: once in second grade when Sister Mary Sean took our class into the building to visit the sister's chapel, and the other time as a sophomore in high school, the day I helped my former choir teacher, Sister Marguerite, carry a load of books. The interior of the old Victorian structure is dark and solemn with ornate woodwork, antique furniture, and heavy curtains. As on my previous visits, I'm struck by how quiet and peaceful the interior of the convent is.

I'm nervous, of course, but that doesn't entirely account for the trembling in my hands. When I considered who I would be speaking with, I passed on my morning cocktail. I have not spoken with Sister Mary Agatha in nearly forty years, and undoubtedly, I will never do so again after today. My respect for this wise, old teacher caused some remaining fragment of willpower to take command and stay the hand that would contaminate my morning with alcohol.

I follow Sister Charlotte through the sitting room and down a narrow hallway to the back of the convent. She opens a large oak door, holds the knob as I enter, and smiles as she shuts the door behind me.

Sister Mary Agatha is seated in a wheel chair, facing a bay window. She's wearing a long gray dress, and a white, knitted shawl drapes over her shoulders. The window affords an interesting and picturesque view of Saint Mathew's Campus. A narrow brick alley divides the scene and is lined on the right by a stand of magnificent oak trees, tinted with autumn colors.

To the left side of the alley is Saint Mathew's Church, adorned on this side by a thirty foot high, stained glass window. The window depicts Mary, the mother of Jesus, bearing a crown and a glorious multicolored robe, sitting on a golden throne with the Christ Child on her lap.

Beyond the church and centered in the landscape, is Saint Mathew's High School, standing proud and tall a century after its inception, unmoved by the intrigue that swirls around it. If the building is ever taken away, a great void will disconnect this peaceful panorama.

Sister Mary Agatha turns and beckons me to sit in a chair that has been placed near her.

"Come sit with me Duane. I can't move too well anymore and I asked to be placed near this window. This is my favorite view of the campus. In the old days, I often had my breakfast here as the sun came up."

"It's good to see you again, Sister."

"Thank you, Duane. I don't get out much and I didn't think I would be well enough to travel. I seem to have the flu more often than not these days."

"Well, sister, I'm certainly glad that you were able to come, and I'm especially thankful now that I finally made it to a reunion because there are many things I've wanted to say to you over the years."

"I want to hear what you have to say, Duane, but first it is I who must speak. There are some things you need to know and perhaps should have known long ago. Shirley Greene called me and told me that you were here so I made the effort to talk to you in person."

"I, I don't understand. You mean Brittany Schuster's Aunt Shirley?"

"Yes, Brittany Schuster's aunt and Sally Schuster's aunt as well."

"But Sister, how do you know Brittany? I just met her myself and don't really know much about her."

"I don't know Brittany Schuster, personally; I only know of her. I knew Sally very well, since, as I'm sure you remember, I oversaw her novitiate. We became quite close then and remained in touch after she left Saint Mathew's."

"Are you still in touch with her?"

"Oh my, no. Sally died many years ago. She took her own life."

"No, Sister, I'm shocked. I would never have thought something like that. I, I don't know what to say. I'm just shocked."

"How well did you know Sally, Duane? I know that you two were quite fond of each other, but did she ever tell you much about her childhood?"

"No, come to think of it, she never did. She seemed real interested in my past, but rarely spoke about her own. She mentioned her mother once in a while, but that was about it."

"Sally's father was a bad alcoholic, and as a child, Sally was abused by her father. Her mother was a victim as well, but at the time, she also drank heavily and was in no position to intervene on Sally's behalf. Sally's father died when she was fifteen, which in many ways was a blessing to both her and her mother."

"My God, I never knew any of this. She never showed it. Sally always seemed so upbeat and happy."

"She *was* upbeat and happy most of the time, but a person doesn't get over an experience like that. Those kinds of scars run deep.

Sally's Mother stopped drinking after her husband died and remarried about a year later to a good man, a religious man, a

Baptist. He was good to Sally, she liked him and even took his last name: Schuster."

"But why did Sally come here? Why did she want to become a Catholic nun? Did Father McGee know about all this?"

"Sally told you very little. I'm not surprised. Yes, Father McGee was well aware of all this. Sally's father was Samuel McGee, Father McGee's brother."

"What? Oh no, Sister, Father McGee is Sally's uncle?"

"Yes, he's Sally's uncle. She loved him and admired him very much. That was the reason she chose a religious life. She saw in her uncle, someone who was good and kind and holy, everything her father wasn't. Sally wanted to be like him as much as possible.

Father McGee was dubious of her decision from the outset. He didn't think she was making the choice for the right reasons, and he asked me for my advice. For better or for worse, we arranged for her to come here."

I struggle not to hang my head as the weight of what Sister Mary Agatha is saying bears down upon me. How naïve I was back then. Now I understand Father McGee's anger the day he discovered Sally and me in the library and I realize the pain he must have experienced last night when he realized what I suspected him of.

"Duane, what happened to Sally isn't your fault. It's no more your fault then it is mine or Father McGee's fault. And you're not the reason Sally left Saint Mathew's. I was already convinced that the sisterhood was not right for her and had been trying to steer her in another direction. The incident with you and her in the library only finalized my decision. I tried to convince her to take a different path, perhaps go to college.

After she left here, she drifted around, and it seemed that each time I would get a letter it was from a different town. Sally was excited about each new job and talked as if she had found what she wanted to do, but each time she wrote, it was from somewhere else and about another job.

Sally lived with a man for a while in San Diego, an artist, a painter. She was very proud of him and thought he was on his way

247

to greatness. They had a child together, but she and the painter parted ways shortly after."

"Sally had a baby?"

"Yes, a daughter. Sally went home with the infant and lived there with her mother and step-father for about six months. I received a letter at the time, and it was vague and, in some ways, incoherent, as if she was telling me a story about someone else rather than talking about herself. Sally talked about what she did during the day, about tending the gardens and walking in the woods with the dogs, but she hardly mentioned her daughter and said nothing at all about her plans for the future.

Not long after that, Sally went alone to a reservoir near her home, a place where her mother often took her when she was young. She drove down a boat ramp into the water and drowned herself."

Now I can't help but hang my head. I feel like it's ready to explode with the barrage of information I'm struggling to assimilate. But amidst the mental turmoil, one more question arises. I raise my head to see Sister Mary Agatha looking at me with a sad and benevolent gaze. I start to ask, but stop in mid sentence as the answer is suddenly obvious to me. Sister Mary Agatha answers anyway.

"Sally's parents raised the child. That's who Brittany Schuster is."

Sister Mary Agatha seems to sense the impact her statement has made on me and so after a moment of silence, she steers the discussion in a more general direction. She draws an analogy between Sally's life and death and the trials we all face on earth. Her perspective on life and loss remind me of my recent discussion with Mr. Liston. Like my former neighbor, Sister Mary Agatha seems to have concluded that how we deal with loss defines us as a person and determines what our contribution in life will be.

I have the feeling that she's directing her comments toward me, although I don't know how she can be aware of what my losses are or of the pathetic manner in which I'm dealing with them. Then she becomes more specific and asks me to imagine the loss

248

to Father McGee when Sally took her life. I try to, and only feel greater remorse for what I suspected he had done to his niece. As if Sister Mary Agatha knows my thoughts, she proposes that it would do the Bishop a great deal of good if he could meet with Brittany.

My meeting with Sister Mary Agatha is shorter than I expected. I think Sister Charlotte intervened when she sensed that the conversation had gone on long enough. I take Sister Mary Agatha's hand and thank her for telling me about Sally and Brittany. I also thank her for the effort she made for me decades before when I was under her tutelage. She chuckles at that, and a kindly, introspective expression comes over her face.

"Duane, you were a great puzzle to Father McGee and me, so much potential that seemed to percolate there just beneath the surface. I tried to pull you along and he tried to push you, but in the end, I learned that you weren't born to follow, and Father McGee learned that you don't like to be pushed. You had to go your own way."

She smiles and gazes up at Sister Charlotte as the young nun prepares her to go. I say goodbye and as I'm closing the door behind me, Sister Mary Agatha speaks again.

"I'm so glad I got to sit here one more time, Sister Charlotte, to see this magnificent view again. In all my years of service to the Lord, none were so wonderful and rewarding as when I was the principal at Saint Mathew's School."

35

I walk away from the convent and turn in the opposite direction whence I arrived, to an alley that runs alongside the Music Room and leads to Pennsylvania Avenue. I decide on an indirect route to Father McGee's office in an attempt to clear my head a bit before I enter into what could be another intense discussion.

The revamped image I have of this man who only hours ago, I suspected of the very worst of sins, will take some time to get used to. How can I look him in the eye after the implications that prompted last night's boiler room break in, especially in light of what I now know?

I cross Jefferson Street and proceed along Shady Lane to Tuesday Alley, the handy corridor that will once again lead me to the high school parking lot. Because of the dense foliage that lines the alley, it's a private route even in daylight. Just before I reach the parking lot, I pause to take advantage of the cover to sip some nerve tonic from my trusty flask in preparation for the trial ahead of me.

As I reach into my coat pocket, I spot a vehicle parked close beside the truck. I'm surprised at first to see someone crowding me in an empty lot, especially when I'm parked in my secure space, but then I realize that the vehicle is Brittany's. When she emerges from the car and walks toward me, I let go of the flask and withdraw my hand.

From the look on her face, I suspect that she's as knowledgeable as I am, concerning the mystery of Sally Shuster and where she, herself, fits into the story. Brittany manages a smile, but can't hide the fact that something is bothering her. She puts her arms around my waist and rests her head on my chest.

"Hi, how'd it go with your aunt?"

"Good, Duane. I love Aunt Shirley, but you and I need to talk. I know you'll be shocked about what she told me. I was so wrong about everything, especially Father McGee."

"Well I just left a meeting with Sister Mary Agatha, and I think I'm already at my shock limit."

"Then you know about everything; you know about me?"

"Yes, I know about you."

"What do you think?"

"I'm still too stunned to think real clearly, but it doesn't change my opinion of you. If anything it makes you more special in my eyes. As sad as what happened to your mother is, she lives on in a way, through you. You're the bright spot in the story."

"Thank you Duane; that's so sweet. I've been trying to convince myself of something like that all the way from Pittsburgh. I even thought that maybe it's why we got together, that it fulfills something my mother, wanted to do. Maybe it's something that should have happened."

"I, I guess I can go along with that. In fact, I like that thought."

Brittany keeps her head on my chest and is silent for a moment, but I sense that there's much more she wants to talk about.

"Duane, Have you ever considered committing suicide?"

"Um, I uh, have, in a way."

"You have in a way, what does that mean?"

"It means I've given it some thought. If you're asking how close I was to actually pulling the trigger, I would have to say, not *real* close."

"You thought of shooting yourself?"

"Oh no, I used 'pulling the trigger' as a figure of speech. Shooting oneself is too violent and messy. I was thinking of something more peaceful and neat like gas or pills, but like I said,

I never came too close. I do have a website bookmarked where a suicide device is sold called a helium hood."

"A helium hood, I've never heard of it."

"It's a charming invention: a plastic bag to cover the head, an adjustable Velcro strip for around the neck and a tube to let the helium in. The helium prevents panic and that nagging feeling of suffocation that ruins many a good suicide attempt. The helium hood comes recommended by many right-to-die groups."

"It *sounds* really charming. But why did you consider killing yourself? Is this something you thought about recently?"

"Oh it's a notion that comes and goes, and I haven't really thought about it much lately. I guess in the year or so after Leah left me, I was most serious about suicide. I wasn't suicidal over her leaving, because in some ways, I was relieved. But it was the way she left, so casually, as if the years we spent together meant nothing to her. She was involved with someone else so soon that it wasn't hard to figure out she had already been seeing him. She seemed to have so little respect for me that I lost a lot of respect for myself.

At the same time, doubts about my work that I'd been wrestling with anyway were magnified. It went beyond just questioning if I was headed in the right direction as an artist—that's the never-ending question—but I became unsure whether I had really done much of anything worthwhile. I started wondering if my whole career had been a mistake.

And then if I tried to look beyond myself for some reason to believe in life, there were always the headlines to dash any last bit of optimism: pollution, greed, poverty, wars. I sat in my apartment above the gallery, drinking, looking out at the world rushing by, and the thought of leaving the picture didn't seem like a bad idea."

Brittany raises her head and looks into my eyes.

"You obviously changed your mind."

"Not really. I don't like the helium hood. It has a weird, techno look to it, and I don't want to be found that way. So I decided on the vodka-drip method. It's slower, but will eventually get the job done."

252

Brittany sighs in a tone of exasperation and puts her head back against my chest.

"My mother must have had lots of doubts about life to kill herself like she did."

I don't respond. My own suicidal musings seem shallow and foolish next to what Brittany has recently learned about Sally. I hold her close and can only hope that she'll never reach a place in life where what I just told her or what her mother did will make sense. I'm relieved when she turns the discussion in another direction.

"I'm glad that you talked to Sister Mary Agatha. Aunt Shirley spoke very highly of her and told me how much she tried to help Sally. Did Sister Mary Agatha tell you about Father McGee and how hard he took Sally's death?"

"No, not exactly."

"Well, apparently Father McGee went to pieces. He took a leave of absence for several years and nearly left the priesthood for good. Aunt Shirley said that he wanted to help with me and to be part of my life, and that's why I have memories of him, talking with my mother in the kitchen.

My mother would have nothing to do with it, of course. She blamed the Catholic Church for what happened to Sally and was determined to keep me as far away from it as possible. To her, Father McGee symbolized the church, and she kept me away from him and everything to do with my past, even if it meant picking up and moving to another part of the country."

"Well, she did a good job of it."

"That's for sure. But you know, even though I don't agree with what she did, I can understand. Like Aunt Shirley said, in a way, Mom was trying to block out her own past. She thought that with me she'd been given another chance, a chance to make up for what happened to Sally."

"Yes, your aunt is right, I don't think you should be too hard on your mother for what she did."

"I need to talk to her though; maybe I'll stop and see her on the way home.

253

Hey wait, I almost forgot. What happened last night? Did you and Mike break in to the boiler room?"

"Uh, yes we sure did, and you won't believe what happened. Needless to say, our theory about the philandering, murdering priest was a little off the mark. But I really don't have time to go into the details, because, believe it or not, I have an appointment with Bishop McGee right about now."

"You're kidding? How did that come about?"

"To make a short story even shorter, he caught Booker and me last night and now he wants to see me in his office."

"Wow, and he knows the reason you were breaking in to the room?"

"Unfortunately, yes."

"Poor Bishop McGee. What a terrible thing to suspect him of. Talk about opening old wounds. We were all wrong about him."

"I don't know if I would go so far as saying *all* wrong. I feel bad about the boiler room fiasco, in fact, I feel like an idiot, but I'm not ready to recommend him for sainthood either. Had he been a different person, not so controlling and condescending and, well, more like a Sister Mary Agatha, it wouldn't have been so easy to build a case against him."

"Is that what you're going to tell him today?"

"Of course not. I'll probably just stand there and listen like I did when I was in high school. And the truth is if I manage to say anything worthwhile, it should be some form of an apology."

"I agree. I think it would do you both a lot of good."

"I'm glad you feel that way, because I think we should spread the good feelings around and you ought to come, too."

"I thought I probably should talk to him, but I don't know if I can handle it. Do you think he'll want to talk to me?"

"Actually it was Sister Mary Agatha's suggestion and she knows him best."

"I wish I could go back to the motel first and . . ."

"Nah, stuff like this is like getting into cold water when you want to go swimming. You can't think about it too much, you just have to jump in. I'll tell you what, you can wait in the hall while I go in and feel him out. If you hear shouting and cursing and the sound of bodies hitting the floor, you might want to reconsider. At any rate, Brittany, I should be getting up there."

"Okay, I'll do it. Let's go.

36

Brittany and I are greeted at the door by an exuberant woman named Eileen Duncan who informs us that she volunteers at the rectory three days a week. Eileen, as she asked us to call her, looks to be in her sixties, and from her attitude and demeanor I get the impression that she is an optimistic and happy person. Eileen is obviously thrilled to have the Bishop in attendance on her watch. She informs us that another party is with the Bishop, but that he wanted to know when I arrived.

We follow Eileen up wooden stairs that double back at a small landing. The landing is brightened by sunlight through a round, stained glass window that I remember seeing decades ago when I traveled this route on my way to my sessions with Father McGee. The window portrays the Holy Spirit, a white dove with spread wings, descending against a backdrop of brilliant golden rays that emanate in a circular pattern from somewhere behind the bird.

A humble perch along a stairway seems to be an appropriate setting for this most quiet member of the Holy Trinity. The Holy Trinity: God the Father, Jesus, and the Holy Spirit, three persons in one God. The three are distinct and yet the concept of God embodies all three persons at the same time. Pretty heavy stuff.

Needless to say, the Trinity is another of those mysteries of the faith that I never quite understood. Yet I accepted it when I was young and I think this was in large part because I thought the Holy Spirit was a cool god, and I wanted Him in the mix with the other two. I liked the way He worked: behind the scenes, mysterious and aloof, but there when it mattered.

Upon reaching the second floor we hear the sound of voices and shuffling feet, signaling that the meeting that preceded us is ending. Eileen says that it will only be a few minutes before we see the Bishop, and I take advantage of the interlude to seek a restroom for the alleged purpose of washing my hands. Eileen directs me to a small lavatory at the end of the hall that is ideal for my purposes.

I stand in front of a mirror, flask in hand, and I feel somewhat cheap and phony. That's probably because I am cheap and phony, not to mention, a liar. How weird, sneaking away to this little room so that I can drug myself with alcohol before continuing my participation in life.

This vodka thing, it started out as a crutch to help me through high anxiety situations such as art openings, or meetings with demanding clients, and certainly this present circumstance, meeting a bishop with whom I have a history of ill will and who I recently implicated as a murderer, ranks up there. But these days, most situations seem to fall into the high anxiety category, even getting out of bed in the morning.

What Booker spoke of yesterday has come to pass: alcohol is no longer a reward in my life, it's a way of life. I may be critical of Father McGee and his brusque manner, but I'm willing to bet he's not sipping vodka right now in preparation for our meeting. And imagine the anxiety Brittany must be experiencing and yet she's facing it honestly and with a clear head. I used to be like that.

On impulse I hold the flask over the sink and consider emptying its contents down the drain, but can't go that far. I do manage to get it back in my coat pocket without taking a drink. My God, it's nearly noon and I haven't had a drink yet!

I find Brittany alone in the hall, sitting in one of two ornate, straight back chairs with plush, upholstered seats. I sit beside her and face a window that offers a close view of Saint Mathew's Church. The scene is of the west side of the church and is dominated by another thirty foot high stained glass window that is on the opposite side of the church from the window devoted to Mary.

This window honors Mary's son, Jesus, the King of Heaven. Jesus' right hand is raised to bless the congregation and in his left hand he holds a golden scepter with a cross on the end. Above His head is a hovering dove, the Holy Spirit (always there, behind the scenes), and on each side of Jesus is a kneeling angel. The inside of the church is bright enough to make the features of the window plainly visible, and from this vantage point, one looks right into Jesus' face.

Eileen had accompanied the party that went before us down the stairs and is just returning as I sit down. She seems a bit confused when I ask her to announce that only I am here, but she acquiesces when I explain that it's a surprise. Brittany pats my hand and smiles as I rise to follow our hostess down the hall.

I approach the office with trepidation. I'm feeling low. I don't feel like a man; I feel like a vermin, crawling towards the door. I probably don't need to open it; I can just scurry under. How do I explain to Bishop McGee the reasoning that led me to suspect him of something so terrible. The true circumstances surrounding the disappearance of Sally Schuster and the explanation for his association with her make my suspicions all the more appalling.

My hands are shaking, but there's no turning back now; we're at the door. Bishop McGee is sitting behind the desk looking over some documents. When Eileen addresses him, he stops and looks over his glasses at me.

"Come in Duane, have a seat, please."

The Bishop motions toward a chair on the opposite side of the desk and then stands as I approach. He extends his hands and we shake before I sit down. It occurs to me that it's the first time we have ever done so. With this friendly gesture, I feel even more compelled to express my regrets for what happened the night before. I only manage to utter a few words when he raises a hand to stop me.

"Let's not dwell on last night, Duane, I've thought it over and I pretty much have the picture of what happened. Carmen got it all started right?"

"Y-yes, I guess that *is* how it started."

"Poor Carmen, he called me the day after he sounded off at the bar. He was falling over himself with remorse and blamed his loose tongue on the liquor."

"I'm sorry, Father, but I never would have guessed that you and Carmen were still in contact."

"Oh yes, Carmen was my eyes and ears in this part of the diocese. Actually, when he was sober, he was an insightful observer and I valued his viewpoint on church matters. Unfortunately, he wasn't sober much toward the end and few people paid attention to anything he said.

That's why when he told me that he had talked about the boiler room, I didn't think much of it. The only thing that sounded a note of concern was when he said that 'one of those *boiler room boys* was there'. Then when one of the boiler room boys showed up here, embedded with a committee of well-wishing alumni, and made a request to enter the room, I suspected trouble."

"And so you were ready for us."

"In a way. I was here working when I saw the light flash on and off. I grabbed Father Walsh's shot gun and thought I would have some fun. The gun was given to him years ago in Indianapolis for being chaplain of a chapter of Ducks Unlimited. It's never even been loaded.

It wasn't a smart thing to do on my part—a gun isn't a toy—but I was fully expecting to confront Bob Macy and crew, not you and Michael Prizza. If I *had* expected Prizza, I would have called the National Guard first."

Father McGee smiles at this statement, and I find myself growing more at ease in his presence.

"How is Sister Mary Agatha? I assume you've spoken with her. I only talked to her briefly before she left the banquet and haven't had a chance to meet with her yet."

"She's good, Father, frail, but still as sharp as ever. And Father, she told me about you and Sally and I just want to say . . ."

"Duane, let's let it go. As far as last night is concerned, I was shocked, of course, but after thinking it over, I understand. There are things that you should have been told a long time ago and I'm sure that Sister Mary Agatha has explained them to you better than I can. What happened with Sally was a terrible thing, the worst experience of my life, and I still have a hard time talking about it, but I moved past that era long ago. So if you don't mind, I'd prefer to do the same in our discussion this morning."

"Yes Father."

"So Duane, tell me, how is your work going?"

"My work?"

"Your art, your wood sculpture."

"Uh, good. Pretty good, I mean. I, uh, I've been a little bogged down recently. I went through a rocky period, a divorce and all, and I'm looking for a new direction, I suppose. I, uh, well, actually, my work isn't going well. I've been spinning my wheels for a few years now; ideas aren't coming anymore like they used to. To be honest with you, Father, for the first time since I started out, I've begun to question what I do for a living."

"Question your work, why?"

"I think it's because I'm not really sure why I'm doing it anymore. When I was young, to be able to create art for art's sake was all the reward I needed. I didn't worry about money, or growing old, or what people thought about me. Now, I seem to worry about all those things and think less about art with every year that goes by."

I stop, surprised at how I'm openly stating something that I haven't fully admitted to myself. Bishop McGee doesn't seem the least bit surprised with my remarks. He removes his glasses and leans back in the chair. He's old now: his hair mostly gray and his faced lined with wrinkles. He no longer is the formidable, looming character I remember him as, and it's obvious in his speech and his mannerisms that he's no longer trying to be.

"How old are you now, Duane, mid-fifties, right?"

"Yes, fifty-five."

"I'm seventy-nine now, so I can't sympathize with you much in the growing old department, but harboring doubts about the path you've taken in life is not so unusual, especially when people reach your age. I hear it often, regardless of what particular lifestyle a person has chosen. I think what happens is that people reach a point physically and mentally where the fact of their own mortality begins to sink in. Whatever their aspirations are, be it family, career, or even a religious calling, everything is viewed from a different perspective when you get older."

"You went through it?"

"Yes, in a way, but at an earlier age. What happened with Sally turned my life inside out and I never looked at anything the same after that. For the first time, I began to question my faith and after that, I doubted everything my life was built upon. I think that's where an analogy might be drawn to your situation. Art is your religion; it's where you placed your faith as a young man and then you developed a lifestyle around it. If you doubt your faith, everything else starts to lose its meaning."

"Well what did *you* do?"

"Me, I started over again. I took a leave of absence from the church and spent some years rediscovering why I became a priest in the first place. I always wanted to serve God, of course, but I wanted to do this through helping people. I wanted to help people live happy, productive, and spiritual lives, no matter what their circumstances. That meant people like Carmen as well as the wealthiest members of the congregation, and I especially wanted to help people like Sally.

So I immersed myself in people: I worked at homeless shelters, counseled teenagers who were in trouble, and did some teaching again. I reestablished my faith in God, but with the emphasis where it should have remained all along, on helping others through my faith."

"But Father, I don't really see how this applies to my situation."

"I think it does. In the beginning you wanted to be an artist for art's sake. Fame and fortune weren't a concern, you were creating works of art for whatever audience was receptive, for whoever would be inspired and elevated by it. It's a great gift to be able to alter people's lives that way and truly a reward unto itself. My guess is that somewhere along the way, you lost sight of that and your work became more about you and your social status as an artist."

"Maybe it has, but that's come about by necessity. You have to make a name for yourself to get any kind of fair price for your art."

"Has it worked?"

"Well, yes, to some extent, but not enough, I guess."

"It'll never be enough, Duane."

"What else can I do now, Father? How would I start over, donate my carvings to soup kitchens? Oh, I'm sorry, that was a dumb thing to say. What I mean is . . ."

"No, that's not a bad idea at all. Why not? Art would be appreciated there as much as anywhere, if not more so. Why not turn your focus back to art for art's sake and let fame and fortune take care of itself? Do you know that Buddhist art is largely anonymous? Artistic anonymity is grounded in the Buddhist belief of working toward the elimination of the individual ego."

"No, I uh, I didn't know that, Father."

"*What*, I thought you were the expert on Buddhism."

I'm caught off guard by the statement, but when I see a smile playing on Father McGee's lips, I recall the last time he and I discussed Buddhism in this office. Whatever apprehension I have about meeting with this man falls away.

"Well, to be honest with you, father, I never really touched on Buddhist art. After you steered me back on track, my studies of Buddhism never went far beyond that paper."

"Hah, I never steered you anywhere. But getting back to your work, what about the abstract pieces you were doing a few years back? I saw them on your website and really thought you were on to something there. What did that lead to?"

"The abstract pieces? Well, I still have some of them. Another piece is in progress. It's been in progress for about two years now, in fact. That's about where it all fizzled out, with the abstract pieces. I keep waiting for some wind from the old days to blow again and lift my sails."

"Don't wait, Duane; stir up a new wind. Forget about age and time. Don't be concerned about the years that have gone by or worry about the years that remain. Focus on the present; attend to the task at hand. One bold era in the life of an individual can change the course of civilization."

I was never so moved by something Father McGee said to me. Decades ago, when I was in his office, I only half listened to what he said, never applying any of it to my life, but now, every word rings true. Now he seems to understand me better than I know myself.

For that reason, I decide to leave the conversation where we are, on art, and go away with the message he's given me. Besides, I want to return the favor to this man who I regarded as a nemesis, but who instead is going out of his way to help me get my life back on track.

"Father, I, oh, I'm sorry, *Bishop* McGee I should be saying, or Your Excellency, right?"

"Duane, 'Father' is fine—for old times sake. But I *am* impressed that you remember the proper manner by which to address a bishop."

"I've been surprising myself this weekend with the things I remember. I hate to interrupt here because I'm finding this conversation very helpful, but someone came with me today that would like to speak to you. She's been waiting in the hall."

"Really, do I know her?"

"Yes, it's Brittany Schuster, Sally's daughter."

"What, how can that be? I had given up hope of ever . . . Are you sure? Brittany is in the hall, right now?"

"Yes, I'm sure, Father, Brittany Schuster, and she wants to talk to you."

I sit back in the chair that Brittany vacated and lean my head against the wall. As I introduced her to the Bishop, her great uncle, I couldn't decide who was more nervous, Brittany or Father McGee, but it was probably me. I felt it was appropriate that I bow out and leave them alone to ease some of the tension, and now that I hear laughter coming from the office, I suppose I was right.

To sit in this quiet spot in the rectory is a welcome respite after such an eventful morning. I gaze out the window at the magnificent stained glass window that adorns the wall of Saint Mathew's Church.

Jesus is gazing back at me from his heavenly throne. His head is framed by long brown hair, highlighted with a golden halo, and His face is a picture of tranquility that belies His earthly trials. From what I learned in religion class, Jesus was in his early thirties when He died and His rise and fall took place in about three years. His story reminds me of what Father McGee just said, that *one bold era in the life of an individual can change the course of civilization.*

37

Brittany and Bishop McGee talked for nearly an hour before they roused me from my meditations in the hall. Brittany decided to stay in town a bit longer and, at her great uncle's invitation, to dine with him and Sister Mary Agatha later in the day. I was invited of course, but I suspected that it was time for me to withdraw from the picture.

Brittany and I spent some time together at the Oak Park Motel as I packed. She was happy and chatted merrily about her meeting with Father McGee. She seemed even younger to me than she did before, younger and more carefree. I feel about the same, like a geezer, but somehow I sense I'm now a wiser geezer.

When I asked Brittany if she'd garnered enough material for her novel, she shook her head and said that in the midst of all the real life revelations, she had forgotten about her book. I almost slipped and made the standard remark that *truth is stranger than fiction,* but fortunately, I held my tongue for once. Because it's not really; it just seems that way. That's because fiction is always influenced by the possibilities in an author's mind, whereas truth is unpredictable and follows no rules.

We both knew that I wasn't going to New Mexico and nothing further was said about it. Instead, Brittany and I parted with a hug and a kiss, a favorite uncle-favorite niece type hug and kiss, and made a mutual promise to stay in touch.

As I move up the long, winding slope toward the East River Mountain Tunnel in southern West Virginia, I realize that I'm hungry and decide to take a break. The timing is good and not only because of my hunger, but because this tunnel marks the halfway point on the journey from Homewood to Janesville. According to the odometer this isn't actually the case, but for me, the mile long passage through a mountain that opens up into Virginia and into the south, is the psychological divide of this journey.

The weather is as glorious as autumn has to offer, and as I exit the tunnel, the afternoon sun illuminates stunning fall colors across a brilliant panorama of tree covered mountains. I procure victuals at a small restaurant just off the interstate, and then proceed to the Virginia Welcome Center, which is only a few miles further. This is an elaborate facility with spacious grounds and dozens of picnic tables. I choose a table that is located in a cluster of maple trees and at a comfortable distance from the swirl of humanity that encompasses the main building of the Welcome Center.

This stop isn't just about nourishment; I need some room to let my mind range a bit more freely. The truck is too confining a space for the expansive thoughts conjured up by the events of the weekend. Among them is a new, impetuous plan, an idea that took seed before I left Pennsylvania and grew to lofty dimensions as I made my way through the hills of West Virginia.

Early on, I tried to dismiss the notion, reminding myself that impulsive decisions have never been a strong point with me. The mental conflict rendered me edgy and uncertain at first, and I reached for my flask. Then I remembered that it was empty and the vodka bottle had been purposely left behind at the Oak Park Motel.

I don't know if it was what Carla said or if it was the fact that *she* said it that made me decide to leave my bottle behind. Carla took a real chance talking to me like she did, and it was a brave thing to do. I need to be brave now as well and take a chance on life again.

The flask is packed in my suitcase beside a small plastic bag of pot that Booker slipped to me earlier in the day when I stopped at his office. I mentioned Carla's rehab suggestion to him at Corky's, and the fact that he acted upon it so quickly, demonstrates as much as his words that he's really concerned about my drinking.

I try to focus my thoughts on the veggie burger that I purchased, but a breeze stirs the maple leaves into a soothing chatter that distracts me. The setting and my state of mind conjure up memories of other times when I was in a similar position: on the road, traveling alone, with change gathering on the horizon.

I watch traffic pass by on the interstate and follow an old van that is heading north. This particular vehicle interests me because as a young man, I owned a similar van and in it I traveled many miles. I rarely used interstate highways back then; I disliked them in fact. Part of the journey was meandering through small towns and talking to people, while the rest of the world rushed by on the interstate.

I watch until the van disappears and out of the corner of my eye, I spot a phone booth. Am I seeing things? This is something left over from the old days: a real honest to goodness, upright, phone booth, with a door and all.

I assume its unlikely appearance is a sign that I must act upon the plan in my head, even before I take another bite of my burger. I rush to the truck for my wallet and scavenge whatever change has accumulated in the cup holder. On the way to the phone booth, I shuffle through the cards that I accumulated over the weekend and find the number.

I know people are watching me, especially young people. They all know that I don't have a cell phone, and are probably snickering about it. What's this? Is that kid filming me with his phone? Great, he's probably posting it on the web right now. Caught on video: *The last Homo sapiens to use a phone booth.*

Of course whipping out some fancy phone would be much more glamorous at a moment like this, but if a man has a *real* call to make, if he *truly* has something worth saying, a good old fashioned phone booth will do just fine.

The instructions on the face of the phone are too complicated for my state of mind, so I dial up an operator. She seems surprised to hear from me, probably hasn't seen the phone booth light blink on in years. I also think she realizes she has a geezer on the line, because she's especially patient and helpful.

"Hello, Tom Liston speaking."

"Mr. Liston, hello. This is Duane, Duane Ryan."

"Duane, hello. I didn't expect to hear from you again so soon. What's that noise in the background."

"Just eighteen-wheelers passing by. I'm talking from a phone booth along the interstate in Virginia.

Mr. Liston, I was wondering if you could do me a favor. You mentioned that a friend of yours is the real estate agent that has my family home listed."

"Yes, Peggy Laurie. As a matter of fact, I just saw her yesterday at the grocery store."

"Would you happen to have her phone number? I've decided that I want to buy the old house and fix it up as my studio."

"You're thinking of moving back to Homewood?"

"Yeah, I, uh, I guess I am."

"Great, that's great; I'm so surprised. That's the best news I've heard in a long time. I don't have Peggy's number right here, Duane, but I'll tell you what I'll do. I'll call Peggy when I find it and tell her you're interested.

As I mentioned before, that lawyer fellow, Thompson, he's looking to get rid of the property, and Peggy's anxious to be rid of him, so I bet we can get you a good price. Get back to North Carolina in one piece and I'll work on it from this end."

I thank Mr. Liston and make my way back to my veggie burger in a happy daze. Am I really doing this, making such a radical move? I don't know if I should worry about being too young for this or too old.

However, now that I've committed myself, I'm anxious to get the wheels rolling at the other end, in fact too anxious to wait until I get back to Janesville. I no sooner finish my sandwich when I'm back in the phone booth, dialing the gallery.

"Duane Ryan Gallery, Hannah True speaking. How may I help you?"

"Hannah, hi, I'm glad I caught you. How are you?"

"Hi boss, I'm good. I was just thinking about you this afternoon. Where are you?"

"Oh, in a phone booth, somewhere in Virginia. Say listen, I was wondering if you could do something for me. I've made some big decisions over the weekend and one is that I've decided to go ahead and put the building up for sale. Could you contact Lenny Taylor and give him the green light."

"Wow, I'm shocked. What brought this on? Are you running off with an old high school sweetheart?"

"No, not exactly. I'll tell you the details when I get there, but I've definitely made up my mind to shut things down and start over again."

"Well Lenny will be delighted. He's wanted to list this building for years. What's the hurry though?"

"I'm just anxious to get things moving before I have a chance to talk myself out of it, and once Lenny gets a hold of this, there'll be no turning back. Besides, I'm not exactly sure when I'll be there. I've decided to get off the interstate and wander through Virginia on the way down, maybe go see my brother, Will."

"What, am I hearing things? Next you'll be telling me you're staying at a bed and breakfast. Have you been drinking?"

"No, believe it or not I *haven't* been drinking. You might just say that I'm high on life."

"Oh come on, Duane, you've always hated that saying."

"Hah ha, I know; I'm just kidding. For now, let's just say that things have changed. So how is everything there? How was business this weekend?"

"Good, we had a few nice sales. In fact, one of your pricier pieces sold, and you'll never guess which one: *The Man in the Room*."

"What, are you kidding me? When did it sell?"

"Saturday afternoon, just before closing; a couple from Charlotte bought it. Their name is Cameron, Bill and Twyla Cameron. I knew as soon as they came in there was potential, because they both loved the gallery and checked out everything real well, but when Mrs. Cameron saw *The Man in the Room* there was no doubt that it was what she wanted. Her husband loved it too."

"I can't believe it, Hannah. You have no idea what a coincidence this is. I was just thinking about that piece. Did they say what they liked about it? Did you tell them the story behind it?"

"They didn't really ask for an interpretation, so I didn't offer one. In fact I did my best not to act surprised that it was selling or even imply that there *was* a story behind it. They were so pleased with their purchase, though, that I couldn't help but be curious as to why they chose that particular piece. So I talked to them while I wrapped it up and tried to get *their* interpretation of it.

I told them that *The Man in the Room* is a piece that draws a wide range of reactions from people, and mentioned that many people thought it was a portrait of the artist. Mrs. Cameron said she assumed that too, but she read more into it than that. Her husband agreed with her, and said that to him it represented a certain state of mind rather then any one individual."

"I like that; that's what I think I was aiming for when I did the piece. So they didn't see a dark side to it?"

"No, not at all. When I told them that some people felt *The Man in the Room* depicts a person who is isolated and alone, Mr. Cameron said, 'oh no, I don't see that. For me, *The Man in the Room* is a portrait of someone who is independent, someone who doesn't mind being alone'.

Mrs. Cameron nodded and said, 'yes, a person who goes his own way in life. *The Man in the Room* is about someone who is at peace with himself'."

The End

www.ingramcontent.com/pod-product-compliance
Lightning Source LLC
Chambersburg PA
CBHW061555170626
46811CB00001B/210